TARNISHED TIARA

The Mysterious Death of an Ingénue

Paul Scopel

To Martha,

Persevere with Joy!

James 1:2-4

TARNISHED TIARA
The Mysterious Death of an Ingénue

Cover Concept: Denise Cassino
Cover image by Shutterstock
Back Page Author Photograph: Jarrod Cecil

Written by Paul Scopel
Visit my website at www.PaulScopel.com

Printed in the United States of America
First Printing: September 2018
Published by: Tom Bird Retreats, Inc.

Paperback ISBN: 978-1-62747-304-0
eBook ISBN: 978-1-62747-307-1

Contents

Editorial Reviews

This is a quite intriguing novel that follows the protagonist, Cece, throughout her entire life — a life that intertwines with a fascinating cousin who is a beauty queen and ingénue who trades on her beauty and love of cats to paint an interesting — and ultimately, sad — life portrait.

Cece grows throughout this novel, from a meek and timid girl and woman to one who is strong and capable at the end, even though her life with Liz, the beauty queen, cost her dearly.

Cece's native intelligence comes to the fore as she helps to unravel the mystery surrounding her cousin's death.

Bill Worth, editor, and author of "Outwitting Multiple Sclerosis: How Forgiveness Helped Me Heal My Brain By Changing My Mind."

The underlying story is gripping, as we see Liz change . . . Ambitious plotting, believable characterizations . . . This author's main passion is details in all their forms — both in narrative and in scene descriptions. He has a tendency to command subjects he writes about.

Idony Lisle, writer and author of "Long-Leggedy Beasties" and "Things That Go Bump in the Night", and Director of Hope Recovery Learning Center.

Dedication

Dedicated to the love of my life, my wife. How very blessed I am to be married to this beautiful lady! Thank you for the advice, patience, understanding, and love throughout the years.

Acknowledgments

Thank you to my wonderful wife, daughter, and son-in-law for your patience, support, and advice on this writing journey. Without your help, I could not have created this work.

Thank you to my friends Janie, Jeanne, Nancy, Marcus, and Therese for your encouragement, advice, and suggestions.

With much gratitude to my coaches for their patience, knowledge, and guidance, thank you Tom Bird, John Hodgkinson (JohnEgreek), Denise Cassino, Hillary Summerton, Sabrina Fritts, and Mary Stevenson. Thank you my writing peers for your advice and support.

To my copy editor, Bill Worth, and style editor, Idony Lisle thank you for your expertise and encouragement in the production of this book.

Most books need a sweetener and I thank the family of my late friend Jansen Chazanof for their wonderful Buzzfield Apiary honey (available at buzzfieldapiary.com).

Thank you to my college English Composition professor who advised that my essay writing was the best she had read. I am appreciative that she encouraged me to excel despite a high school English teacher's rebuff of my writing efforts.

Author's Comments

This book attempts to portray its characters as persons within the Deep South of the United States. Often their dialect appears in the form of contractions and slang to reflect authenticity. As with each region, the natives have their own dialect stemming from a learned pattern of speaking.

As the lives of my characters unfold over years, events and relationships occur that leave a lasting mark on their psyche. I tried to convey their thoughts and feelings as I expected them to react given their personality styles.

My selection of passages from Scripture, poetry, and children's rhymes and songs consists of inspirational or memorable quotes collected in my brain over the years.

Don't delay getting your affairs in order. You don't know the time or place. . . .

Major Characters

"Cece" Cecilia Perkins Turner – *wife of Ross Turner*
"Liz" Elizabeth Perkins – *first cousin of Cece*
Ross Turner – *Cece's husband, a professor*
Bill and Nancy Mayer – *college friends of Liz*
Charles and Camilla Perkins – *Liz's father and mother, Cece's uncle and aunt*
Ben Perkins – *Cece's birth father, Charles' brother*
Molly Brinkman – *detective, Mary's Island, SC Police Department*
Joey Broyer – *Liz's live-in boyfriend*
Harold McCracken – *Cece's stepfather*
"Izzy" Isabelle Perkins McCracken – *Cece's mother*
Kerry Tyler – *Director of Zoning, City of Mary's Island, SC*
Carl – *Liz's fourth husband*
Reverend Matt and Marie Turner – *Ross's father and mother*
Jack Perkins – *Cece's brother*
Mary Ann and James Evans – *sister and brother-in-law of Ben and Charles*
Richie Evans – *Son of Mary Ann and James, Cousin of Cece, Jack, and Liz*
Suzy – *Liz's Pageant Chaperon*
Kent Sullivan – *Liz's secret fiancé*
Dr. John Brashon, III – *Liz's first husband*
Sharon and Tom Lee – *Undertakers*
Rufus Jasper – *Liz's Attorney*
Harry Caisteal – *Cece's Attorney and college friend*
Joe Anthony – *Sergeant, Georgetown Police Department*
The Honorable Judge Janie Bonham – *Probate Judge*
Kay – *Manager, Georgetown Animal Rescue Center*
Allen Schafer – *College friend of Liz*
Lloyd – *In-Charge Caretaker at Santee Delta Medical Center*

Prologue 1

Reflections

Spring 1999
New Orleans, Louisiana

Cece Turner nestled into the rugged leather writing chair that faced the green natural setting of her backyard. On the table, next to Cece, three freshly cut magnolia blooms overpowered the room with a sweet fragrance of lemon and vanilla. Competing with the blossoms, spicy aromas wafted from a simmering iron pot on the stove filled with Cece's recipe of Cajun jambalaya. At a time like this, she relished comfort food, with recipes she long ago carried from her native Baton Rouge. Despite the love for her hometown, she had succumbed to the good life and charm of the Big Easy.

Jolting Cece from her lethargy, one of her three rescue cats pounced into her lap seeking a tender touch. Stroking her pet gently, Cece's heart contemplated the years of happy times along with the difficult ones. Cece was unsure the good outweighed the ghastly bad events. She thought regardless, *I'm ready for this sordid mess to go away.*

Prologue 2

Carefree

1955
Charleston, South Carolina

Higher and higher, the timeworn swing ascended, only to sweep downward again. Over and over, the child's shoulder-length golden curls waved carefree in the flow of the breeze. Now, age five, Cecilia "Cece" Perkins clasped her petite fingers snug around the smooth chains of the swing. In this moment, Cece's childish brain perceived the smooth sensation of soaring. She imagined flying like the bluebirds she watched at her home in Louisiana, each winged creature owning their flight path. In a regular cycle, she perceived the familiar tug of Mother Earth coaxing the swing's return. Upward she and the swing rose, as she pumped her dangling bony legs and relied upon gentle propulsion guided by her babysitter, her fourteen-year-old cousin Elizabeth Perkins.

Everyone called Elizabeth "Liz" most of the time. Despite their age differences and that Liz and her parents lived in South Carolina, far away from Cece in Baton Rouge, the two girls bonded during that family vacation. The youngsters' fathers being close brothers further shored up the relationship of the two favorite cousins.

Cece loved to swing. Between Cece's rosy dimples, the two corners of her red lips joined in an infectious grin. The rows of white enamel emerged under her lips. A pulsing twinkle in Cece's piercing green eyes attested to how real her smile was. The toothy grin revealed a happy life in the little one's soul. Cece sensed Liz's overwhelming love and unconditional acceptance. The older girl repeated Cece's favorite nursery rhyme.

Liz rested after the last stanza, but the demanding child pleaded, "More, more, higher, higher, Lizzy."

Every girl who takes to a swing in a park chants this ageless appeal to her companion. Up and down the swing cycled. Liz chanted the lyrics to *Five Little Monkeys* repeatedly. She relished being the focal point and envy of her little charge. Liz's voice lessons equipped her to power the enunciation of each word with inflection and energy.

Five little monkeys jumping on the bed
One fell off and bumped his head
So Momma called the doctor and the doctor said
No more monkeys jumping on the bed!

The two girls laughed and giggled as one less monkey remained each time Liz recited the cadence of verses. Spellbound, Cece shook her own head and wagged her finger as she aped the doctor's disapproval of the monkeys' misbehavior. Countless times, Liz restarted her rhythmic chant of the old English folk song. Cece's countenance lit up with her pleasant toothy smile. Liz chortled to herself as she realized her own magical charisma.

Even at this early age, Cece is a watcher. Cece's bewitching eyes took in everything around her. As her swing soared, they opened wide to capture the heavens. Above her, puffy white clouds drifted across the blue sky. On the downward motion, she squinted her eyes to sense the full effect of earth's pull. With her swift movements, she felt the humidity and heat of the coastal city permeating her skin. Whiffs of the piquant tang of salty air teased her nostrils. Then, an overwhelming display in the gardens caught Cece's eye as she reached the bottom of the swing's arc. Random islands of red, pink, and mauve azalea shrubs punctuated the green spaces of White Point Park. Fragrant floral scents of South Carolina wafted to the two girls. As her green eyes darted back and forth, Cece seized the panorama in her little heart and mind. Her senses took in the turquoise sky, green fertile flora, and the sounds of the other children playing in the park. Cece captured every move of Liz, her sugary words, and the children's songs that she sang. Her fully charged senses enjoyed this revelry, yet at this age, she had no clue of the gruesome future that awaited in the moments or years ahead.

The youngsters' families gathered together two or three times each year. Visits were rare due to the thirteen-hour drive between Louisiana and South Carolina. When a visit occurred, it was pure joy for Cece to be with her cousin. Thoughts of sweet Liz surfaced often in Cece's memory chest. Years later, Cece's sharp mind replayed and repeated her next few steps, but she still cherished this day forever. Her snapshot memory of Liz portrayed a teenaged girl who transformed from the gawky, clumsy stage to a gorgeous brave icon. A cygnet transformed to be a regal protective swan. Cece adored glamorous, fun-loving, courageous Liz.

Tiring of the monkeys' perpetual dilemma, Liz tried something new. She shifted into a traditional French song sung by children around the world. She crooned "On the Bridge of Avignon" about an old bridge on the Rhone River, with her lyrics first in French and then English. She focused on the melody as she dropped her hands to her side while letting the swing slow. When Cece noticed the shift in speed and Liz's voice transitioning from lyric recitation to playful singing, she wanted off the swing. Cece slid out of the rubbery seat and plopped down on the mown grass. The words in a language she had never heard enthralled her. Her silent little face looked with inquisitive puzzlement at her cousin. She puckered her lips to mimic the funny words Liz intoned. Liz switched to the English version, bringing back the sparkle in Cece's eyes. She exposed her little teeth in contentment.

On the bridge of Avignon
They are dancing, they are dancing,
On the bridge of Avignon
They are dancing all around.

The familiar word dancing recited several times resonated with Cece. She stood and twirled her agile body in time to the music. Alert to Cece's interest, Liz repeated the refrain. As if a top, the little girl spun as she danced. Liz took her hand as she whirled.

Within a few minutes of silly non-stop swirling, Cece made herself dizzy. She dropped onto the grass again. As the spring sun descended under the jagged tree line, Liz glimpsed at her silver wristwatch.

Liz said, "Cece, everyone should be back at our house now. We need to go home soon. Dad is serving a Low Country boil for dinner."

Both girls disliked that the carefree playtime was ending. However, the prospect of boiled local shrimp, new potatoes, freshly shucked corn, country sausage, and Old Bay seasoning spread on layers of newspaper tantalized their taste buds. Liz's dad, Charles, usually prepared and served the Carolina specialty outdoors under the shade trees to placate his shrewish wife's penchant for cleanliness and a proper kitchen. She would not tolerate the smell of shrimp inside their pristine home.

Out of the corner of her eye, Cece captured the movement of a white pickup truck driving on the park grass. A city maintenance worker drove to the tables near the swings. The short man jumped out and slammed his door shut with a bang. He carried a coiled water hose as he approached the tables. Cece watched his ritual of washing sticky picnic tables and removing contents of shiny steel garbage cans.

Cece rose in fear of the stranger's intrusion on their territory. She motioned toward a grove of azalea bushes not far away.

As Cece pointed, she begged, "Let's take those flowers to Aunt Camilla and Momma."

In her sweet Southern lilt, Liz exclaimed, "What a splendid idea, Cece." Giving the child a warm hug, Liz announced, "What a lil' darling you are!"

Cece amazed Liz with her stroke of wisdom. Liz had learned that a peace offering helped when her mother, Camilla, came home in a foul mood. The quarrels happened more often as Liz, an only child, aged. That afternoon, Cece and Liz's parents played golf at the country club course. Liz expected the two tired mothers, Camilla and Izzy, to return exhausted from walking the eighteen-hole round. The two dads, Charles and Ben usually invited the ladies to enjoy a round of drinks at the Nineteenth Hole club. Alcohol seemed to sour Camilla's demeanor more. Liz shrugged, *Why should today be any different?*

Cece skipped on one leg, then the other, on the concrete sidewalk next to Liz. In her usual spirit, Cece watched everyone else and said little. Her quietness obscured her intelligence. Yet on the entire jaunt over to the azaleas, she chattered non-stop. Cece gained so much confidence from Liz. The older girl's warmth and endearing spirit stimulated and delighted Cece. She loved Liz and cherished the moments with her idol.

A moat of taller grass surrounded the grove of azaleas. Liz thought, *This grass needs mowing soon.* Fallen tree limbs mixed with other plant debris on the grass. Within reach of the nearby colorful bushes, Cece smelled their fragrance. The two girls tugged on the long woody stems teeming with leaves and blossoms.

Liz said, "Let me show you where and how to bend these twigs to make a clean break. We must avoid injury to the plant."

Cece watched Liz snapping a branch. Liz giggled as she placed a small bouquet of blossoms in Cece's curly hair. Cece slapped her hand behind her head aping poses of flirty models in her mother's fashion magazines. With hips gyrating, she sashayed around the next bush. Self-absorbed in her playing, and captivated by the colors and scents, Cece moved out of the sight of Liz.

Suddenly, placid Cece screeched out a shrill scream that resounded across the park. A sudden swirling movement startled her. The little girl saw the frightening creature three short feet from her. A menacing auburn and bronze snake rose in a threatening position. Three more steps and Cece would have stumbled onto it. While screaming her lungs out, Cece froze in fear. Liz reacted as fast as a lightning strike. She swooped down and scooped up the child as the viper aimed and struck at its target. The serpent missed both girls and recoiled. In a pure adrenalin rush, Liz hustled Cece to a resting spot a safe distance away. Shaken, Cece, out of control, wailed. The waterfall of tears required Liz to dry Cece's tears using her own expensive silk blouse. Her mother would be furious, but under the circumstances, Liz could care less.

The park worker ran over to Cece and Liz. His relaxed brown eyes opened wide while exuding sheer terror. In a guttural cry, he bellowed, "Is anyone hurt?" Pointing to a place near where they were standing, he added, "Y'all stand over there and keep a close eye on it. Uh oh! Look at them telltale markings and rings."

The girls eyed the pattern of chocolate kisses in a row along the serpent's back.

He continued, "That one is a danged copperhead. Those critters have been bad this year."

He repeated, "Is anyone hurt?"

"No, no snakebites, but frightened to death," a calm Liz replied.

The workman returned with a ragtag assortment of tools. The collection included a sharpened hoe, a long shovel, and an ancient leaf rake. Liz pointed at the slithering creature that moved several feet farther away. She volunteered at a veterinarian's clinic where she learned about snakes. Liz told Cece that the copperhead acted in self-defense from fear. Cece did not care. She felt she deserved this territory as much as that snake did! As she sat on the ground, Liz crossed her legs and pulled the quivering child to her in a tight embrace. They watched as the caretaker placed the squirming body of the headless snake in a garbage can. Cece's heart pounded like a bass drum. She squeezed against her cousin. Liz looked up and thanked the city worker for removing the serpent.

"There, there, honeybun, we won't let anything get you," Liz whispered.

Bit by bit, Cece calmed down, and her sobs lessened. Her viselike grip on her cousin's arm softened.

Cece whispered, "I love you, Liz. Thank you for protecting me!"

"Oh sweet little angel, I love you too!" Liz paused, thinking what to say next. "Now let's go find you an ice cream cone at home! What will you have, chocolate, or vanilla?"

Liz did not mind taking heat from her mother for spoiling the child's dinner.

Cece hesitated, and then murmured, "Chocolate."

Liz wiped the residual moisture from Cece's face as they arose. Cece tugged with tension on Liz's hand while motioning toward the azaleas.

Liz thought, *Did Cece want to return to the scene of her scuffle?*

The child whimpered in a raspy voice, "We can't leave the flowers."

Cece kept her eyes focused on the ground. Just in case she ran into another Mr. Squiggly. The two each collected the dropped blossoms. Liz noticed Cece's face and body lacked her earlier animation. The two walked in silence on the long sidewalk toward Liz's home. The rose-stained sunset illuminated the pathway. Cece's tight grip bonded to the older girl's free hand.

Brave Liz gained her cousin's unrelenting loyalty that day. Cece held the frightening but dear memory in her heart over the years.

Prologue 3

Seeking a Tiara

Six Years Later
Columbia, South Carolina

Cece surveyed the mass of people gathered in the cavernous auditorium. Her wide eyes focused across the patchwork of glittering formal dresses and black tuxedos. Cameras flashed and spotlights whirled in the suspenseful moments. As the emcee announced her name, each contestant glided to her assigned place on the stage. Guests cheered for their favorite. Cece's cousin Liz floated step-by-step to her designated stage marker. Seated in the elevated loge, the entire family gazed with pride on their preferred candidate.

Liz achieved high marks in most things she attempted due to her God-given gifts and despite her mother's goading. Beauty outside, phenomenal vocal talent, and a relentless drive for success, she had it all. Her personality drove her to treat life, even the simplest meeting, as a social event. Mundane occasions morphed into a party revolving around her. She craved attention and desired the spotlight more than most people. Compliments and praise were the fuel feeding the flames of her fragile ego.

Liz's peaceful smile conveyed supreme confidence flowing out of her soul. Her heart swirled as she prayed that the coveted crown would be hers. Her mind argued that the preparation, the fuss, and the work were worth the effort. The emcee prompted each finalist to take their stroll to the distant end of the stage platforms. Poised, Liz glided over a hundred feet of runway out into the approving crowd. Looking up, she caught Cece's eye and gave her a loving wink. Slowly revolving in place, with her chin pulled slightly over her right shoulder, Liz pitched a flirty smile to the judges. Her eyes sparkled. This was the moment to shine. Anticipation and suspense flooded into the tense audience as they expected the imminent announcement of a winner.

With hope for her cousin's success, Cece grabbed her mother's hand, as she heard, "Now is the time to announce the top three contestants and crown your new queen. May I have the envelope please?"

Chapter 1

Trouble in the Night

Monday, May 4, 1998
New Orleans, Louisiana

Half a lifetime passed. Now, Cece snuggled next to the love of her life, rugged Ross Turner, in the comfort of their rice-carved bed. They had enjoyed twenty-six years of marriage. Cece matured into a gorgeous brunette with twinkling emerald eyes. Her mysterious eyes assessed and grasped details of her surroundings. She watched, absorbed, and reacted to each movement within her world. Her cupid smile reflected a contentment she never dreamed she could reach. Her life was better than she imagined it could be. The Turners now called New Orleans, Louisiana, home.

They lived in a quaint brick cottage in the posh St. Charles Avenue district for twenty years. Gas lamps flickered warmly above their placid street. There the Turners embraced a devoted circle of neighbors. Cece, a trusted and loyal chum to her friends, showed her caring disposition by offering steady encouragement to others. She sent hand-penned notes and cards to co-workers, neighbors, and friends. Within the notes, she exposed her generous heart for the welfare of people. A dinosaur in the emerging computer world, she used email only for work projects. She possessed a sterling character and a sweet disposition. Cece dispensed fragments of her tender caring heart to touch many lives in the community through her volunteering spirit. She displayed quiet leadership in civic, social, and church organizations. As good a person as she appeared outside, inside she felt less than perfect.

She and Ross relished their move to the birthplace of jazz, the capital of gastronomy, and the home of Mardi Gras. They were believers in the Saints football team in the early days, although Cece secretly rooted for the Dallas Cowboys. Oh, how they enjoyed the town's offerings of unique eateries. Occasionally venturing into the gritty bowels of the urban jungle through its dark sides and blighted areas, the ride seemed worth the risks so that they could enjoy the ethnic and diverse cultures, cuisine, and music. Navigating street corners crowded with vampy hookers, homeless folk, and crack heads and other druggies, the couple experienced the underbelly of the old city in search of their latest restaurant discovery.

Cece blossomed in her prior professional work as an actuary. Her mathematical bent sharpened by her education at venerable Driesh College aided her in problem solving. Her analytical mind enabled her to perform an efficient schedule. She asserted herself in a quiet, sweet, yet stubborn way at work. Her instincts guided her to avoid trivial matters when choosing her battles. For issues close to Cece's heart, her associates learned her hot buttons and avoided them. Uninformed people thought Cece did not exert herself in a crisis, so they misinterpreted her quiet, watchful personality. She could conceal her Herculean efforts like a camouflaged reptile. She was not a braggart. When struggling with a dominant bossy person, Cece's quiet, stubborn nature protected her, like the hard shell of a tortoise.

When pressed under demanding conditions, she kept a calm facade despite her gut bursting with butterflies. Her internalized butterflies remained bottled-up until the troubling situation passed. In a crisis, Cece's exterior appeared placid as if she were a mallard floating on calm water. But on the inside, she looked like a duck furiously paddling her feet hidden under the water's surface. As distasteful events troubled Cece, red-circled eyes and tears gave clues to her emotional state. In her early years, her lack of self-esteem, meekness, and sense of privacy inhibited her from verbalizing her moods and sensations. Cece remained emotive in a quiet manner, yet she became more expressive verbally as she matured.

She left the work force the prior year, intending to pursue her personal interests of gardening, volunteering at charities, socializing, and being with her husband. Cece was not getting any younger and she wanted to enjoy this time of life.

Cece went to sleep, exhausted from a long yet fulfilling day and evening.

She began that day working the dirt in her flower gardens amid armies of annoying mosquitos. Over several hours, she placed three flats of blooms in finely sifted beds of soil. A steaming and relaxing bath in her new freestanding tub rewarded her hard work. As she pulled the soft towel of Egyptian cotton to wipe dry her tender body, Cece counted the angry welts from the bites of the little critters. She saw seven bites rising from her pale skin, despite her precautionary spray of DEET repellent. *The annoying skin bumps are a small price to pay, but the front-yard was presentable.* That afternoon, the neighborhood book club met in the Turner's home to discuss a new mystery book filled with intrigue, Wall Street mergers, and murders.

As she put the dishes away after the gathering, Cece smiled about her planned expected activities of the evening. Ross and she flamed the fuel of their

marriage with a date night each month somewhere
in the gritty neighborhoods of old New Orleans. Their
dates usually occurred on a Monday night to avoid
the tourist horde, which invaded the hoary city on
the weekends. The ancient streets had activity nightly
but the couple preferred tamer evenings. When Ross
arrived home from his work, the two drove the short
distance to the Vieux Carre. Ross parked next to the
old St Louis Cathedral and the couple walked across
Jackson Square. As they headed toward Royal Street, a
mix of buskers entertained the couple with improvised
jazz. One memorable youngster blasted a trumpet
while accompanied by a trio of brass musicians. Cece
and Ross tarried in front of a young lady sitting on
the sidewalk. The twenties-something woman with
hippie grade hair flowing to the middle of her back
strummed a red acoustic guitar. On her lap, a black
lab rested his head as the vocalist crooned a soulful
country ballad. Cece nudged Ross in the ribs while
she nodded at the open guitar case lid containing tips
from onlookers. Ross reached over and placed several
dollars carefully in the case. Cece and Ross unwound
from the day's cares at their favorite penthouse bar
atop the historic Monteleone hotel. A theme of antique
carousels saturated the nostalgic club. In the center,
they stepped onto a full size revolving Merry-Go-Round
bar. The revolving counter beckoned patrons to its
seats with a view of the surrounding patrons, the
bartenders, and a panorama of the city. The room's
perimeter of seamless windows afforded a romantic
vista of flickering lights. In front of the patrons stood
framed placards proclaiming, "Laissez les bon temps
rouler!"

The couple compared the hubbub of their busy
day. Cece scratched her bites as she engaged Ross
with a summary of the interesting new book her group

discussed. Mysteries involving Wall Street captured Ross's interest, as he taught finance as a tenured professor at the small private Iberville University located only a few blocks from the Superdome.

Turning philosophical as he scanned the glittering city below, he then mused to Cece, "Ah, we have it good here, don't we? Life is spinning like a balanced carousel, isn't it? What more could we want out of life?"

Cece thought hard about it. *How about a modern kitchen Ross.*

"Drink up. Let's move to the main course. I made dinner reservations for twenty minutes from now."

He pointed at the placard and added, "As this sign says, let the good times roll!"

They exited the old hotel to the refrains of *When the Saints Go Marching In* played by a jazz band directly in front of them. The members of a wedding party streamed out of the hotel and formed the first line behind the musicians. Two people led the procession while raising aloft black and white umbrellas as if drum majors. Behind the wedding party a second line formed, comprised of family and friends. The crowd shook excitedly to the beat of the jazzy music. As the tempo sped up, Ross nodded at Cece.

"They're going our way, let's join them."

Cece winked at Ross as she whispered, "But Ross, you know I am not always a saint."

Along Royal Street for two blocks, the Turners sang, clapped, and cheered. Cece learned from one of the twenty-somethings in the crowd that the wedding was a destination affair thrown together by an eloping bride and groom. She quickly dismissed a flashback to a similar event in her cousin Liz's past. Soon the party arrived at Brennan's, their favorite Creole restaurant. Cece's mouth watered as she anticipated the tasty file gumbo and succulent seafood the historic restaurant offered. The entertaining evening unfolded just as she had wished with good food, drink, music, and most of all, her rock, Ross. Three hours later, they arrived at their home, satiated from the treats of the evening.

She lay motionless in their vintage bed at 11:00 pm when the bedroom phone rang. The ring shocked both Cece and Ross from their deep slumber. *Who would call at this hour?* She climbed out of bed in a fog. She took small steps toward the blue princess phone on an antique dressing table. Cece had inherited the oaken heirloom and her prized bed from her grandmother. She sensed the aches of the day pulsing through her torso as she reacted to the pain. The mosquito bites itched with relentless distraction.

She lifted the blue receiver and said, "Hello, yes, Cecilia Turner here. Yes, I am one of her first cousins. Who is calling? No! Why, please tell me, what happened to Liz?"

A pause and then Cece screamed, "Oh, God no, how terrible! Yes, No."

The caller's litany of puzzling questions continued. Cece's green eyes spilled droplets on her cheeks. *No, this could not be her Liz that she adored and loved. Tell me this heartbreak is not happening.* The shock of the instantaneous report of her loved one's death overpowered Cece. Her heart pounded as she tried to spill out her sense of loss.

Emotionally, she sobbed as she continued to listen. Liz's two lifetime friends, Bill and Nancy Mayer, explained an unfolding tragedy. The couple calling from Charlotte once attended Blaketon College with their classmate Liz. The small prestigious college was nestled in the Appalachian foothills in tiny Blaketon, North Carolina.

Nancy said, "Yes, one's worse fear. We expected you did not know, Cecilia. This is so unfortunate! Liz and

I first became friends in the freshman Shakespeare class. Our friendship continued to grow after we pledged our sorority. We still socialized after graduation. Ah, gorgeous Liz. I remember her beauty pageants. She was such a rare and gifted person."

Cece smiled for a moment. In her mind, she pictured when she had seen the glittering rhinestone tiara atop Liz's head. How it had sparkled! Cece and her family attended the prestigious pageants as moral support for dear Liz.

"Please call me Cece. When did she die?"

In a long slow Southern drawl, Bill explained, "Two days ago. After a 9-1-1 call, the local Mary's Island police and EMTs came in to retrieve her body on Saturday morning. A detective explained to us that a friend found Liz submerged in her hot tub at home. Have you ever been to Liz's mansion in South Carolina?"

Cece replied, "Yes, the first time was eight or so years ago. We usually visit when we go to the beach there. But, over the years, we've shared a boatload of letters and cards. We talked on the phone a lot."

"The detective described the scene as horrific, in fact, pretty unbelievable."

Liz's classic home sprawled in the center of a posh golf and beach resort called Mary's Island. The idyllic community teemed with pricey mansions, beach houses, quaint golf cottages, and boxy condominiums. The planned development rested on a natural atoll south of Myrtle Beach. A village-like atmosphere reminded Cece of both Liz and her aunt's refined taste. A bevy of quaint shops awaited discriminating shoppers.

Bill continued, "The detective researched names in Liz's address book and called us to see if we could help. She asked if we knew any family. It took time, but we found your number a few minutes ago in a list Liz had shared with us. This was a tragic ending to this beautiful woman's life."

Nancy asked, "Can you call us about the funeral arrangements? I'm sure I can spread the word to Liz's friends and former classmates."

The prospect of planning a funeral, much less one so far away in South Carolina, seemed daunting. Cece requested the Mayer's contact information.

Cece asked if they knew whether Liz still nurtured a relationship with a long-term boyfriend. She heard morsels of information from family scuttlebutt after Liz's four divorces. *How deep was this new connection? Did it still exist?*

Bill replied, "Yes, the boyfriend found her lifeless body. His name is Joey Broyer, yet his phone number is not on this list. Hmm, I suppose they could have become an item after she prepared the list. Why don't you contact the local authorities in Mary's Island? The detective gave us her office phone number."

"Yes, I need that number."

After she wrote it in a scruffy blue notebook, she recited the phone number back.

A tsunami of questions made Cece's head swim. Where do we have a funeral and how to pay for it? Which cemetery? How elaborate? What about a will? Would there even be enough cash for a proper funeral for the former beauty queen? What are the chances this might be somebody else's responsibility? Why now? Cece knew the Blaketon alumni, especially the Greeks, were like family. Someone from Liz's family must do the heavy lifting to arrange the burial. She remembered now she had promised Liz years earlier she would help when the time came.

Cece pondered, *Surely I can handle this crisis.* Naïvely, she remained clueless in the moment.

She hung up the phone as she said, "Good-bye, I'll let you know."

Her rigid and perplexed husband sat upright with both feet on the floor. Ross Turner scratched his balding and graying head as he wondered aloud who disturbed them at this god-forsaken time of night. Cece sobbed big tears, which alarmed stoic Ross. His powerful body displayed panic. With wide-open blue eyes, and a quizzical look on his furrowed brow, he stretched to relieve his tense muscles. As she blubbered through Bill and Nancy's conversation, he reached to embrace her. He told her how sorry he felt for her loss.

Then he whispered, "I love you, Cece."

As he eavesdropped, he had felt an intuitive alarm. From the disturbing phone call, he felt his emotions move through a descending scale of distress, dread, loathing, and revulsion. Unsure of where these contemptible feelings arose, he confessed to her he did not relish this new challenge. Yet, they must do the right thing! He longed to make his sweet Cece happy. Repeatedly, a thought reverberated throughout his soul: *This does not sound good.*

Chapter 2

Scratching the Surface

The Next Morning
Cece's Kitchen

Seated in her happy place at the bay window in her worn kitchen, Cece hoped her handy-man husband might modernize it soon. It was her nest where she read the morning *Times-Picayune* newspaper and watched the outside world. In this cozy niche, she relaxed and studied busy squirrels, an air corps of colorful, chirping bluebirds, and lush blooming foliage. Meanwhile, she sipped steaming coffee in her over-sized indigo mug. The hot liquid poked holes in the morning haze of her mind and coalesced her random thoughts. She savored this favorite morning routine. Nothing, not the gym, not bridge, nor telephone chats with friends, surpassed it. Nothing topped living in this moment, except maybe having Ross here. How secure he made her feel!

The ceramic cup belonged to Cece's late father, Ben. The mug was a souvenir he had brought back from his time in the war. The two brothers, her father and Liz's father Charles, had served in the Army Corps of Engineers in Asia during WWII. Her dear mother had remembered to save this treasure for Cece after he died. Daily, she met her first few waking moments savoring the tantalizing aroma and rich flavors. The simple ritual reminded her of earlier times at the kitchen table surrounded by the wisdom spoken by her dad. *Oh, how she yearned for his wisdom now.*

Cece's breakfast remained untouched on her plate. She nursed a glass of chilled orange juice alongside a bowl of raspberry yogurt. Fresh strawberries with a touch of Buzzfield Apiary honey glistened in a yellow Fiesta ware cereal bowl. Cece dialed her small cell phone. Seconds later the Nokia device connected to the Mary's Island Police Department.

A female voice rattled out, "Police Department, do you have an emergency?"

The voice was pert, and insolent. Cece's brain registered, *This woman has an attitude.*

"No, no, may I speak to Detective Molly Brinkman?" Cece countered.

"She's not in now; this is the dispatcher, do you wish to leave a message or call back?"

"My cousin, I understand, died there. I have several questions I hope your department can answer."

With a kinder, gentler tone, the dispatcher replied, "I'm sorry for your loss. And who is your cousin?"

"Liz, ah, Elizabeth Perkins."

A noticeable pause elapsed, and then Cece perceived a sigh.

"Poor Liz. I will have Detective Brinkman call you. What phone number is best to reach you?"

Cece recited her phone number and ended the call.

She thought, *Well this call was not very fruitful, but it is a start! Hmm, the locals knew Liz; or maybe the dispatcher heard the story. Mary's Island paled in size to her beloved New Orleans. Everyone on the island knew everyone else and his or her house cat.*

Fifteen minutes later, as Cece refilled her coffee mug and sat down, her phone rang in her pocket, which startled her.

A sharp staccato voice said, "Detective Molly Brinkman here, Mary's Island Police Department. Did you call me?"

Cece whispered, "Yes, I did."

"I understand you want information about Liz Perkins. Who are you?"

Cece clarified her long relationship with her late cousin. She added details on the family members. To add credibility to her call, she added that she was a professional, an actuary. She hoped it might garner her more information. Cece ended her fruitful career after twenty-five years at St. Charles Life Insurance Company. Desperate to get the skinny on Liz, she became more direct in her queries to the detective.

She asked, "Do you know of funeral arrangements for Liz? How did she die?"

Detective Brinkman divulged only the bare facts as she responded, "We are sorry ma'am. There are no funeral arrangements yet. Family members of the deceased must call the morgue. The family arranges the release of the body to a funeral home. Then morticians take it over from there. Release of a cadaver occurs only after payment of the storage fees. Our team is still investigating how Ms. Perkins died. We are awaiting toxicology tests and the autopsy data. Plan on at least twelve weeks before the autopsy results come back."

Cece interrupted. "Can't you tell me the cause?"

"Since this investigation is active, I cannot comment on the cause of her death. We gathered sketchy information from witnesses who described activities preceding her death. The case is still inconclusive. I will tell you her living conditions were disgusting. From what I saw and have heard, you had best prepare yourself."

Cece felt a lightning-fast streak of terror run up her spine as she blinked a tear from her eye. *What does disgusting mean, in that gorgeous home? Cadaver . . . sounds so impersonal. Don't local taxes pay for the morgue services? Why do I have to pay storage fees? Goodness, by the time we retrieve her, surely her beautiful skin will have turned purple. She will be all wrinkled and crusty. Should Liz have a closed casket or cremation?* Cece's heart pounded.

Cece was relentless. Detective Brinkman offered that a friend, a boyfriend named Joey Broyer, discovered Liz. The boyfriend said Liz fell into her hot tub and when he found her, he called the police who summoned the EMTs and the fire department.

Cece interjected, "I so am thankful for his being there to find her."

"Since her passing, Mr. Broyer has been living in the house while taking care of cats that were Liz's or his pets."

"How can I reach this Mr. Broyer to inquire or help with funeral arrangements?"

"Hold on, let me look in her file. Ah, here's his cell number."

Cece scribbled his name and phone number. She planned to call him later, but not now. She could not face it yet. Her interminable inquiry continued.

"How many pets are there?"

"Joey told us there were twenty-two. In the house, our team found sixteen cats alive and two deceased. That is eighteen. More outside but that is what we found when our team investigated. Mr. Broyer insisted Liz had asked him to care for the cats. That many cats running loose, you see how unpleasant the place is. We removed the dead ones, and he kept the others."

Cece gasped. Her imagination went wild at the detective's description. Deep in her heart, she loved cats so much that she had adopted three rescue cats. Her two Persians and a Tabby owned her now. She loved them almost as much as she loved Ross. First hand, she knew caring for any extra pets presented problems in the form of more residue and mess than she tolerated.

Detective Brinkman continued, "So, where do you live, Mrs. Turner?"

Cece observed that Ms. Molly Brinkman is not from the South. Not that she was judging. Cece thought Southern women as herself chose their words and added a touch of sugarcoating.

"We live in New Orleans, too far away to respond on one-day's notice."

"Until you called we have not connected with any family. Are you her only relative?"

"I am sure I am her closest kinfolk. She had one other living cousin. Her immediate family has passed, all of them."

Cece held back one question. *Does it look accidental to you?*

"Our city's Director of Zoning needs help. His note requests that Liz's family sift through her personal items. He recommends the securing of family heirlooms, keepsakes, and valuables. Evidence of the house restoration must be available soon. If you will help, please call Mr. Kerry Tyler who oversees the serious violations of the city code. Mr. Tyler is out of town until next week. You or someone else in the family needs to connect with him."

Cece held her measured breath, clenched her jaw, and tightened her glossed lips. She reviewed the detective's comments. Her dusty brain replayed a long-ago conversation when Liz had asked Cece to bury her. *The request carried a new complication. Liz's simple burial wish had morphed into home repair and cleaning out of the estate.*

Butterflies fluttered in her abdomen as she added the phone number in her notebook. She displayed a calm demeanor on the outside, while her thoughts registered internal doubt about how, or where to begin.

"That's all I have ma'am. If you have no more questions, I will call at this number if I need information."

Cece asked, "Yes, and may I call you?"

"Anytime."

Cece pressed the end call button, rose from her chair, and moved to a red and gold sofa in the living room. As her face pressed into a pillow, copious tears flowed. She cried her worn body to sleep.

Chapter 3

Differing Opinions

Friday, May 8, 1998
The Highway to Baton Rouge, Louisiana

F riday arrived, gloomy and stormy. Torrents of chilling rainwater gathered in pools on the Turner's lush lawn. The old street in front of their cozy home overflowed. Impulsively, Cece wanted to visit her mother Isabelle and stepfather Harold again in Baton Rouge. Despite the nasty weather, they planned to leave before the afternoon rush hour. Cece thought the four of them could mull ideas and resolve their dilemma. As the closest ones left in Liz's family, they had to do something.

While she prepared for the trip, she mused over her semi-annual childhood visits to see her Carolina relatives. Her parents had packed their old Ford with a blanket, pillows, food, luggage, and a gallon thermos of water. These long drives, before interstate highways, wound through the five states from Louisiana to the Atlantic Ocean. The poor rural roads and distance limited the frequency of their visits. As a result, personal contact with the distant family between trips relied on expensive telephone calls or snail mail.

The closeness to the white sandy beaches enhanced the time spent in South Carolina for Cece and her family. Remembrances of those past trips filled Cece's nose with a smell of the salty ocean air. She sensed ocean ions magically attracted to her body. She imagined reclining on blue canvas beach chairs under a bright multi-colored umbrella. The crash of the frothy waves ran between her toes as she dug foot-sized caves in the sand. Steel-gray gulls and squawky terns retreated and advanced over the wet sand in search of sea morsels.

Cece snapped out of her temporary trance when Ross returned from work. Today, Ross and she would drive merely a fraction of the Carolina trips through Louisiana's bayous to Baton Rouge, Cece's childhood home. They packed his Mercedes Benz SL 500 and pulled out into the rain-soaked street around 4:00 pm, later than she wished. Ross loved the feel of the black convertible as it hugged the open road. Heavier clumps of the storm had moved on, yet ponds of water remained on the shoulders and at dips in the highway. The rain rhythm on the ragtop roof lent white noise to their journey. Raindrops coalesced in beads on the polished surfaces. Northbound, the drive took an hour and a half in good traffic, but not today. Cece yearned to make this travel time productive. She kept in her lap several magazines to read over the weekend. By her feet lay a sack of birthday and friendship cards. She addressed them to put in the mail. The inclement weather and snail-paced traffic due to wrecks impeded their progress. The afternoon sky remained dark. Ominous storm clouds moved over the slow stream of vehicles. When Cece sealed her last card, she delayed the next and only chore remaining. Her worse trait besieged her again. She sabotaged herself with procrastination and deferred completing distasteful tasks. She swallowed, and then dialed the number on her cellphone. A twinge of innate resistance hit her as she did not look forward to hearing an account of Liz's demise, but she had to do it. She waited for Joey Broyer to answer. She sensed mystery and even darkness. *How will this man react? Thus far, he's an enigma to me.*

He answered on the fourth ring. At first, the chatter seemed civil enough. They exchanged general information. Mutual condolences, names, relationships, even Cece's cell number. Cece let Joey ramble as he described what happened that awful night. The more he talked, the less sense Cece could make of his babbling. Cece noticed the angry sky had morphed to pitch black. Random flashes of intense lightning lit the heavens. The car wipers struggled to keep pace with the new deluge.

He muttered, "Yeah, Liz had mentioned you. Did you know she and I had become close? Do you have any clue how heartbroken I am? I loved Liz with all my heart. She and I reveled the night before she left us, and the next morning I found her."

He sobbed something unintelligible. For longer than Cece could endure, a depressed Joey threw himself a pity party. He dove into pointless self-introspection. Cece interrupted Joey's lamentations by shifting the focus off himself to Liz. Liz's death saddened Cece and broke her heart too. With teardrops on her cheek, she queried what thoughts he had for her burial.

Joey said, "I want to never bury Liz. Her body should stay above ground. Don't you believe that if you bury a person in the earth, they are dead? I mean, really dead! Why, then it is really over, right? Instead, if we place her body in a mausoleum, she can live forever. Do you catch my drift? If she is above the ground in a sacred room, I know that she and her beautiful presence will live on with us."

Cece raised her red, stressed eyes.

She glared open mouthed at Ross and then pronounced a prolonged and dubious, "Okay."

She remained speechless as she reflected, *Joey sounds drunk . . . or depressed . . . or both.*

Cece tried to reason, "But she is dead, Joey. We must get on with a funeral."

She rolled her eyes as she thought, *Joey, get a grip!*

Distraught Joey ignored her plea. Since Liz's death, his sense of reality had deflated to grief and delusion.

Ross lifted his intent gaze off the I-12 expressway and turned his rugged face toward Cece. He kept one eye on the road. With the other, he detected her facial movements coupled with more salty teardrops. She pulled the phone from her ear. Her hands rotated in a motion that appeared as if she were choking the gray cell phone.

She ended the call saying, "Thanks for your time, too."

Cece was frantic. She shook her head with near violence. With her fingers on the phone, she clicked off the call before he spewed more nonsense in their conversation. Exhausted, Cece squealed out a blood-curdling scream.

Ross glanced at her again, this time aghast. While paying attention to his driving, Ross's brain registered a random thought. *Man, the only time I remember Cece screaming this loud was when our old home caught fire. What did this dude say?*

"Tell me about it honey; do I need to pull off the road?"

Between sobs, she muttered, "No, no, he is so . . . different!"

Another thought followed immediately. *He sounded incoherent. What issues does he have?*

She unfolded the jumbled train of illogical dialogue that Joey hurled at her. Liz, her death, his vague interment plans, and his ideas of the afterlife.

"He will not make any real final arrangements. Claims he is upset. Since he remains immobilized, we have a job to do. I will call the attorney whose name he mumbled. He said Liz consulted the firm for a legal matter."

Cece sighed with the realization she stepped up to face her worse fears and had made the phone call. While the conversation raised many more questions and answered none, at least it provided an opening for her to go ahead with Liz's burial. *Somebody has to!*

The rain subsided. They passed the bottlenecks created by several accidents. The traffic improved to a more normal flow as they neared the Baton Rouge city limits. Cece lifted the cell phone again to call her mother about their impending arrival. When they pulled into the circular driveway of Cece's childhood home, Cece saw her mother and stepfather sitting in rocking chairs on the covered porch. The long roof overhang gave ample dry outdoor space at the humble saltbox cottage. A light precipitation continued, which blurred the windshield image of the aged couple. Petite, silver-haired Isabelle waved at the arriving passengers. Harold McCracken, gray-haired and thin as a rail, towered as a giant over "Izzy". Both were seventy-five years old. Harold and Izzy married one year after Cece's dad died in 1990. Like her niece Liz, Izzy wasted no time remarrying either. She had known Harold since their college days in the 1930s when the two of them reigned as homecoming queen and king.

Cece and her mother hugged. The daughter sobbed as they consoled each other. Izzy opened a new package of tissues. Each dried their swollen eyes. Ross and Harold unloaded the convertible as the women dished out a hot savory homemade dinner. Isabelle scooped steaming chicken and dumplings out of a blue antique tureen. Each place setting had a small bowl of cooked turnip greens. On a wooden cutting board sat a loaf of homemade sourdough bread, soft butter, and homemade fig jam. A coconut cream pie with real meringue awaited them on the old dining room sideboard. Isabelle knew her daughter's favorite comfort foods. After Harold's simple prayer of grace, the four lifted their cloth napkins. For two hours, Cece held the elder couple spellbound with her dilemma until she announced, "Let's have some of that pie!"

Chapter 4

Phone Calls and Dreams

Monday, May 11, 1998, 7:30 am
The Highway from Baton Rouge to New Orleans

Ross and Cece prepared to return to their home in New Orleans early. Dark skies pregnant with rain threatened them. Cece did not relish the work ahead, but she felt encouraged. The wise counsel from her experienced parents emboldened her.

In her usual shotgun seat, Cece motioned to Ross that her abdomen ached with queasiness.

She breathed, "I cannot call that Joey Broyer again."

She cracked the tinted car window for fresh air, since it was not yet raining. Ross pondered a moment. *What is up with Cece? Did she eat spoiled food? Is she going to foul my car? Is she pregnant?* As the morning unfurled, she explained that she was a basket of nerves. He noticed her increased moodiness since the Mayer's disturbing phone call about Liz.

Cece commented, "Here goes."

Ross saw on her notepad a scribbled phone number for Kerry Tyler. His blue eyes alternated between the highway and the car's digital clock. It was an hour later in the Myrtle Beach time zone. He deduced that the director of the County Property Zoning Office should be at work by now.

Anxiously, Cece glanced at Ross, the interstate highway traffic, and then dialed her phone. When the phones connected, a gruff male bass voice resounded, "Hello."

"Hi, please let me introduce myself. This is Cece Turner. I am a first cousin of Liz Perkins, who died last week. I understand you want to talk to someone in her family."

"Sure, Mrs. Turner, this is Kerry Tyler, the zoning department head. On behalf of Mary's Island, please accept my sympathy to you for the untimely death of Mrs. Perkins."

"Thank you. How can I help you?"

"Thank you for your cooperation. We have several things we must discuss. Can you send us a record of Liz's next of kin, to get the family's help? Second, we need to brief you about the condition of her property."

"Mr. Tyler, do you mind if I put you on speaker phone? Can my husband Ross listen to your comments?"

"No problem, ma'am."

Cece fumbled with the tiny keys on the device. After a moment, her red-painted index nail depressed the speaker button. Ross observed her fingers shaking.

"You can start with me. I am her closest first cousin. We have one other cousin, but I am sure there has been no interaction between him and Liz for years. For one thing, she never talked about visiting with the other cousin and I know he's not much into family affairs. Liz's parents, Aunt Camilla and Uncle Charles, are dead and she had one sibling who died as an infant. Thus, you could say she grew up as an only child. She had several husbands, four to be exact; those marriages have ended."

"Can I email you our forms to document the family as you know it? Complete and notarize them, then return them by snail-mail."

"Sure, I can do that."

After the two exchanged email addresses, Kerry continued.

"Thanks, I'll send the forms when we finish this conversation. Last night, one of Liz's meddling neighbors tried to enter a side door of her house. They never kept it locked. She took a step in before she encountered an awful stench. The overwhelming odor overcame her, so her husband called 9-1-1. After our local police investigated, they called us."

Puzzled, Cece reacted, "Mr. Tyler, how does that concern me?"

Kerry stammered. "Mrs. Turner, I find it difficult to tell you this, but I must. Ms. Perkin's house is uninhabitable and borders on biohazard status. From the evidence, we concluded the occupants were both object hoarders and animal hoarders."

Ross and Cece glanced at each other with puzzled looks on their faces. Ross shrugged.

Kerry continued, "I will spare you the details for now. You or other family members need to collect the keepsakes, jewelry, and valuables. Store them somewhere for safekeeping to distribute to the rightful heirs later. Otherwise, there may be theft or pilferage."

Cece interrupted, "Do you mean someone needs to come to Mary's Island?"

With a sense of urgency in his comments, Kerry replied, "Yes, ma'am. Please let me continue. My description cannot convey what we have here. I am assuming that you knew she kept many cats."

"I just learned about the cats from the detective, last week."

"The cats made their messes. General squalor covers the entire house. You might say the house is in total chaos! The situation is far worse than when the police removed Liz's body earlier. Last night the police encountered Joey Broyer on the floor of a bedroom. A Scotch bottle and empty beer cans encircled his comatose body. Counting all the empty cans, he had consumed a half-case of beer over some period. His small refrigerator contained more unopened beer cans. Spilled booze, blood and feces mingled on the carpet. The EMTs diagnosed the victim's initial problem as a diabetic coma. While drinking is not a crime, his abuse endangered his health. The EMTS also noticed that the cats. . . ."

Cece cut off Kerry in mid-sentence. Her mind replayed her wretched conversation with Joey three days before.

"I am sorry Mr. Tyler, but Joey and I talked this past Friday, and it was freaky. This conversation is making me relive that creepy experience. Why was he there? What do you know about the cats?"

"Sometimes Joey lives out of his travel trailer and his van at remote sites. After Liz's removal, he had taken over Liz's house, claiming to care for the many cats. We are not sure who owns them. The assumption is that they were in her house; hence, they are hers, eh? When the EMTs picked him up last night, we removed twenty live cats in the house. Don't forget two dead ones were taken out last week when Liz's body was discovered."

Cece nodded, "Twenty-two?"

"Yes, ma'am, dead or alive that accounts for twenty-two critters."

Kerry continued, "We cannot guarantee that Joey will not return to the house. We are offering you an opportunity to protect valuables that should go to the family such as silver, clothing, and antiques. We have sealed the doors to prevent theft. Inside the house, the things in it will continue to deteriorate."

"Where are the cats now?"

"At the Georgetown Animal Rescue Center. Most of Liz's cats are sick. The vet said many would not survive. The clinic is charging ten dollars per day per cat as the base overnight boarding cost. Specific medical care is extra."

Always quick with math, Cece thought, *Twenty cats times ten dollars per day.*

She gasped and shouted, "Over $200 a day for boarding and medicine? This is so overwhelming! How will we ever work through this?"

"At our official request, we ask that you or a designee put the keepsake assets in a safe place for the family. The house itself is substandard per our zoning codes. The heirs must correct the issues and then decide what to do with her property."

Cece saw in her mind, *Hundreds, maybe thousands, of dollar bills flying out a window.*

When a light sprinkle of rain fell, Ross turned the car wipers on an intermittent setting. Cece watched Ross continue his self-imposed silence.

Kerry declared, "I cannot give you legal advice. Find out if she had a will. The family can ask the judge to let someone administer her estate and probate her will. Then get the home up to code, sell it, and distribute her estate. The restoration company might recommend that you level it.

"Regardless, someone must come over to Mary's Island as soon as possible. Whoever comes will need protective gear such as facemasks, gloves, antibacterial hand lotion, boxes, and tape. Either bring it with you or buy it here. Bring an old pair of shoes to wear that you can throw away. Mrs. Turner, I will go over more details when you or the other cousin you mentioned arrives here."

Remembering that Joey had mentioned a lawyer's name, Cece also asked Kerry to reveal what if he knew anything about the attorney.

She probed, "Do you have any idea who Liz's attorney may have been?"

"No, check the legal papers and mail in the house. You might detect helpful clues."

Cece asked curiously, "Where is Joey now?"

"He is a sick man. We took him to the hospital."

"Thank you for the information, Kerry. I suppose I will be the family representative. Ross and I can get to Mary's Island next week. Is that soon enough?"

Cece looked at her Day-Timer calendar and asked, "Can I see you at 9:00 am on Monday, May 18?"

"Yes ma'am, we are very sorry for this inconvenience to you. Since you're helping us, you can bring the completed forms with you. Thank you for helping us."

"Good-bye."

"Good-bye."

Cece hung up the phone. She shrieked another blood-curdling scream.

She thought, *Poor Liz! We have to give her a proper burial. In addition, what must I do for those poor sick cats? They pose a huge health risk and their condition may be too expensive to continue their care.* Exhaustion and doubt enveloped Cece.

Cece realized she had committed Ross's time and help without asking him. Yet, she held to the adage it was easier to do something, then beg for forgiveness instead of requesting permission in advance.

As she stared at Ross, she said, "You heard we need to gather up Liz's valuable things. Can you go with me next week? Why don't we plan to stay a couple weeks near Mary's Island to air out?"

Cece did not realize how prophetic her comment was.

His head spun as he tried to remember what was on his calendar and what he needed to do. Ross repeated the words to himself, *Everything is happening too fast.*

He analyzed what was in his memory in the short term and replied, "I'm not busy at work. We don't begin the summer session for three weeks. None of my consulting clients are clamoring with projects."

He had only one major task to finish this week; that was posting his students' final grades. As a persistent problem solver, Professor Ross Turner attempted to answer complex issues without drama. Unlike emotional Cece, he coached and advised others while he exhibited little sentiment. He was a true stoic. Time and efficiency were important to him. His highest priority was Cece, followed by his work, and his students. He poured himself into these, without frivolous distractions. New acquaintances might say he bordered on being boring, but no, he was deep. Whatever made Cece happy became his mantra, even at the risk of his health, his finances, and his own sanity. The two of them were opposites. She knew everybody's business without effort. He often wondered how and why she did that. Then he remembered that Cece watched and listened, her best traits, unlike Ross and most other men.

As they made their way to New Orleans, Cece yawned several times. Over the past week, Cece's sleep patterns changed, starting with the phone call she received from Bill and Nancy Mayer. She used to sleep eight hours in undisturbed peace. Even Ross's noise while preparing for work seldom disrupted her sleep. Since Liz's death, she internalized the tragedy, reducing her nightly sleep to four hours. Anxiety, restlessness, and insomnia pierced her psyche. She experienced a continuum of pleasant memories to disturbing dreams and nightmares.

Eager to return home, Cece looked at her wristwatch. A large green sign on the side of the highway announced sixty miles to New Orleans. The raindrops grew into a steady flow. She closed her heavy eyelids. Her ears registered the monotonous click-clack of the windshield wipers. A slight vibration of the tires on the weathered highway rocked Cece. As Ross rounded a gentle bend in the road, Cece's head rolled to the left side. Exhaustion overcame her and cast her into a deep dream focused on her first visit to Liz's mansion on Mary's Island. Cece's mind reverted to eight years earlier, after her birth father died.

Her dream panned the difficult life event for Izzy and Cece. She regretted not getting to say a last good-bye to the one they loved so much. He had collapsed with a severe heart attack while mowing grass in the front yard. A neighbor saw the elderly man fall as he clutched his chest. Milliseconds later, Ben Perkins was dead.

The close-knit family gathered for his final rites. But Liz and Carl, her final husband, were absent. Liz's current marriage with Carl continued as the longest with any of the four husbands, almost twenty years. Camilla, Liz's mother, shared that the couple were away on an anniversary celebration trip to Italy.

After the funeral, Aunt Camilla remained with Izzy for two weeks before returning to her home in Charleston. Herself, now also a widow, she felt compelled to tell Izzy of the benefits and risks of widowhood. With the many opportunities to gossip, Camilla filled Izzy's ears with snippets of Carl's shortcomings. During her last night at Izzy's, a tipsy Camilla divulged more details. She acknowledged that Liz had asked a lawyer to start secret divorce proceedings when they return from the Italy trip. Camilla blamed Carl for the failure of the marriage. Camilla pleaded for secrecy as she filled her sister-in-law's listening ears. Izzy winked with assurances that the secret remained safe with her. The next weekend, the hush-hush news passed like a baton from Izzy to Cece. Cece was under strict instructions not to share it with anyone else, including Ross. Izzy then told Cece they both needed a break. She announced she planned to use a minuscule fraction of the generous life insurance benefits to treat them to a family vacation at Myrtle Beach.

Izzy rationalized the idea to Cece, saying, "You and I relish the fresh air and wide sandy beaches. The Carolina shore will help cure our blues and grief."

A few weeks after Izzy's announcement, Ross, Cece, and her mother started the long two-day drive to Myrtle Beach. Their automobile propelled over miles of bayou waters, rolling hills, flat cotton fields, and the low country. Finally, the three reached the evolving landscapes of sandy beaches and crashing waves south of Myrtle Beach.

During the tedious drive, nosy Izzy confided to Cece that she wanted to meet and see Liz's fourth husband first hand.

Cece replied, "I remember when Ross and I visited them as newlyweds. Carl seemed to be a nice chap."

The three pulled into their oceanfront condominium and unloaded the car. Izzy called Liz to confirm the dinner plans that night.

Liz begged, "Aunt Izzy, please join us here instead of at the restaurant. Mama made an unexpected drive up from Charleston today."

Izzy raised her eyebrows and smiled.

To feign a weak protest to Liz, Izzy said, "Isn't that too much bother for you?"

Besides meeting Carl, she wanted to see Liz's palatial digs Camilla had bragged about, as she was prone to do. When she hung up, Izzy informed each of them to bring a change of clothes for a fun time in Liz's pool and hot tub.

Izzy quipped, "Why miss a pool party with Liz?"

Only five miles from the condominium to Liz's home, they drove through the picturesque village of Mary's Island. The trip carried them past schools, the city hall, and charming shops that beckoned to Cece and Izzy.

Ross turned the car into a lengthy driveway. Cece and Izzy envied the ancient massive live oaks draped with gray Spanish moss. Several grottos of wind-gnarled trees framed the classic tobacco plantation mansion made of red brick with white wooden trim. Wrought-iron benches under the trees provided a place of reflection. Dual symmetrical white wrought-iron stairways descended from the second-floor balcony. The stairs curved outward, then inward to meet at the bottom steps. The home portrayed Southern elegance and privilege.

Aware of her own humble living conditions, Izzy asked Cece, "Why this massive house for two people?"

Cece surmised Liz must have cleaned out the financial resources of her earlier husbands. In spite of her love and earlier admiration for her cousin, Cece's respect of Liz plummeted over the years.

Carl and his mother-in-law Camilla met the visitors at the front door and ushered them into the formal living room.

Izzy attempted to size up Carl's personality based on her first impressions. She tried to relax despite the propaganda Camilla had fed to her a few weeks earlier.

Overwhelmed by the opulence of the place, Cece's mother commented, "Those trendy home décor magazines should feature your beautiful home."

The walls, carpet, and furniture in the home featured muted shades of ecru, even the chandeliers in the living and dining rooms. While studying the twin chandeliers, Cece noted they featured the sole accent in either room. The ecru iron chandeliers had small pale pink metal bows on each of the eight arms.

With aplomb and visual fanfare, Liz staged a dramatic entrance. Framed by an arched doorway, Liz sparkled in her pale pink chiffon dress, accented by a liquid silver necklace holding a solitary pink sapphire stone. The soft dress form fitted her curvy hips, long tanned legs, and full bosom. Despite the years and failed marriages that marred her psyche, she maintained her stunning features. Cece stood in amazement. She recognized that Liz was the focal ornament of the entire house. Everything else was sterile and colorless, except for her radiance, necklace, dress, and the iron bows. Only a few new pounds betrayed Liz's outward looks. Her glossy platinum blonde hair shone brilliant as ever. Liz's soft radiant skin glowed in the dim light. Her lips glistened with a fresh coating of shimmering pink lipstick. Liz still had spunk, determination, and a flash in her eyes, but these features now dulled in comparison to Cece's earlier remembrances.

Up to this point, Liz's path had been as up and down as it gets. She had traveled the zeniths and depths of existence while she trekked the world and experienced life. Her professional career as a motivational speaker and ad personality had slowed, however she could find work when she wanted it. Lately, Liz's path sped downward more often due to her creeping age and her own demons.

Associates differed in their attitudes towards Liz. With many acquaintances, but not friends, she struggled to recall their names as she once could. The most common exposure of this fault occurred when she ran into these people at the store or at social engagements. She greeted them with loose Southern terms such as sweetie, honeybun, or sweet pea. Occasionally, this loose greeting offended people who considered it superficial or insincere, but she brushed their reaction off. Others thought her flashy conduct screamed *look*

at how amazing I am. But most of her friends did not
dismiss her as a showoff. Cece did not because of their
mutual childhood experiences. She had experienced
Liz's brave and loving heart. She remembered Liz's
talent and integrity. Despite another pending divorce,
Liz's flourishing lifestyle outwardly appeared to Cece
to have few boundaries.

To Ross, Liz appeared ethereal, as if a buxom angel
floating into the room. He beamed as he gave Liz a
hug and a prolonged kiss. Cece recognized that he
savored the moment, so she smiled as she kept her
eye on him.

Ever gracious, Liz exclaimed, "How nice to be with
you again! It has been far too long. Aunt Izzy and Cece,
I am so sorry for our loss. It was so sudden, no? I wish
we could have been with you for the funeral. Mother
told you we were in Italy, right? We can look at our
photographs later. Let Carl and mama show you the
rest of our home. I need to work on dinner."

Liz excused herself and retreated to the kitchen.
She wanted dinner to be ready to serve in thirty minutes. Carl and Camilla continued to guide the guests
over yards of ecru-hued carpet in each room.

Izzy commented, "I bet those carpets are tough to
keep clean."

As they entered the spacious two-story great room
next to the open kitchen, one sensation after another
tantalized them. First, the aroma of Liz's cooking captivated them. With admiring eyes, each person saw an
imposing pageant portrait of Liz centered above the
mantel of a massive brick fireplace. While a myriad
of candles on the mantel and hearth flickered under
the colorful painting, Izzy perceived the setting as a
shrine to Liz. The artist captured Liz's features, even
the detail of her glittering tiara. Years before, Liz had
competed for both state and national titles. Cece and
her entire family traveled to both events. Filled with

pride, Liz absorbed the accolades about her portrait from her position in front of the kitchen stove.

Izzy remarked, "Why you haven't changed from your princess days, Liz."

Liz retorted, "Oh, if you only knew Aunt Izzy, if you only knew."

Another wall contained rich walnut shelving filled with hundreds of books. Ross stepped up to the extraordinary library. He admired the large collection and searched for a good read during their time at the beach. Books ranging from classics to sweet savage love novels to Arthur Conan Doyle packed the orderly shelves.

Aunt Camilla eyed Ross looking at the books and crept up unnoticed behind him. She surprised him as she cleared her throat and placed her bony fingers on his shoulder.

Surprised by her touch, Ross felt he jumped three feet high. He exclaimed, "You startled me!"

She whispered, "Oh, I'm sorry. I have five signed first editions in there Ross. It has been a struggle to declutter my home in Charleston. My eyesight is not what it used to be, so I shared my library with Liz. Lord knows what I have placed in those books."

His curiosity piqued. Without asking, Ross pulled out a Sherlock Holmes hardback. In his left hand, he let it plop open. Three twenty-dollar bills fluttered to the floor. Ross reached and picked up the currency and offered it to Camilla. She smiled and took the volume and the money from him and re-shelved the book. It was an awkward moment for Ross. He was both surprised and embarrassed by his curiosity. He felt he had violated Camilla's secrets by appearing to pilfer through her library books and her makeshift piggy bank. He remembered his own aged grandfather's obsession with hiding packets of money. When he died, it took weeks to find the old man's treasures in unusual places. Ross speculated to himself whether Camilla was exhibiting the same sign of dementia.

Ross apologized, saying, "I'm sorry I dropped the money, Aunt Camilla. I am impressed with your collection of books."

Camilla cackled, "No telling what else you might find, Ross."

Liz stayed in the kitchen preparing her gourmet meal. Meanwhile, Carl and Camilla ushered the visitors outside to the gardens and a massive oval pool. Dozens of white flowering hydrangeas and gardenias provided a fitting backdrop. A circular hot tub large enough for eight lay between the house and pool. Mosaics and tiles from Asia trimmed the pool and spa. In the twilight, the colored lights played optical tricks in the swirling waters. The immense spa beckoned bathers to enter. In a crowning touch, a row of three imposing Buddha statues peered over the swimming pool.

Cece thought, *Boy! This rivals the proverbial Garden of Eden.*

Camilla, said, "You may remember that Carl served in the Navy for his career. While stationed in Viet Nam and Korea in the late 1960s, he found the Buddha statues and stored them until they built this place. For good luck, I rub the belly of this fat one often!"

They laughed. Carl invited the visitors to settle into comfortable lounge chairs around the pool. He served each guest his jazzed-up cocktails. Liz heard the laughter and stepped from the kitchen to investigate. She never wanted to miss the fun or a drink.

Six feet from the diving board a path with flat stones meandered through the gardens. Cece followed it around two ponds of koi and short mounds covered with lush plants. Liz intended for her back yard to resemble a Chinese tea garden. Farther back, a high red brick wall framed the rear property boundaries. Occasional random eight-inch wide openings in the wall allowed a breeze to flow from the ocean. Liz noticed Cece, timid and careful, pacing around the bushes as she stared intently at the ground.

Liz laughed and said, "Oh, Cece, you don't have to worry. There are no copperheads here. Frogs yes, but no snakes."

Her own comment prompted Liz to share the childhood story of their park scare. And it gave Cece an opportunity to heap praise on Liz for her bravery.

The weather had cooperated by granting them a comfortable evening. In the late afternoon shade, Liz served her feast by the pool on a massive glass and steel table. At his chair, Carl carved a steaming beef tenderloin.

Liz exclaimed, "Oh my, perfect!"

Within the rare meat, Liz had concealed a central pocket of melting blue cheese and juicy mushrooms. Cece overheard Ross compliment Liz three times, as he declared the meal one of the best he had consumed. Each time he smiled at his own wife. He claimed Cece had inherited her own culinary talents from both Izzy and Liz.

Camilla chortled, "Cece, you married a charming politician, didn't you?"

After dinner, the six changed into swimsuits to relax in the hot tub. Cece could not wait. She watched as the steam and circulating waters coalesced into a rolling boil. First of the group to step in, she felt a cool ocean wind gust chill her exposed torso. She submerged to her aching shoulders. Her back nestled against a pressure-point jet. The powerful stream blasted her tight shoulder blade muscles with mixed sensations. Waves of comfort, warmth, twinges of pain and pleasure enveloped her in a well-deserved treat after her long ride for the past two days. Her watchful eyes glanced up and gazed across the dreamy stars. *My, this spa is heavenly! I want one of these someday.*

Carl broke the enchantment of Cece's personal paradise by asking, "Another drink?"

Cece knew her limits for both the alcohol and the sugar effect. With full-blown Type 2 diabetes, she monitored her sugar intake. She balanced it daily with three types of injections.

She replied, "No, but thanks for asking."

More stars twinkled in the advancing indigo night. A lively banter flowed among the group. Cece, water-logged, rose out of the spa into the chilled air. Liz met her with a pink cashmere bathrobe. The soft sensation of the fabric caressed Cece's figure.

She winked at her husband and begged, "I need one of these. Put it on my Christmas list, Ross."

Liz reminisced about their mutual childhood experiences as she escorted Cece upstairs. The two women went to her bedroom to change and freshen their makeup.

Out of earshot of the others, intoxicated Liz whispered, "Shush! Can you keep a secret? I have filed papers to divorce Carl. I cannot take his physical and mental abuse any longer. He has drained my bank accounts and added nothing to make this marriage work. My heart is empty. After his actions all these years, I do not love him anymore. I hoped our trip would help, but it did not. I am not getting any younger."

At the mention of her secret, Cece maintained a serious straight face. *Why expose her earlier conversation with Izzy?*

"Let me ask you something. When I die, will you handle my funeral? I want to leave mother's house and remaining antiques and my assets to my first cousins, you and Richie."

Awestruck by her promise, Cece nodded and sighed, "I am very sorry for you and Carl. And I hate to think of you ever dying. Yes, yes, I promise to arrange your funeral, Liz. You honor us with the kindness of this generous bequest."

The ladies hugged. As her tears flowed, Cece's analytical mind went to work. Her conscience registered a twinge of guilt for it. Camilla's house in Charleston contained wall-to-wall antiques. She guessed at the value of both mansions. She forgot there might be savings, insurance, stocks, and bonds too. Sadness and delight filled her heart to hear she would be a modest heir someday.

Chapter 5

First Impressions

Monday, May 11, 1998, 9:30 am
New Orleans, Louisiana

Bump! Bump! Ross's car rolled over the tracks of the St. Charles streetcars. The commotion awakened Cece from her nap and her dream about an inheritance vaporized. Despite her stupor, she recognized Ross had altered the route to their home, but she discerned his destination immediately. She knew both his habits and the impulses that often beckoned to him.

Ross found the closest parking spot to the entrance of a beignet bakery in their neighborhood. Just a hole in the wall, but they were the best beignets near their home. Tolerating the light rain, he ambled into the store. Cece yawned and stretched while remaining in her bucket seat. Melancholy feelings returned. She trembled. *How did Liz change so much since our childhood? Did she really change? Was Liz always like this?* A few minutes later, Ross returned with a white takeout box. The steaming scent of the fresh beignets escaped the foil and seal of the carton.

Ross exclaimed, "Half of them are dripping with warm praline sauce. The rest are plain. Plus she included her customary lagniappe."

The French term lagniappe captured the New Orleans tradition of adding a bonus for free, in this case, an extra beignet.

Cece's mouth watered, as she smelled the delicacies. She licked her red lips. She would allow herself an indulgence, only one or two of the treats without praline sauce. Yet, she considered it fair game if some of the viscous nutty sauce escaped to taint her plain beignets.

Ross winked, "Well you seized a catnap, didn't you?"

Cece laughed at her husband's cleverness and added, "For sure Ross, I must have been in la-la land. It is peculiar how memories can replay in dreams. When we get home, I will describe it to you. You will remember most of the details."

Only a short time passed before Ross turned the car into their driveway and drove to the garage door. He carried their small luggage to the front door of their cozy home. Cece followed him as she shared the vivid details. They dropped off the bags in their bedroom and scurried to the kitchen for a lazy breakfast.

Cece hummed and sang her own improvised ditty, *Hot beignets are waiting; time is a wasting!* Feeling a chill in the comfortable kitchen, Ross clicked on a small gas-log fireplace with a remote switch. The two had much to discuss before Ross headed to the university. Cece pulled out her chair and slid up to the table. Ross brewed a pot of aromatic New Orleans coffee laced with chicory. The strong beverage complemented the warm beignets on the table. Cece loved her coffee, and she loved it hot. Cece's chatter focused on her dream. She talked and opened Saturday's mail that a neighbor had piled on the kitchen table. While handing Cece a full mug, Ross pulled up his chair. The pungent steam filled Cece's nasal passages. She pressed on with details about Liz's promise to bequest her possessions.

"Ross, her specific words addressed her estate. She wanted to leave her valuables and property to her two first cousins."

Ross interjected, "Your inheritance is a no-brainer, Cece. Wow, I remember Liz, the mansion, Camilla, even the hidden money in the library. As if it occurred yesterday. Where did the years go?"

Turning to the present, Cece replied, "I don't know how this will play out, Ross. We need to make plans now. If we are going to Carolina next week, we should drive instead of flying. With such a short time before we leave, the airline prices are likely prohibitive."

Thrifty Ross added, "Driving would save us the car rental cost for the entire two weeks. We'll just need a van overnight to transport Liz's keepsakes to a storage place. I don't want to mess up my car."

She leaned over to kiss his forehead. Cece cherished her Ross. She coveted his steady ability to cut through to the smallest details.

He glanced at his half-empty coffee mug. He whispered, "Thanks, hon, do you remember the first time I met Liz and Carl? How long ago was that? Has it been twenty-seven, twenty-eight years? Remember visiting them during my family's trip to the beach?"

Cece smiled at his flashback and nodded, "We were single then, just two silly college students in love!"

Ross Turner of Sumter attended Lexington State College in central South Carolina years before. As an industrious senior, he pursued double majors in accounting and finance. He chose not to apply elsewhere because his father said so! That is, if he wanted his father's financial help. No one in Ross's family had ever attended another college.

Cece, originally from Baton Rouge, was a senior at the private preppy Driesh College in Columbia, where she majored in actuarial science. The origin of her school in the early 1800s stemmed from the desire of the benefactor to instill the tenets of his faith within the Carolinas. A wealthy Scot philanthropist founded

Driesh and named his institution after an ancient granite munro he had climbed in the Scot Highlands.

Cece's first exposure to Driesh occurred during Liz's participation there in the state beauty pageant. At age eleven, she fell in love with the school. Liz's family, including Cece, attended a formal tea hosted by the college for the pageant contestants. During the program, each speaker repeated Driesh's sterling reputation and national academic ranking. The image of fountains and lush green lawns stuck with Cece. The forested genteel campus matched Cece's style and remained etched in her memory until she had to decide on a college. A venerable institution, it remained her first choice although she visited seventeen other campuses before choosing Driesh. You could say she analyzed everything thoroughly.

In the summer before their junior year of college, Ross and Cece first met on the same foreign exchange program. Both traveled to New York City as a precursor to departing for Europe. Cece often referred to their first meeting in the 42nd Street hotel elevator as a divine appointment. After frolicking around in five countries together, the two kids returned to the U.S., where they continued their relationship with visits, telephone calls, and love letters. Ross's family beach trip would be the first opportunity for Cece to meet his parents.

Cece felt blessed as she sipped her now lukewarm coffee. The synapses in her brain were working double-time. The memories of long ago flooded her thoughts. She remembered it was during this beach trip that she also first noted the early red flags of Liz's slow demise.

Liz and Carl married only six months before the two college kids headed to the beach. The newlyweds settled in Liz's white-brick apartment in Pawley's Island, a perfect place to start their new life together. Cece called Liz to plan a dinner at a restaurant upon their arrival.

Liz told Cece, "I want you to come enjoy our cute little place. Carl will cook steaks and blue crab! Can you arrive at 7:00 pm?"

"Yes, we'll see you then."

Cece wanted to see the newlyweds' pad. Ross's family, the Turners, planned a rendezvous at a nearby beach house for the week. She looked forward to meeting his parents. The older couple would not arrive until later that night and planned to stay up to meet Cece. She rationalized, *Ross and I can have an early dinner with Liz and be back early to meet them.*

Sunburned from an afternoon on the beach, Ross and Cece rang Liz's doorbell. A cacophony of dogs barking proclaimed their arrival. Carl answered the door, accompanied by three Jack Russell Terriers. He welcomed the young couple into the spacious three-bedroom apartment. The high-strung purebreds barked, growled, and ran between their feet.

Carl said, "Great to meet you two. Liz has told me of your fun as kids, Cece. Liz will be here soon. You know the drill, last-minute makeup. Meanwhile, let me show you the apartment. I'll guide you on the fifty-cent tour."

They smiled at his humor as he snaked them around the flat. Unopened boxes of wedding presents filled two bedrooms. The cartons provided the dogs a maze to negotiate as they yelped in excitement. Ross liked Labs and Irish Setters; however, he liked other dogs less. Three dogs seemed too many. He tried not to show his discomfort. Two of the rambunctious dogs settled on the carpet each with one eye remaining open. The other dog, more curious and annoying, came up to Ross and sniffed his crotch repeatedly. It annoyed him. He thought, *Try that one more time Fido!*

Liz entered the room carrying herself with the grace and look of royalty.

♛

Ross placed his empty mug on the table as he commented to Cece, "Man, Liz mesmerized me! Hmm. What a honey! Sure, she had oddities, but her good looks and charm made up for her foibles. I thought glamourous Liz could pass for a composite of Marilyn Monroe and Jayne Mansfield. I loved her sultry pout, that sweet smile, her shimmering platinum hair, and, well, those buxom boobs. She engaged you in her conversations with her syrupy voice offering Southern hospitality at its prime. It's no wonder I liked Liz. She could relate to people. I felt so welcome. How did Carl go wrong with all that?"

♛

Liz's entrance provoked another round of anxious barking. There was no way an intruder could accost their master or mistress. Liz commanded quiet, and the dogs obeyed.

Ross inquired, "Why so many dogs?"

With pride, Liz responded, "Oh, they are rescues, a family. I got them from a clinic that insisted we not break up the siblings. You know I can never stand to see a poor animal suffer. They and I have K-9 classes three times a week. When Carl is on reserve duty for weeks, I get lonely. So now Carl, the dogs, and I are family. Mother still has our three poodles."

Ross perceived Carl to be affable and generous. He offered the young couple their choice of cocktails. The terriers paced around Cece and Ross as Carl pulled ingredients from the stocked bar. Ross thought, *Am I dreaming? These mutts are on a foxhunt and I am the fox.*

"A cosmo for me," piped up Liz.

Cece added, "I'll have the same."

Carl prepared the cosmopolitans at the bar and carried the crystal glasses to the ladies. When he returned, Carl asked Ross what he wanted.

Ross asked, "Do you have any Scotch whisky?"

He added that he was learning to tolerate single-malt Scotch. He liked the slow burn on his throat, however the smoky, peaty flavors of whisky from Scotland's western isles were not yet to his liking.

Carl said, "I have just the thing. Try a Scotch old fashioned with these appetizers. This is an easy way to acquire the taste for it," Carl added as he spooned bitters into the concoction.

Ross sniffed and then savored the tang as he swirled the magical potion in his mouth.

"Hey, I dig this."

Carl invited Ross to the balcony where they found refuge from the dogs. Ross asked Carl to share his experiences on board an aircraft carrier. Carl opened as if he were a book. He missed the fun aspects of a naval officer's life, including the camaraderie and solidarity. Ross paid rapt attention to Carl's description of the intricate operations of the mammoth ship.

Her stomach growling, Cece wondered, *Would we ever have dinner?*

At 10:00 pm, Liz opened the door of balcony saying, "Time to put the potatoes in the oven. Carl, dear, can you grill the steaks later? We need them ready in an hour and a half."

Carl nodded.

Ross's palate drooled at the thought of grilled steak and fresh crab. He was an athletic and often hungry

college student. Meanwhile, Cece's stomach growled
and fluttered as she worried about getting to the beach
house too late to meet Ross's family.

An hour later, Carl announced it was time to grill
the meat. Liz watched Carl and Ross leave for the
apartment complex's barbecue grills. Cece perceived
that Liz wanted to say something. Now facing the
cabinets and pretending to look for an item, Liz had
turned around to avoid Cece's eyes. A tear rolled down
Liz's cheek. Cece hesitated to ask what was wrong.
She did not suspect a repeat of the pattern of abuse
experienced with the first three husbands. But she
noticed Liz's countenance change before her eyes.

Next to the swimming pool stood three large gas
barbecue pits. With a gas grill turned on, Carl lit a
match and held it in place. The over-sized black grill
responded with a poof of fire and heat. As four ribeye
steaks sizzled, the men's conversation evolved to the
intensification of the war in Southeast Asia. Ross was
a decade younger than Carl. They agreed the carnage
wasted much of Ross's generation.

At 11:30 pm, Liz and Cece carried the steaming
feast to the balcony. Seated around a wooden table,
Liz proposed a toast.

She raised a flute of champagne, exclaiming, "To my
dear sweet Cece. Here's to a bright and romantic future."

The four raised their glasses and sipped. The gourmet spread included the tender steaks, boiled blue
crab, loaded baked potatoes, roasted romaine, tomato
salad with Stilton cheese dressing, and creamed
spinach.

Carl commented, "Not bad for a newlywed, eh,
Ross?"

Ross ignored the comment and others Carl had
made that evening. The condescending tone sounded
raw to him. He breathed in the aroma of the steaming

steaks as Liz filled each dinner plate. The conversation turned to Liz and her mother's health. Emotionless, Liz quipped that Camilla had fallen and undergone a serious hip replacement.

"The old coot is doing fine, still as dominant and obstinate as ever."

Cece thought, *My, what an unusual remark from Liz.*

Liz and Cece discussed the predicaments and ailments of the remaining family members. Meanwhile, the two men focused on the ports of call Carl visited in the navy. When Liz observed that the guests devoured the contents of their dinner plates, she begged them to have a second helping. Both declined.

She asked, "Are you were ready for my signature dessert?"

The two youngsters exclaimed, "Sure!"

Carl hummed a verbal drum roll as Liz presented a magnificent chafing dish of flaming Baked Alaska. Ross and Cece relished the treat. After the meal, Liz and Cece gathered up the dishes. The three dogs ran circles around the women, hoping for a scrap to fall off the plates. With the dishwasher closed with the last plate, Cece relaxed in a chair. Cece abstained after her second drink. She feared her doctors warning about her diagnosis of adult onset diabetes. Instead of more booze, she requested a low-cal soda.

She appreciated the time alone with Liz. Now Cece could pose her questions to ask about her growing love with Ross. She might dig into how Carl and Liz's relationship was going. For most of the evening, Liz had controlled the conversation while Cece listened.

If anyone knew the skinny on husbands, it would be Liz.

Carl and Ross remained on the balcony where they overlooked the vast Atlantic Ocean on a bright moonlit night.

Carl pulled out two cigars and said, "Ross, time for El Presidente!"

They puffed on their cigars and sipped pricey brandy. Their lively discussion turned to the chaotic college football season. They opined over who would win the conferences, and the coveted national championship trophy. As they spotted shrimp boats heading out to sea for the next day's catch, the haze of a gentle fog enveloped the full moon. Carl refilled both crystal snifter glasses.

Ross's head swirled at the thought of another brandy. *Even his frat parties were not this excessive.*

Ross soon found out he could not tolerate the excesses of that evening. When they said their goodbyes, he struggled to walk to the car. He was clearly inebriated. In the parking lot, before he opened the car door, he lost his whole dinner, and drinks. He vowed never to do this again. Oh, how his head hurt.

Cece chuckled to herself. She thought, *Silly boys.*

In the passenger side of the car with his window open and his mind in a fog, Ross pondered, *These two people love to entertain but, man, they numb their guests. Both of them have drinking issues, don't they?* At the least, it raised a question in Ross's mind. As he described his thoughts to Cece, she concurred. She did not share she had learned the newlyweds were at odds with each other and Liz's mother.

He was glad it was only fifteen minutes from Pawley's Island to the rental beach house. At 3:00 am, Ross and Cece pulled into the driveway. Cece had driven the distance praying the entire time that state troopers would not see her and Ross.

Every light glared in and outside the beach house. The imposing silhouette of Ross's father, Reverend Matt Turner, filled the doorway. His tan complexion and stature told of his years of work in the dwindling textile mills. To supplement his wages, he served as a part-time pastor of a small Methodist church near their home in Sumter. His endearing spirit and patience were his strengths.

Cece was incredulous. *This is the wrong way to meet Ross's parents. They are waiting up for me. What do I do now?*

Cece entered the kitchen where Ross's mother Marie sat at the table shelling fresh black-eye peas. Rie was an attractive medium-build woman with a pleasant smile and a head of natural curly brunette hair. A white canvas apron covered her navy culottes and floral beach blouse. Rie stood up.

"Hello, I'm Cece. It is very nice to meet you. I need to go to bed!"

She slept until 10:00 the next morning.

Chapter 6

Memories of Christmas

Thirty Minutes Later
New Orleans and Charleston

Four beignets remained on the plate. Not motivated, Cece hesitated to begin her daily activities. Her energy zapped by the drive from Baton Rouge, she wanted to remain inactive. In fact, she considered climbing into her bed.

Ross asked, "Another cup?"

Cece nodded. In her kitchen, she sat entranced as another childhood memory surfaced. In this recollection, the entire Perkins family came together over the Christmas holidays. Family celebrations were big events for the families of the two Perkins brothers, Ben and Charles. Their sister, Mary Ann, and her husband, James Evans, often drove down from North Carolina with their son Richie for reunions. The loosely woven extended family gathered together several times a year.

Cece remarked to Ross specifically about one of the times Liz's parents hosted the holiday celebration in Charleston. She asked herself, *Was that 1960?*

In those days, the roads crossing much of the Deep South were primitive compared to the efficient interstate expressways populating the landscape in other regions. Despite the distance, Cece's parents completed the marathon trip in only two days. The drive began in the Cajun backwaters and ended in the Low Country of the Carolinas. Cece and her only brother, Jack, rode in the back seat. Jack was the consummate protective older brother, six years older than Cece. She so looked up to Jack. Cece remembered the two kids repeatedly quizzing her dad, "Are we there yet?"

Thinking of the long drive alongside Jack, these holiday memories melded with thoughts of a fleeting tragedy. Jack had met with his premature death in a mishap involving a drunk driver. It had shattered her world. The crash happened near Lake Charles when he was twenty-three. She was only a junior in high school then. She repeatedly asked herself, *Why did Jack's death happen.* At this moment, Cece pondered, *How can I cope with all of Liz's problems? She needed Jack's help now.*

Cece's mind returned to the more pleasant Christmas memories. She could see, smell, and taste the gatherings at Aunt Camilla and Uncle Charles' home as if it were yesterday. The mansion in the East Battery district of Charleston had a dramatic view of the Atlantic Ocean. In tasteful displays, Camilla's collection of period antiques filled the spacious living quarters. An imposing carriage house served as a four-car garage and rental apartment. Camilla's investments in more antiques occupied three bays in the garage. Cece loved to wind her way through the aisles of vintage furniture, china, silver, and crystal. The overflowing and packed-to-the-gills labyrinth provided Cece, Jack, and Liz a venue for playing hide-and-seek. For hours and hours, the three ran haphazard patterns among the antiques as if they were rats in a maze.

Stuff she thought, *but nice stuff!*

Slaves had built the majestic three-story home in the early 1800s. In the antebellum style, a widow's watchtower topped the third-floor corner. The domed turret exposed a commanding view of the surrounding ocean and nearby Fort Sumter. Cece remembered running up the stairs with Liz to peer out the curving windows of the tower as if watching for invading pirates. Later, pretending they were princesses in a fairy tale, Liz and Cece awaited Prince Charming's rescue. Aunt Camilla claimed the tower for her study. Here she held court over the decisions of her household and Liz's life. The matriarch knew which strings to pull and which buttons to push, especially in her daughter's psyche.

Camilla exposed her snarls and talons in reaction to protests from Liz and other people. She had a discreet way of meddling in everyone's business that created discomfort. She was not shy to raise her voice to assert superiority. No one outdid Camilla.

As challenges arose to her social status, Camilla faced them to prove herself and show she was in charge. Her pride and drive for dominance led to forthright aggression. No one challenged her plans or ideas without retribution. She looked for opportunities to win each battle. Whether bragging, boasting, or offering condescending, unfiltered comments, Camilla controlled the landscape, always on top, always the best. With her air of faux royalty, she had critics. She would laugh them off and ignore them. An adversary's pain or misfortune fueled her for the next battle. In her contentious mood, she was like a towering polar bear that trekked the ice to conquer or defend against her predators. Indeed, ice water ran in her veins.

Yet, Aunt Camilla had a contradictory sweet side in her role as the Southern matron. Cece remembered the gourmet Christmas meals her aunt created. She prepared Southern fixings: Turkey and dressing, Curry Farm country ham, and a standing rib roast. An excess of entrees, but it was the Southern way. Complementary sides of sweet potatoes, Brussel sprouts and chestnuts, gravy, biscuits and sweet cornbread overflowed the china platters. Sweet tea, spiked eggnog, and many desserts completed the feast. She arranged the entire meal, her way with two maids jumping at her orders.

After Christmas dinner, she sent the maids home while the men washed and dried the English porcelain dinnerware by hand. Then, the family moved into the cavernous cherry wood-paneled den. Around the massive glittering Christmas tree, the three families exchanged gifts. As usual, each person gave presents within his or her own immediate family. Each person brought another gift to exchange with someone in the other families. Weeks before, Camilla conducted a lottery to decide who gave to whom. That year Cece had drawn Liz's name.

When the time came, Cece picked up a long package wrapped in gold paper. She placed it in her cousin's hands.

An excited Liz exclaimed, "It's a box from Neiman Marcus. Oh, thank you, Cece!"

She tore the wrapping and opened the box. Under a bolt of tissue lay her gift. Liz ran the feathers and sensuous silk through her smooth hands. She draped the gown over her body.

"I love it, Cece," Liz exclaimed.

Proud of the gift she purchased on Cece's behalf, Izzy announced, "You can sleep in it during the state pageant next year. Don't you love the feathered neck? I have nothing with so many dangling pieces. I bet they will tickle when you sleep."

Everyone laughed. Izzy avoided saying she had never previously purchased items from the famed store. A veiled competition existed between the two sisters-in-law, Izzy and Camilla.

As Liz hugged her cousin, she chortled, "Thank you Cece. When I wear it, others will mistake me for Zsa Zsa."

Another round of laughter followed as Liz and Cece parodied movie actresses in glamour poses.

With a sip of coffee and a nibble on a beignet, Cece wondered why Jack and she were the only normal ones in the original brood of four cousins. *Whatever normal was.* On the surface, this extended family did not appear dysfunctional. Yet, how dissimilar were the four cousins who shared the same grandparents.

The cousins, Cece, Jack, Liz, and Richie sat on the floor by the tree. Both boys tried to ignore the girls playing with Liz's dolls. Richie was the family geek. Something electronic or mechanical always filled his pockets. Transistor radios, a slide rule, walkie-talkies, or other devices lived there. In his white long-sleeved shirt pocket, a plastic protector held three pens of different colors. Cece noticed early on that Richie was, well, different. He seemed to be a smart, quiet guy, but still a geek. Richie planned to attend a college near his parent's home in two years.

Liz developed an extreme obsession surrounding animals. In her high-school days, Liz volunteered during summers at a veterinarian's clinic. She often brought home a stray puppy or cat. She begged and pleaded with Camilla to let her keep the animals. But her mother forbade pet adoptions. Liz enjoyed a special kinship with the vet's animals. Unlike humans, they offered unconditional love. Unlike her mother, the animals offered acceptance. Camilla relented and allowed Liz to adopt a rescue family of four poodle puppies. She confessed that they were so cute even her rigid heart did not resist. Later Liz gave one of the puppies to Cece. Liz's triad had full run of Camilla's elaborate home.

Tiring of exploring the idiosyncrasies of her relatives, Cece's mind continued to flash back to the warm Christmas gathering. She remembered sitting on that floor with Liz while they sang an old song.

Over the river and through the woods, to Grandmother's house we go. . . .

Because Liz had a voice trained for classical music, she carried the tune. Everyone, even Camilla, joined in the song. As it ended, the family reveled in the bond of the moment. Nostalgia and cozy memes flooded from every niche in the massive room. The fire in the old hearth crackled as Uncle Charles stoked it. He tumbled more wood into the fireplace. A bed of coals released glittering splinters of sparks up the flue. Flames consumed the oak wood. The greener wood released moisture as it hissed, crackled, and popped.

As Cece delighted in her memory of this melancholic moment, into her mind crept a constant dark cloud that troubled her. *Who would have guessed what lay ahead in future years for this family? She detested the squalid mess of Liz's mansion, the unrelenting web of red tape, the mystery of Joey, the shrew-like Camilla, and the weird tone to it all.* Cece forced herself to return to more pleasant flashbacks.

Cece stared at Camilla's Christmas tree that featured glowing bubble lights. The lighted tubes of liquid gurgled when warmed. The unusual trimmings chalked up another new experience for Cece.

Izzy whispered, "You can always count on Camilla to have the latest decorations."

That Christmas celebration was a sacred memory of warmth, family, and love for Cece.

Aunt Mary Ann suggested, "Liz and Cece, lets sing Christmas carols."

Liz sat down at the piano while Cece turned pages in the songbook. When the last carol ended, Aunt Camilla began a bragging session. With too much eggnog under her belt, Camilla's proud mama buttons had burst. She recited an impressive list of Liz's achievements. On and on she droned.

"Did I tell you she's a sophomore at Blaketon College, my alma mater? She is majoring in classical voice. The largest fraternity chose her as their sweetheart and her freshman class elected her princess for homecoming. She pledged her favorite sorority. Did I mention her grades?"

When Uncle Charles detected that his wife had said enough, he put his arm around her and joked, "The woman is proud of her daughter, isn't she?"

Cece's mother exclaimed, "Give Liz a stage and she will fill the theater."

Camilla responded, "For sure. And we want y'all to join us in Columbia to see Liz in the pageant in May!"

Chapter 7

Encounter

1935
New York, New York

Camilla completed her bachelor's degree in theater at Blaketon College. Diploma in hand, she was intent on a career path on Broadway. Off she went, against her mother's better judgment. She enrolled in a theatrical college in New York to earn a master's degree. She craved the challenge and set a goal to prove herself. With rigor, she sought casting calls across the theater district. Camilla loved the city, the theater, and the professional training she experienced. People in the city viewed her as tough and strong. New York did not intimidate Camilla. Naïve at heart, she sought new thrills, often in risky environs. She, too, was a daring beauty in her college years.

After two years, Camilla neared the end of her classes. She took a shortcut through a park square as she walked home from the school theater one night. During the day, the park bustled with a lively street market and teemed with people. She always felt safe in the milling crowd. However, the night's cloak of darkness hid trouble. As she neared an unlit street corner alone, her torso tensed. Camilla observed two moving shadows. One burst out of the inky blackness. With a seductive whisper to her face, the savage hands groped her. She found herself accosted on the street by a fetid goon. Aggressive at first, she fought his challenge. The physical strength of the attacker was overwhelming. She feigned death until she no longer could hear his footsteps. She let out a piercing scream. Within moments, several people came to her aid. They summoned the police.

Angry and shaken, Camilla moaned. Her lip was bleeding from a hard slap. She lashed out with obscenities at the attacker. She wanted the perpetrator castrated on the spot. However, he had disappeared. When she told bystanders of her attack, her body trembled. Shame, hurt, fear, and rage boiled in the cauldron of her mind. This chance meeting soured many benefits of her education and professional experience. She left New York for two weeks. When she returned, the city lost its panache to her. Over the years, Camilla repressed the bottled-up demon, but it remained with her. As her daughter matured, she vowed to keep her from falling into the same trap. Camilla's dominance often clashed with the daring personality of Liz.

Meanwhile, Liz's father, Charles, advanced as a career U.S. Army officer taking assignments around the world. When World II broke out, during the early years of Liz's life, he served with the Army Corps of Engineers in the Pacific theater. Despite his distinguished military career, he cowered to Camilla's control. Following Liz's pageant competitions and first wedding, he died of a cerebral hemorrhage. However, most people attributed his death to a broken heart.

Chapter 8

A New Tradition

1953
New York, New York

The period between the end of WWII and the Korean War carried a slow healing process for the wounds inflicted on the United States. Communities buried and remembered their war dead. Veterans with injuries healed in homes and hospitals. Healthy soldiers sought employment in droves. Even before the Korean War ended in 1953, bank accounts grew flush with money saved during and after World War II. During the World War, women had "manned" the war production machine. Women signed up for work in the industrial factories and the armed forces, but not in combat roles. They earned enough money to support their households plus savings. The male military forces shot the guns, flew the planes, drove the tanks, and steered the ships. Eisenhower strengthened the U.S. and world economies through foreign relief programs. Lower and middle class mobility became easier with a new expansion on Main Street America. Peace and wealth became prevalent. Americans unleashed their economic machine with their surplus of cash savings. New housing starts soared across the country. Businesses rushed to sell automobiles, major appliances, clothing, and furniture. Vacation travel moved from a novelty to a common occurrence. However, women of all ages found themselves shoved back into their pre-war traditional role. Most stepped up to become the ideal mother in the ideal family with an average of 2.3 kids. Women worked in the home, or in a noble but lower paying career. Some women educated children in the nation's schools, pursued nursing, or landed a job with little mobility and pay. Of course, there were rare exceptions.

Management told women, "Nope, you cannot take the more desirable jobs that belong to the returning soldiers."

Postwar gender roles favored males. They populated and led the executive and management ranks in major companies and the media. The guilty ones poured fuel on the stereotype of women as the weaker sex. Regardless of the motivations of fear, prejudice, misogyny, and warped humor, most wanted to protect their own jobs, and keep the good-old-boy networks. Others said they wanted to work in a zone free of petty female issues or a place that expressed their male code of condescension and deprecation of women. These crude notions furthered the idea that women cannot do a man's job. The citizens of the United States forgot an important factor that helped them win the war. Women had focused their efforts to run the successful productive machine of America. Woman power had forged the Allies' war victory by providing needed supplies and armaments.

Yet, manager after manager said, "You are not strong enough or capable to endure the pace."

Something repeated enough could alter the mindset of a nation. Untruths recited repeatedly led society to accept the false notion as truth. Evil or misleading people misused good tools to create problems for other groups. A fabrication arose that women shunned work or that a full day at the office or factory overwhelmed them. Untrue, but the prejudiced culture of the day held that they should stay at home and have children. With the barriers, it was difficult for a woman to explore a different calling. Professional careers remained off-limits to females. Instead, working women became typists, stenos, nurses, clerks, tellers, and girl Fridays, not CPAs, CEOs, attorneys, doctors, surgeons, nor land and skyscraper moguls. Only a few women controlled or inherited wealth and directed opportunities for themselves. That is just the way it was.

On a chilly spring day, a dozen businessmen met at the Waldorf Astoria. Those in the meeting intended to brainstorm ways to lure bucks and people to New York City. As they huddled around a conference table, their goal aimed to garner a greater share of the surplus supply of money.

Excited, the meeting chairman interjected, "Our tourist sites and empty hotels need help. This plan is perfect. Our city has languished long enough."

He cited maladies the boroughs of the city had suffered for years. The perceptions of urban blight, crime syndicates, prohibition, tenements, and unacceptable masses of immigrants marred the city's aura. He wanted fresh, new, imaginative, and bold ideas to change the city's image. A single event would not be enough. He urged for a coordinated and sustained approach by the city and businesses.

The dozen leaders invited a marketing team from Madison Avenue to share their designs. They proposed ideas to attract a cross-section of people from the forty-eight states and Canada. New faces destined to visit the city and to enjoy its best experiences.

For two weeks before Thanksgiving, the city ushered in the holiday season. The consultant's promotion aimed to shower the period with special events, sales, parades, and more, all focused on the newcomers. The city leaders listened to the proposals of crafty advertising in the summer aimed to entice travelers in the fall through splashy ads filling magazines and newspapers, the new medium of television, and the trusted radio.

As he invoked a dare-to-dream challenge, one marketing executive remarked, "Consider the personal touch. Imagine thousands returning home for the holidays after experiencing New York as a safe and fun place to be. Word of mouth is your best salesman. Your tourist numbers will be up in a short time. And bottom line that means dollars for your city."

Beside the monetary discounts and heavy advertising, the scheme had other facets. The marketing team proposed a beauty pageant, which included women from every state competing in the spectacle. The large entourage accompanying each contestant added more masses of people to enjoy the city. Their following included the families of the participants, their friends, support teams, well-wishers, and sponsors. They joined with curious everyday tourists flocking to the city from the media emphasis. The coffers of the New York City business machine awaited dollars arriving from across the country. On the heels of the new money, the assembled leaders expected new hotels, new streets, improved housing, the revival of Broadway shows, a new bridge and transportation tunnel across the Hudson, and new local taxes.

In closing his discussion about the pageant, the consultants' leader invoked a plea to the gathering, "Now is the time to lead by showing respect for what women have done and will do for this country. We, the city with the symbol of freedom in our harbor, can and must encourage women. Unbind them and unleash their talents. They did a major part to preserve freedom in the war, now do something for them. Imagine the beautiful women of America at their best."

From the simple plan, the Miss American Glory pageant grew in stature over the years. The concept was similar to other prestigious and older national pageants, which propelled many young women to gain exposure and access to new careers. Educators at universities and colleges added their voices and coursework to improve women's futures. The terms "empowerment" and "taking charge" entered women's vocabulary. The government added a protected working class law with the implied warning: *Thou shalt not discriminate against women!* A day of feminine "can do" dawned. With her life soaring like a Mercury spacecraft, Liz was a part of the new wave.

Chapter 9

Liftoff

May 1961
Columbia, South Carolina

Excited, eleven-year-old Cece studied her pocketbook calendar. Nightly, she crossed off the calendar day before she fell asleep. Five months had passed since the prior Christmas gathering. The week of the "Miss South Carolina Glory" pageant had arrived. Every year, the city of Columbia hosted the gala event. Cece had traveled from Louisiana with her mother Izzy and father Ben, and her brother Jack. They met up with Liz's mother and father, Camilla and Charles, at their downtown hotel. During the week, the family attended the focused events on the Driesch College campus. On the night of the pageant finale, Cece anticipated seeing "her" cousin, Elizabeth Perkins compete. Liz's family entered the area reserved for them, one of many loge balcony sections within the Civic Center. Doorways of the skybox sported drapery of maroon fabric. The box contained plush chairs of maroon velveteen that rested on legs of dark wood. Cece settled into her seat and rested her eyes as the conversations rose to a crescendo in the great hall. Her eyelids opened wide to the swirling spotlights moving across the huge room.

As the emcee introduced each contestant, Cece waited for her cousin's turn. When Liz stepped onto the stage, Cece captured Liz's every move as if she were a spy camera. Liz could do no wrong! Then, the emcee announced the top twelve semi-finalists, one of whom was Liz. The swimsuit contest started a new round for the twelve women, followed by the talent, evening gown, and interview competitions.

The contestants wore one-piece bathing suits in the latest styles from California. As she crossed the stage with confidence, Liz floated to the center and walked the long runway into the audience. A multitude of spotlights flashed around her as she moved. She looked up to the loge section and smiled. Her biggest asset had to be the confidence she felt.

Observing the buxom figure, Izzy chuckled to herself as she remembered the story Camilla told them on the way to the pageant.

"Liz held a sleepover party at our house when she was in junior high. It was just too quiet. I grew suspicious; something was going on, so with stealthy steps, I headed downstairs where the girls were. When I got into the room, I smelled the smoke. Six of Liz's friends were in their finest pajamas watching the Ed Sullivan show. A pile of short butts filled the ashtray. I paused and thought, *Oh dear, what do I say?*

"I laughed and whispered, 'Girls, I don't mind if you smoke cigarettes, but remember that if you smoke, you will be flat-chested!' As far as I know, Liz never smoked again."

As she ended the tale, Camilla cackled with laughter. Cece rolled her eyes. Then she smiled and thought, *Smoking really did not hurt Liz any!*

Cece sat back in her plush chair and wished so hard for Liz to win the title.

Since its start, brunettes had ruled as the first eight winners of this state pageant. Their talents varied from baton twirling to dance to drama to country music solos. Liz did not fit that mold. She brought sophistication to the contest with her looks and talent. Liz was a striking blonde performing opera.

Liz had entered the pageant for the second time. The prior year, she won first runner-up to Miss South Carolina Glory. The near-win established her as the new front-runner. In retrospect, she was thankful she did not win the title before because she wanted to engage in her activities at Blaketon. The title commitment continued not just for the week of the pageant but involved a yearlong contract of public appearances, plus the national competition. The state's organization did not have funds or volunteers to transport her intrastate, or to coordinate the frequent speaking engagements, school appearances, and media interviews. The appearances depended on the titleholder's resources alone. As a freshman, she did not feel mature enough to have an accolade-filled year at school, keep her grades up, date, and allow the commitments to sap her resources. She wavered between changing majors. A jump from music performance in the classic vocal style to engineering or business seemed treacherous. Either new major launched the graduate to careers considered off-limits to women. Liz expected the technical and additional new prerequisite coursework to consume more time than any courses she had taken. The insurmountable hurdle surrounding a change in majors rested with her mother's unlikely approval. She knew her old-school mother preferred the fine arts fields as the acceptable majors for a woman's future.

For her talent, Liz sang her favorite aria which she heard the diva Maria Callas sing, *O Mio Babbino Caro,* by Giacomo Puccini. The title translated to *Oh My Beloved Father.* She sang it as a tribute to her dad, poor henpecked Charles. She nailed the runs in the classic piece. The crowd went wild in appreciation of the perfect and unique performance.

In the talent and evening gown competitions, no candidate could match Liz. The other contestants had chosen the safe "old school" route of traditional layered gowns with petticoats. Instead, Liz chose the new style of an elegant empire ball gown. The popular new First Lady, Jacqueline Kennedy, set the trend in Washington with similar designs by Oleg Cassini. A wrapping of fitted ecru taffeta accented the creamy translucent, light tulle of Liz's gown. The dress hugged her buxomness and waist while portraying Liz as a princess of graceful movement with a flair for modernity. Jackie's style was one thing on which she and Camilla agreed.

The state pageant drew to a climax. Liz placed in the top five finalists. *Only Liz herself can lose this now,* Camilla thought. The last event before crowning the new queen was the important interview phase.

The emcee asked, "Name a person you most want to meet. And what would you ask or tell them and why?"

When Liz's turn came up, she smiled and without a pause said, "I want to meet Alan Shepard. I would ask him how weightlessness feels."

Shepard had just piloted the first Mercury spacecraft to become the first American in space.

Liz added, "I hope to be the first woman astronaut. I have studied Astronomy at Blaketon College. Exploration of space will create new opportunities for men and women."

As she stressed the word *women,* her penetrating gaze connected with each judge. The audience sat in silent, stunned amazement. Audible gasps, whispers, and laughter chilled the auditorium. The crowd pondered the novel idea. *No; NASA will not allow women in space. But why not?* Liz sensed an uneasiness about the crowd's delayed reaction and the laughter. Then the silence gave way to a tidal wave of thunderous applause.

Oh no, too risky, she thought as the votes were being tabulated. She studied the judges assembled at their table. She displayed her nerves by biting her lip. Liz found no one to make eye contact with to read his or her reaction. None of them looked at her. The murmuring audience compared their favorites to win. In the loge, Camilla was sobbing because she knew Liz had ruined her big opportunity. Izzy took her hand to comfort her. As the emcee came onstage to proclaim the winner, a hush came over the crowd. Similar to the moments before Alan Shepard's rocket launch, the countdown of finalists began.

"It is time to announce the top three contestants and crown your new queen. May I have the envelope please?"

He paused raising the anticipation. Then he read the name of the second runner-up. It was not Liz. He gave the young lady a kiss, a scholarship envelope, and a bouquet of white magnolias accented with the state flower Yellow Jessamine.

Only the final two positions remained. Liz still had a chance!

"The first runner-up is very important. If the winner of the title Miss South Carolina Glory does not complete her one-year reign, the first runner-up will assume the title."

The remaining finalists, all brunettes except Liz, held hands. Liz's eyes swept the audience as if she was looking for someone.

Smiling, the emcee announced, "First runner-up is Judy Haines, Miss Sumter Glory, and your new Miss South Carolina Glory this year is Elizabeth Perkins of Charleston."

Realizing that she won the pageant, Liz raised her left hand to her mouth and gasped. Instantaneously, her right hand slid to her forehead where she patted

her brow. She peered into the crowd, serious and solemn only for a moment, and then followed up with a
big smile. As if in a panicked state, both hands moved
within inches of her face where they started to flutter
like wings of a butterfly.

She graciously mouthed, "Thank you, thank you,
thank you. . . ."

The triumphal movements all unveiled in seconds
as she and her coach had rehearsed.

Applause broke out as the crowd rose to a standing
ovation. After a kiss and a hug, the emcee presented
Liz with an ornate bouquet of red roses fastened to a
two-foot-long scepter. The rhinestone scepter rotated
from winner to winner each year. The winner of the
prior year anchored the keepsake glittering tiara upon
Liz's head as best as she could. Then, the sash proclaiming "Miss South Carolina Glory" found its place
across Liz's bosom.

Liz beamed with beauty and pride as the spotlights
rotated on her and the crowd. She stepped onto the
runway. The orchestra and emcee broke into a jazzy
rendition of the official state song. She experienced
a magical moment! High above, a suspended silver
mirror ball cast a thousand diamond lights over the
main hall. Cascades of yellow and white paper confetti
wafted from the ceiling.

Cece smiled from ear to ear. Liz blew a gentle kiss
motion to young Cece.

The young one said to Izzy, "Who knows, maybe
Liz can earn the crown of Miss American Glory too!"

The contest was six months away. Cece understood
the enormous consequences of the event.

She asked, "Can we go to New York?"

Camilla entangled herself in a mess of nerves. Yes,
she was proud of her daughter's accomplishment. It
enlarged her own persona and bragging rights. But

the prospect of returning to New York City revived the memorable demon of her attack in the park. Throughout the next six months, she exchanged bouts of anxiety and depression. With Liz away at school and performing her queenly duties on weekends, Camilla's wrath poured nonstop on her husband Charles.

Chapter 10

Preparation

The Day After the Pageant
Columbia, South Carolina

A divide existed between each successive pageant on the local, state, and national levels. Volunteers and merchants in the contestant's sponsoring town provided guidance before the state pageant. They stressed realism and for the contestant to be herself. When the state organization crowned a new titleholder, she joined their domain. The state-paid "professionals" worked their magic to reshape the new winner. The two weeks that followed were as intense as the pageant itself. During the first week, non-stop personal appearances and interviews with the press and local television stations filled the calendar. Liz's life was no longer her own. The week ended in a private meeting with the white-haired governor of South Carolina. It was heady stuff for a twenty-year-old.

The next week the state people quarantined Liz in Columbia for an intense debriefing and top-to-bottom re-branding of the contestant in preparation for the national pageant. Liz surmised that her new pageant coach was hell-bent to change everything about her.

The intimidating commands were "No, you need to move your talent a notch to the more popular side. Sing something less pretentious than opera. Ditch your wardrobe. Get a hair makeover, less curly. Change your makeup."

The re-branding reminded Liz of life with her mother. She felt like a poodle at the pet groomer. She had little choice in decisions affecting herself.

Chapter 11

The Next Level

November 1961
New York, New York

Six months passed. The leaves had fallen in Central Park. The chilly breeze blowing through the open hotel window awakened young Cece. Exhaling a gasp, she realized, *Oh, boy! I am in New York! Oh my! To be eleven in New York City! What a thrill!* What once existed as a dream world she read about, now sprawled out in the big city beneath her hotel window. She had never seen anything as tall as the city's skyscrapers. When she looked up, she felt she would topple over herself.

Liz's entire family stayed in the Plaza Hotel beside the famous park. In the north wing of the hotel, the relatives had a splendid view of the forest within the city. However, pageant officials sequestered the contestants themselves to a no-distractions view in the south wing, protected by strict security.

Liz and her support team flew to New York City on the expense account of the state pageant. Cece and her family in Baton Rouge departed from New Orleans for the long journey by train. The countryside zoomed by as the Southern Crescent wound its way north in one long night and day. The express train amazed Cece! She never traveled so fast in her life.

Before arriving in New York City's Grand Central Station, the passenger train seldom stopped. Cece, Jack, and their parents, rode in a first-class Pullman car. Most of Liz's remaining family including her parents, Camilla and Charles, and his sister Mary Ann and her son Richie, boarded the same train car in Charlotte. As they wound through the Appalachian Mountains, Cece peered out the panoramic windows. She saw Fraser fir trees, which reminded her of the last family Christmas celebration. When the journey became boring, she, Jack, and cousin Richie would duel each other in a game of War with playing cards. Over time, the clack-clack of the train cars on the rails lulled Cece to sleep.

While Cece slept and others had gone to the dining car, Izzy noticed her sister-in-law Camilla seemed anxious about something.

"What's bothering you, Camilla?"

She retorted, "Nothing, why do you ask?"

Secretly, Camilla's mind was replaying the scene in her mind of her attacker in New York. Years ago, she had put it out of her consciousness, but with the advent of this trip, the old pangs returned. Her mind's recorder replayed the tragic park scene repeatedly. Inside, Camilla felt defeated and tarnished. How she loathed that city. It seemed strange to her that after all these years that the rape memories still affected her so deeply. Fear enveloped her whole being.

Meanwhile, the frigid air and the brightness of the November morning poured through the windows of Liz's room in the Plaza Hotel. Her rehearsal schedule would challenge even the hardiest of women. Most of the agenda was fun, glamor, bright lights, makeup, hairstyles, photographers, and interviews. The behind-the-scenes work required discipline to keep one-step ahead of the next competitor.

Liz overslept on that first day of four competitions. The effects of her contraband booze from the prior night fused to her brain cells as if they were a film of fresh molded plastic. Suzy, Liz's pageant chaperon, entered the bedroom and tapped the arm of the sleeping beauty.

"Miss Liz, Miss Liz, you must get ready, swimsuit preliminaries begin in two hours. Here, here, I will help you get it together."

Through the veil of fog, Liz gazed at the round black dial of the travel clock with luminescent green numerals. It was 7:00 am. An hour for travel to the auditorium and an hour for preparation remained. She thought, *It is too early for a competition.*

With a quick layer of makeup and a scarf over her hair, Liz hurdled the steps of the hotel to the taxi stand. Her professional fashion team waited to take over when she arrived in the pageant dressing room. Within her itinerary, she noticed breakfast treats were available, and a seated lunch followed the preliminary. Her stomach ached with hunger.

"Take me to City Auditorium on 32nd Street. Be quick about it. I'm running late."

The driver of the yellow taxi screeched the tires. With every minute that passed, Liz made impulsive glances at her watch. It seemed like the taxi was circling the blocks due to the maze of one-way streets blocked by road construction. Fifty minutes later the taxi arrived at the destination.

"Drive me to the back. We check in there."

She ran in and flashed her credentials to the bouncer and welcoming hostess at the entrance.

"Welcome Miss Perkins. We have been waiting on you. Continue to the end of that hall."

Her start that morning was more harried than she wished. The nervous clack-clack-clack of high heels on marble reverberated in the hallway much as Cece's train scaled the tracks on its way to New York City. Liz's noisy shoes betrayed the confident posture of a professional at her best. She calmed herself as she saw the other girls in the same stage of preparation as she. Her coach warned her not to play the comparison game, but she was human.

Liz entered the first room to present her credentials. As she glided from checkpoint to checkpoint, she cased the earlier arrivals. She smiled as she met her rivals and ticked her mind through the assets and talents that each was to highlight this week. She had studied the pageant orientation materials and each person's biography and picture. In her mind, it was as if the condescending voice of her mother, Camilla had whispered. Liz noted to herself, *How in heaven's name did these hillbillies make it here? From what turnip truck did they fall? I guess even a barn looks better with a new coat of paint.* Assured she was in a better condition, but not overconfident, Liz conceded that when she took the stage, she faced a battle.

She fumbled the document and gazed at the raised print "Miss American Glory" surrounding the pageant logo of the Statue of Liberty. Her momentary dreamlike, trance settled on a scene in a crystal ball in her mind as she waved to a pretend audience cheering her advance on the runway, her crown in place. Her pageant coach had imprinted the picture of success on her mind. *Oh, if only she could win the coveted title! Winning may alter other plans, but she would deal with that when the time came.*

The brash accent of a native of middle New Jersey interrupted Liz from her temporary magical spell.

"Papers, please" the worker demanded.

Liz commented to herself, *Do you think I am a poodle?*

She handed over a form and gushing she said, "I'm Miss South Carolina Glory, Elizabeth Perkins."

Behind her, a lass from Michigan shouted, "Oh say it again, that was so cute; how do you people talk so slow-w-w?"

With her warmest smile and in a pouty drawl stretching every syllable, Liz played along, "Wey-ah I come from, our front porches are wide, and our words are long!"

The desk woman handed back to Liz her document, a binder, and a bag of goodies and directed her where to meet her team for wardrobe, fittings, and makeup. Liz thought her main swimsuit competition would be Sara Richards, Miss Virginia Glory, a tall, gorgeous, and leggy brunette.

Yet, Liz's stunning blond hair, ever-present smile, and luscious body earned her good marks, too.

She gulped, *This will be a tight race!*

Liz's support team went to work. Her pageant coach, hair stylist, makeup artist, and wardrobe consultant stood by her dressing table. Each one performed their tasks in a scripted order. They washed, dried, and curled her hair, applied base and finishing makeup, mascara and eyeliner, rouge, and lipstick. Then, the team molded Liz into the one-piece royal blue bathing suit and silver high heels. With a few splices of tape in the right places, the coach announced "show-time" for Liz's first preliminary. She didn't mind exposing herself in a bathing suit. She had worked hard to get her torso into shape and this was the time and place to be proud of it. She endured the grueling four-hour session. Afterward, the pageant organizers released the women to eat lunch, and then to rehearse for the next day's talent competition. That evening an envelope slid under her room door. She tore it open.

Miss Elizabeth Perkins,

You placed in the top five contestants in the swimsuit preliminary. We are very proud of you. Good luck in the next preliminary. Be ready for Talent, tomorrow.

Best of luck,
The Judges

Elated with her ranking, she slept well that night. To the delight of her chaperone, she woke up before 6:30 am. Liz again met her support team for their kid-glove treatments at the auditorium. She slid into a knee length red dress for her talent and headed to the stage.

At the end of her song, she changed into a three-piece suit provided by the pageant sponsors. All the contestants appeared in a ticker-tape parade meandering through Wall Street and the financial district that afternoon. The boisterous crowds, streamers, bands, and convertibles carrying each girl thrilled Liz. The young ladies received a gift certificate to use after the parade in a shopping spree at the high class department stores clustered on Fifth Avenue in Midtown.

Liz asked her challenger from Texas, Marylou Martin, to join her for a peek at a posh jewelry store known for their trademark gift-wrapping. Marylou noticed Liz spent an inordinate amount of time trying on engagement rings. That night the Texan wrote in her diary, *Liz looked dreamy-eyed today. I wonder what is up with that.*

In her room, Liz glanced at the floor by her door and found another envelope.

Miss Elizabeth Perkins,

You placed in the top five contestants in the talent preliminary. We are very proud of you. Good luck in the next preliminary. Be ready for Evening Gown tomorrow.

Best of luck,
The Judges

At the final round of preliminary judging, Liz displayed the new evening gown her sponsors picked to highlight her best qualities. When she and Camilla went to the fitting session earlier in Charleston, Camilla expressed her disdain for the bold color lines. The fashion coach parried every snide comment with a strong rebuttal.

Camilla interjected, "She looks like a fashion doll, not a beauty contestant."

The coach parried back, "I want Liz's dress to scream contrast, pizazz, panache, and flair. Trust me, this Bob Mackie gown will make the statement that Liz is in charge and knows where she is going."

Camilla squealed, "These are not colors I would use."

"Tough, isn't it lady?"

The morning of the preliminary, Liz stepped into her new empire-style ball gown. Her flashy hues and accents differed so much that it took Liz a moment to adjust her mindset. The dress wrapped her in fuchsia satin, accented with wide hot pink and lavender vertical lines. A long train of fuchsia tulle cascaded to the floor.

At 9:00 pm, another envelope appeared under the door. Liz breathed heavily as she opened it. She hoped for more good news. She had a chance!

Miss Elizabeth Perkins,

You placed in the top five contestants in the evening gown preliminary. We are very proud of you. Good luck in the finals, tomorrow night.

Best of luck,
The Judges

While Liz endured the tedious and wearying pace of the preliminary phases, her family scheduled visits to New York's tourist icons. She was disappointed that she could not share her good news with her loved ones. Contest rules prohibited contact between the contestants and their family or anyone not on the contestant's support team, or pageant staff. As Liz passed in the ticker tape parade, the family gazed at her from a distance of forty feet. They could see her but she had no clue where they were standing. That was their only interaction during the week, until the finals.

Young Cece, her brother, and cousin Richie talked non-stop about their visits to the Empire State Building and the Statue of Liberty. Cece's mother reminded the kids that their great-grandparents processed through Ellis Island as legal immigrants. For the youngsters, the trip exposed them not only to their cousin's greatest moments, but also to history, architecture, foods, and a different way of life.

Chapter 12

The Finals

The Next Night
New York, New York

On the last of four days, the pageant final competition arrived. Each contestant strutted out as the tuxedoed emcee proclaimed their title, name, hometown, and college, if they had one. Liz waited her turn behind a petite four-foot-ten-inch Miss Rhode Island Glory. Every ten seconds, the producer's assistant cued the next person and motioned them to get moving. Then it was Liz's turn. She postured herself, smiled, stepped, and floated across the stage. The battery of multiple spotlights blinded Liz as she reached the end of the long runway. Her mind recalled her coach's acronym for this very moment: B-A-B-E-S. She remembered *Boobs forward, Arms at side, Butt in, Eye connection, Smile.*

"Miss South Carolina Glory, Elizabeth Perkins, Charleston, South Carolina, Blaketon College."

With perfect posture in her torso, she relaxed. Her eyes riveted on the audience, and they roared back in unrestrained applause.

The ovation cemented her smile in place. What fun this was! She lived for the approval of the crowd. Her five seconds to pose expired. As the producer pointed at her to move, she revolved, gave a flirting twist of her head, and glided to her assigned spot. The representative from the next state took her place.

Based on the preliminary results, the judges' votes

culled the fifty to the top ten semi-finalists. One by one, the lucky women who placed in the elite ten paraded to center stage. The emcee ticked off the first eight in the group from Mississippi, Michigan, Texas, California, New York, Florida, Tennessee, and Nebraska.

Aunt Camilla frowned with a fear in her heart. She shook her head. With her program, Izzy fanned a breeze toward Camilla to cool her. Jack watched intently. Richie fidgeted with his slide rule. Cece lay in her chair. Her nervous legs stretched forward on the floor and she crossed her fingers with her eyes closed. Cece wished. She prayed. She hoped for Liz's success. Camilla nervously barked at Cece to sit up straight with proper posture.

In his ninth call out, the emcee bellowed, "Miss South Carolina Glory, Elizabeth Perkins."

Liz strode to the rightmost position in the line of the other eight. She peered into the cheering audience. She looked to the ceiling and whispered, "Thank you, Lord!" As Camilla rose to her feet cheering, the rest of the family followed her lead. With raucous applause, the spectators agreed.

"Our tenth semi-finalist tonight is Sara Richards, Miss Virginia Glory."

An equal round of cheering and clapping exploded from the audience to the rafters.

During the evening, the ten women competed anew in the four categories of swimsuits, talent, evening gown, and interviews. Each area counted twenty-five percent. With a miscue in one category, the contestant might make up for the lapse in another stronger category. The earlier preliminary competition scores meant nothing. The women had entered a new game. It was time for Liz to make it or break it.

In their swimsuits, the graceful contestants paraded on the stage again. Izzy sat back in her chair and mused to herself, *These one-piece monkey suits are the pits. Will they ever wear the new style bikinis? They look more interesting and flattering.*

The state pageant director had changed so much of Liz's persona with which she won the state title. Her hair was longer and straighter, and the makeup more pronounced. For her talent, her board insisted she sing something more contemporary. At their urging, she sang *Somewhere* from the popular musical *West Side Story.*

Upon her last note, mixed feelings circulated through Liz about her performance. While she was singing the song with emotion actually to someone in the audience, she wondered how events would unfold for the two lovers. As she left the stage after her performance, Liz shook her head. She sang it less than perfectly. With a bad case of nerves, she did not have the same sense of accomplishment as she did at the state pageant.

When Liz stepped onto the stage in her fuchsia evening gown, the crowd roared their admiration for her boldness and beauty. She was a hit. She floated the length of the runway and fortunately remembered B-A-B-E-S again as she paused for more applause. Her coach had drilled in her that a temporary loss of focus was possible and would be devastating. She nodded and smiled at the judges. As much as she could muster, she portrayed confidence.

After a musical break, the emcee announced four of the top five finalists. Sara Richards, Miss Virginia Glory was the first name he proclaimed. Two more candidates came forward to the finalists circle. Then a fourth, Marylou Martin, the redhead with big hair from Texas, stepped forward. Liz still had a chance. She looked at her family, saw Cece, and winked.

The emcee paused and shouted, "The last contestant to reach the finals is Miss South Carolina Glory, Liz Perkins."

As the crowd cheered each of their favorites, the five beauties held the hand of the contestants beside them.

The final event in the pageant featured a personal interview. Navy escorts in dress-white uniforms ushered four of the five finalists into a large windowed and soundproof booth until their turn, to prevent them from hearing the answers of earlier contestants. The emcee posed the same question to each lady. Sara Richards moved to center stage for her turn. Then, one by one, the emcee called the candidates from isolation. When Liz's turn arrived, the finalists who answered before her formed a semi-circle behind her. Her heart was pounding. The emcee's question did not surprise Liz. She had prepared.

Chapter 13

A New Platform

Camilla and Liz's board of advisors urged Liz to ditch the astronaut idea. They thought it to be preposterous. They said the contestant must consider the platform she presents as serious, since it sealed her title hopes. It must be something realistic. Liz was serious about soaring into space but the culture of her time resisted women's progress. Liz remembered her volunteer work at the veterinary rescue clinic in Charleston. She once had a passion for her duties at the clinic. The rescue facilities were small, compared to those in Charlotte and Atlanta, but she and others made the facility work. Liz could not stomach suffering by any animal. Every stray, rescue, mutt, or tomcat that came in she welcomed with kind words, and a gentle hug for the animal. If it did not have a collar with a name on it, Liz gave the animal a name. Each one was her child. Liz found strength in caring for these creatures that had an unsure future. As she reflected on this experience, Liz created her new pageant platform. What did children and family issues mean to her? She did not see herself being a mother soon. She had no passion for motherhood. She ticked through her options of health, sports, the new women's-rights movement, and politics. None of them excited her. One afternoon, after she looked through some old photobooks, she settled on her new platform.

The emcee said, "Who is your hero, why, and how would you seek to emulate them?"

"My hero is a veterinarian in my hometown of Charleston. Under Dr. Estes' wise instruction, I volunteered every summer during high school. With his help, we nursed different animals to good health, and we saved many of them from their premature death by euthanasia. Nothing can replace the love and unconditional acceptance these animals gave me. Dr. Estes is my hero."

A polite round of applause followed her answer. Liz had rehearsed her expected response as prompted by her coach. She wanted the audience to relate to her as a real person. While she loved animals and the love they returned, it had been so long since her volunteer days she had lost her fire and zeal. She was not sure she convinced the judges of her long ago passion.

Chapter 14

Exposed

Minutes Later
New York, New York

The suspense in the huge auditorium was over-whelming. The emcee asked for the envelope listing the winners, He read the first name.

"Our second runner-up is Marylou Martin from Texas."

The emcee handed Marylou a bouquet and kissed her. The audience cheered their approval. Izzy clenched Camilla's hand in support.

"If for any reason, the lady who is selected Miss American Glory cannot fulfill her duties, the first runner-up will succeed her. Good luck ladies!"

He continued, "Now I will announce the first runner-up."

Then, a pause followed, cracked by a dramatic drumroll. Surprised, Cece, recoiled in her seat.

"Elizabeth Perkins from South Carolina. And the winner, your new Miss American Glory, is Sara Richards."

The previous titleholder anchored the sparkling tiara on the new queen's head. The emcee handed a bouquet to Liz and a larger floral arrangement of roses to Sara. He kissed both ladies. The crush of finalists and contestants mobbed their new queen. Liz congrat-ulated Sara with a peck on the cheek. Moments later the new Miss American Glory paced down the runway while the spotlights circled her and the audience. Liz thought, *My, she is gorgeous!* The contestants gathered at center stage for a short photo and media session. Then, Liz said her good-byes amid hugs and kisses. She gathered her makeup and clothes in the dressing room with her support team. More good-byes mixed with tears as she exited the auditorium. Outside, no tears fell. Feeling sorry for herself for not winning was far from her mind. Alone, she motioned for a taxi.

"Take me to the Plaza Hotel, please."

At the hotel, Liz paid the taxi driver and ran into the lobby with an aging doorman lagging behind by three steps. Inside, in a hidden alcove, Kent Sullivan reclined on a leather armchair. He stood as she ran into his arms. They embraced in a tight hold for a long moment. Kent gave her a prolonged kiss.

"You were stunning."

At both pageants, he had observed her in the general admission section away from the family.

He added, "I can't wait for you to be my wife."

"Kent, I cannot continue to live without you. What have you found out?"

She glanced around the room. She saw none of her family or her chaperone in the lobby.

Kent said, "I've got your ring and I will get our license next Tuesday at the Beaufort County clerk's office in the courthouse. The damn law requires us to wait one more day so we cannot get married until Wednesday. Our wedding appointment with the probate judge is at 3:00 pm."

Kent was a Private First Class in the United States Marine Corps. Liz had a "thing" for military men and he fit the mold: tall, tan, and handsome in dress blues, Kent Sullivan was her dream man. They had met the prior year at Blaketon. When his freshman year ended, Kent decided instead he wanted to honor America by joining the leathernecks. She compared his photo to pictures of her own father when he was in the army. She thought, *Here is the man who I want to marry!* Now she had found her own Prince Charming.

Kent planned for them to go to his post in Beaufort, South Carolina, where they would elope and take a short honeymoon trip to St. Augustine. Liz told her mother she planned to drive to Florida the next week, as she needed to decompress after the non-stop activities of the pageant. Her alibi was that she needed a break.

Liz did not see young Cece waiting in the back of the lobby for her. The bewildered little girl hid behind a heavy curtain. Cece had never seen the strange man who was embracing Liz as in the movies. She heard Kent whisper the word marriage. Cece ran back to her mother's hotel room and banged on the door.

Izzy said, "What is all this noise about? Where have you been?"

Cece blurted out, "Liz is getting married!"

Cece did not notice Aunt Camilla primping herself in front of the mirror in the bathroom. Camilla poked her head out the door. Her countenance took on an evil distortion as she looked at Cece. Aunt Camilla's eyes moved up from the little girl's feet, then her knees, her yellow frilly dress, her chest, and met Cece's emerald eyes.

In her most insolent voice, Camilla shouted, "What did you say, child?"

Cece whimpered as she recounted verbatim what she heard. Camilla's anger explosion hit at once, as if a ball peen hammer struck a nail solidly. Aunt Camilla was livid. She had other plans for Liz. Not even waiting to tell her husband Charles, she left the north wing of the hotel. In a rage, she argued with the security guards in the hallways of the contestants' quarters. Camilla busted past the guards and spotted Liz saying goodbye to Marylou.

The fuming mother ordered, "Take me to your room now! We need to talk."

The two women screamed at each other for a few moments when Camilla shrieked, "You are never to speak to this soldier again. If you do, I will write you forever out of my life!"

That night the emotion overwhelmed Liz. With tears streaming down her face, she wrote Kent a "Dear John" letter. It was 3:00 am before she stopped crying. She had not won the pageant. But she cried because she could never see her dreamboat again.

Chapter 15

The Wall

The Following Week
Charleston, South Carolina

Liz pulled a letter from her mailbox. It was from the Reality Shampoo Company and addressed to her. RSC's products ranked as number one in the nation for premier hair care. While the beauty contest awarded scholarships, pageant sponsors offered endorsement opportunities and advertising gigs. The windfall helped college students cover school costs. With her mouth wide open, Liz read the letter.

Excitedly, she exclaimed, "Oh, my goodness."

Dear Miss Elizabeth Perkins,

Please allow me to introduce myself as Max Greenman, Vice-President of Marketing of Reality Shampoo, Inc., headquartered in Hollywood, California.

My team and I followed your participation in the Miss American Glory pageant with extreme interest. I want you to know you were my staff's favorite contestant. You impressed us with your glamourous hair and total persona. Your voice and image fulfill our criteria for a new spokeswoman. It is my pleasure to offer you the opportunity to be our first "Real" woman. We propose that your distinctive image appear on labels of Real Shampoo and fine beauty products. Our company will compensate your services as a representative for our products in television advertising and at special appearances. In addition, we offer you a salary, an all-expense paid trip to Hollywood for photo and video production, and an advance stipend of $2,500. Use this bonus for your future college courses or other expenses. For each unit of our fine products sold, if you accept, we will pay you a generous royalty. Each year we can revisit this agreement to make sure it meets our mutual needs. If our offer pleases you as we think it will, call my assistant Gladys Loving at phone number 323-732-5489 by June 5. She will coordinate your visit and contract signings. We are excited to present you this opportunity to collaborate with us!

Truly yours,

Max Greenman

Overjoyed, Liz showed the letter to her mother. With her lips sealed for the moment, Camilla avoided another explosion as in New York just days ago. Her heart could not handle it. Inside, Camilla knew Liz was not going to Hollywood. *It was not her plan for her baby girl.* Camilla wanted to continue to call Liz's shots.

The night before the deadline to call Mr. Greenman, Camilla said, "No Liz! You are not going. And that is final!"

Liz opened her mouth to protest as Camilla walked out and slammed the door on her daughter's opportunity. This completed an indestructible wall separating a mother and her daughter.

Chapter 16

For Better or Worse

The Months After the Pageant
Charleston, South Carolina

Kent was not the only serious boyfriend in Liz's life. When Camilla issued her edict not to see Kent again, Liz found others. She made sure that her mother never heard mention of them. Liz shielded herself from her mother's shackles by continuing her studies at the out-of-state school.

Camilla's own plan for her daughter hatched. She found a local suitor. It came together one wintry day at the country club. Betty Brashon, Camilla's bridge partner, had an eligible son, John, a medical resident in Columbia. Liz knew of John when they were younger, but there was no chemistry between her and the frail older nerd. Being a geek, he did not possess the brave persona or machismo of Kent as a kid. However, now he was a doctor, available and soon to be rich! The two dated for almost two years while Liz finished her music degree. Before graduation, Camilla and Charles announced the engagement of their daughter Elizabeth Virginia Perkins and Dr. John Brashon III. The betrothal kicked off a season of society parties in Charleston. Then the wedding day arrived.

Camilla employed an army of skilled decorators to array their home, the church, and the country club in everything traditional, ostentatious, and Southern. She repeated the theme of magnolias, white roses, and bolts of draped imported tulle fabric to decorate the three venues. The Perkins spared no expense. If Camilla wanted it, consider it done. A full church celebrated the event. In the radiance of sunlight pouring through stained glass, brass candelabras provided a warm glow to the church gathering. The wedding party advanced on a white runner amid the long aisle. As Liz's maid of honor, Cece led the procession. She beamed at her Uncle Charles in the narthex of the cavernous cathedral. A stringed orchestra played Vivaldi's first movement of *Spring* as the ten bridesmaids advanced. As she reached the altar, Cece glanced at Aunt Camilla on the first row. Her aunt nodded her approval. Throughout the procession, the mother of the bride thought, *Today is my show.* True to form, Camilla had chosen her daughter's wedding dress. Resplendent in the gown of satin, lace, pearls, and glittering rhinestones, Liz paraded as if on a runway once again. Her fifteen-foot train gathered at the waist in a gentle bow. Instead of the traditional veil, Camilla opted for her daughter to wear an oversized white hat. The groom, in a formal morning suit, met his bride at the altar for the exchange of vows. On and on the festivities continued, day and night, at the church, country club, and the Perkins' home.

After their extended honeymoon on a cruise to Aruba, the young Brashon couple settled in Columbia. Their century-old row house stood only a few blocks from his practice. In a short time, the couple's stature rose in the community. They often hosted post-event socials in their townhome.

The ugly secret that the Perkins did not know earlier is that at age twenty-nine, Dr. Brashon fought chronic alcoholism. One evening, after the well-fed and satiated guests left, Liz and John continued an intense argument that had erupted during their party. Liz confronted John, telling him to clean up his act.

With his back to her and muttering something under his breath, the doctor pivoted. As he turned around, he held aloft a huge butcher knife. Liz was sure his intent was not surgery! She ran out of their perfect home. She tripped on the front steps and fell face first on the brick sidewalk into the grass. Her knee was swelling, and she was in excruciating pain. Liz groveled on her hands and feet to the neighboring row house. As she crawled behind lush bushes and sobbed, she noticed John standing in the open front door of their home. With a burst of adrenaline, she stood up, hobbled up the steps to the neighbor's front door, and banged on it. She looked back over her shoulder. John had not come after her.

The neighbors opened the door, allowing a sliver of light to shine on her contorted face.

"Help, help. I need the police and the EMTs. My husband attacked me. I am in fear of my life."

The elderly couple pulled her inside and slammed the door. In what felt like an eternity, an ambulance and a fire truck finally pulled up to the house with flashing red lights and screaming sirens. Behind them were two Columbia Police Department sedans, ablaze with blue lights. A few neighbors turned on their outside lights and peered through their windows. The ambulance whisked Liz to the nearby Catholic hospital emergency room. Nurses dressed in black-and-white habits scurried in and out of the ward. Liz, heavily sedated, endured several hours of X-rays and scans by the new state-of-the-art CAT scan machine. The ER doctor diagnosed her injury as a partial tear of her right anterior cruciate ligament. He prescribed biweekly therapy, a regimen of opioid pills for the pain, and consultation with an orthopedic surgeon the next week. While the injury was painful but not life threatening, the on-duty doctor kept her in the nuns' care overnight. She moved to a private room for observation and protection from the stress of her abuser.

At their row house, the police handcuffed Dr. John Brashon III, for assault and battery, and domestic violence. Within the hour, John's attorney had posted bond and the Palmetto County jail released him.

The next day, Liz balanced herself on crutches as she entered the offices of Lorrison, Lambert, and Keith, Attorneys at Law.

Paul Lorrison, a middle-aged, ruddy, and gentrified Southern attorney, wore white slacks with a blue blazer. Liz chuckled and thought, *If he were not married, I would make a move for him.* They discussed her trauma that occurred the preceding night. Paul opened the closet in his office and pulled out a box.

"When you appear before the judge, I want you to wear this brace on your ankle and knee. Between it and the crutches, we will engender sympathy and we can demand even more than alimony alone. Your injury and marriage will not be easy to overcome and we will make him pay for it, okay?"

With an incredulous look, Liz questioned, *That ugly thing on my leg?*

He asked, "When do you want to pursue the divorce proceeding?"

She shouted back with determination, "Yesterday!"

Chapter 17

The Enemy Within

1992
Myrtle Beach, South Carolina

In covert ways, Liz aged into an empty suit. An outward shell with nothing inside to protect. Yes, she had the package of looks and charisma, yet her mother ripped Liz's self-identity from her. She remained a fragile child who never escaped her mother's tentacles. While desperate for approval, she craved real love more. She could not find the evasive lasting love she hoped for from her mother, her dead father, or a suitor. Continuous companionship and intimacy remained outside her grasp. When she found tolerable mates, they remained in the relationship a short while, then they evaporated off the screen as if black dots on Cece's childhood Etch-A-Sketch.

Liz never let go of the fear of her exacting mother. Her life reflected actions dictated by others, seldom what she thought she should do. She sought the positive influence of others. Their own expected return is that her Midas touch might rub off on them. Only a precarious thread held Liz's self-esteem and her fears of failing together. It was a balancing act.

Liz amassed plenty of cash over the years. She plowed it into blue-chip investments. Beside alimony and antique sales, she gleaned stipends from her public speaking tours and commercials. As age crept in, she maintained her silky voice, voluptuous figure, and glamorous looks. Wherever she went for speaking engagements, she praised the benefits of positive self-esteem. Liz influenced the lives of women and school-age girls. How ironic it was that she peddled encouragement despite her fragile ego.

The career duties Liz enjoyed most occurred when she starred in television ads with pleas to rescue dogs and cats from imminent death. Intertwined with foreboding music, the dramatic pictures flashed scenes of feline and canine suffering. Amid distress, starvation, and squalor, the ads exposed the cursed animals. Then the lens moved into a softened close-up of Liz's sad face. She implored the audience to act now to save the animals. Her sweet syrupy dialect proved convincing. The final scene zoomed in on the celebrity's face as she patted her cheek with a tissue and wiped away a tear. She still maintained convincing stage presence.

Liz rode a train of four marriages. She recovered from her first marriage, but not from the injury. For the rest of her life she walked with a noticeable limp. A pulmonary physician in the military followed John Brashon III. Immediately, the new groom's beating assaults began. Then divorce. The third husband, adept at sales of his product and himself, was a once productive real-estate broker. He encouraged Liz to develop her own agency. Early in her new career, she learned he siphoned off her cash to fund his recreational drug habit. Liz stayed clean, but the spouse's drug problem led to physical abuse when she cut him off from her earnings. Divorce, again. At age twenty-nine, after three failed marriages in seven years, she married Carl, the career navy officer and the caboose of the train. Their marriage lasted twenty years, while repeating the pattern of an abusive relationship. She hesitated to admit failure again.

There had been no children involved in Liz's life. Even though she had four virile husbands plus many boyfriends, she did not have the luck, yearning, or blessing to have children. Instead, Liz's children spread over decades in the form of the animals she rescued personally — poodles, Jack Russell terriers, and cats.

She rested on a couch in the shrink's office as the mental professional droned a familiar message. The round table next to the leather couch held a ballpoint pen, paper, and a box of tissues. She heard the doctor talking to her directly, but it was as if she were in a fog, some distance from him.

"Liz, you are your own worst enemy. You continue to seek love in relationships with men you hope mimic your father. Falling from the apex of your youth, your self-esteem is now low."

Her mind flashed back to the swing Cece sat on in White Point Park in Charleston years earlier. The swing's movement mirrored her emotional health plummeting from a zenith to the bottom of the arc.

"Understandable. These strong militaristic or commanding types control you and steal your power. It is easy for these men to cause you to collapse to their demons. You told me your past partner choices had these repetitive traits: Narcissism, physical and verbal abuse, isolation, accusations, control, misogyny, taunting, disrespect of your person, and risky behaviors. These deeds ruined your marriages. We both know you have worth and have made huge personal contributions to the good of our society. Nevertheless, poor choices counterbalance the good. We need to explore how to fix this destructive approach to ensure a brighter future for you. Here are my recommendations to consider."

He handed her a list of her difficulties and his treatment plan. When she had walked the runway in the pageant many years ago, the life that played out was not what she expected nor desired.

Liz wept. *Her fairy tale life was not to go this way. She was still a young woman.* The doctor leaned over, handing her the box of tissues. At that moment, Liz determined she never wanted another husband.

Chapter 18

Assembling a Puzzle

Monday, May 11, 1998, 11:00 am
New Orleans, Louisiana

Cece lifted the mug half-full of lukewarm liquid to her lips. She had her day's fill of the rich full-bodied Louisiana coffee. A sugar rush enveloped her, stemming from the two beignets she nursed during her reminiscences of Liz, the pageants, her husbands, her pets, and this mess. Cece's mood worsened due to the mix of coffee, sugary food, distant memories, and the reality of a full schedule. She was glad that Ross went to work to get the grades posted for the classes he taught this semester. It gave her more time to develop a plan, gather information, and to execute her ideas.

She called Alfred Bobbin first. He worked at the Delta Funeral Home and Crematory in Baton Rouge for thirty years. His father had been an undertaker at the same funeral home. Alfred owned the flower shop across the street from the funeral home, too. An old family friend, he befriended Cece's parents at their church. Cece had gone to school with his daughter Linda. She had confidence in Alfred's sound advice on how to arrange a proper funeral for Liz. He informed her it would not be difficult to transfer Liz from the morgue and to inter her in the cemetery plot next to her deceased parents. Distance was not a problem. He confided the usual hurdles that Cece might need to leap. Alfred recommended Cece decide on a funeral home in the Charleston vicinity to handle the embalming or cremation. Further, she needed to prepare for the large outlays to the morgue, the cemetery, and funeral home. This entailed confirming the cost for each and coordinating a schedule with them. Meanwhile, he said the cemetery keeper had the records, which could tell her if Camilla and Charles's plot had enough room for Liz. After thanking Alfred, she hung up the phone and looked over the list of insurmountable tasks.

It was necessary to use money from Liz's estate for the funeral. Ross and Cece wanted to use their own savings for a phased renovation of their home. They had no idle cash sitting around, whether $15,000, $10,000, or even just $5,000. What would it all cost? She ran through a mental list of the expected costs for the funeral home, cemetery, transportation, and morgue. Other costs surfaced. The amounts were overwhelming.

The morgue came up next on her call list. The agent stumbled through her protocol to make sure Cece was a family member. She explained the family must pay the storage fee before release of Liz's body to a funeral home.

"Do you have an estimate how much that will cost?"

The clerk replied, "We base our fee on the actual number of days of storage at a rate of twenty-five dollars per day."

Since the time Liz died and until she could organize the funeral, she expected a month to pass. Cece did the math. The estimate of the morgue bill was close to $800.

The agent added, "When the county receives payment, we call the funeral home of your choice. They handle the rest."

"Okay, I'm guessing we will get you the money in two weeks, after we arrange the funding. Let me ask you something else. Do you know if she . . . uh, is Liz turning purple yet?"

Cece shuddered at her own morbid question.

"No, not likely at those temperatures in the freezer."

"Thank you for your help. Good-bye."

Cece felt a sense of accomplishment. Next, she examined listings for cemeteries in the Charleston vicinity. Among the ads, she eyed the name of the final resting place of Liz's parents. The Cooper River Gardens opened in 1950 as a funeral home, chapel, mausoleum, florist, crematorium, and cemetery. She realized, *The full-service facility is as old as I am.*

She dialed. A kind woman with a silky voice answered.

"Hello, Cooper River Gardens, Sharon Lee here. How may I help you?"

Cece explained first, who she was. Then she added details about Liz's title, prominence, and her death, and Liz's parents having a plot there.

"My first question is whether the family plot has adequate space to inter Liz."

She added, "With these considerations and a funding problem, how much will it cost to bury someone?"

Sharon replied, "We want to do the best for our family, don't we? My first thought is that since you are, well, um, short of money, we can offer you our pine box coffins for paupers. That is only $4,000."

Cece screamed, "Mrs. Lee, surely you cannot bury a Miss South Carolina Glory in a pine box. What does an upgrade cost?"

"Can you hold on the phone a minute Mrs. Turner, please? Let me check with the director."

Silence, and then Cece heard voices speaking in the background. The wait lasted what seemed forever. Mrs. Lee returned and said, "You need to talk to the director. Please hold. Thank you."

A moment later, a deep bass voice resounded through the receiver.

"Hello, I am Tom Lee. My wife explained your dilemma. We are so sorry you experienced this tragedy. I tell you what, we offer a VIP Courtesy Special for people with notoriety in our state. We can do this plan for $6,000. You can choose from three or four floor demo coffins for women. Just like new, but a lot cheaper. For that price, we cannot offer free flowers. This fee includes the cost of opening the grave. The service would be a simple graveside service and you can buy the blanket of flowers for the casket and supply your own preacher to preside. You must understand that any added services or elegance such as a chapel or limousine for the family would add to this special offer. But, we extend this service if you need it."

His words encouraged Cece. *This just might work.*

She asked, "Is the cost of embalming included? It has to fit in the budget we give to the court."

"We included embalming in the fee. Moreover, our records show that the Perkins plot has three people interred, two adults, and an infant. The plot could accommodate two more people. And a zero balance exists on this account."

"The only other question I have concerns how much it will cost to transport Liz from the morgue to your cemetery."

"You are in luck, Mrs. Turner. For any relocation within one hundred miles of us, we transport free. It is company policy. In such a difficult time, all of our services remove pressure from the bereaved."

"Okay, Mr. Lee. You have convinced me. Can you please email a contract and a detailed cost estimate I can take to the court next week?"

Tom said, "Yes, Mrs. Turner. Let me get your information. After you return the papers, we can proceed with the services. If you have questions, please call me."

The phone clicked off. Cece had another brain-storm. Ross's father was a retired preacher. When Ross returned, she would have Ross call his dad to ask him to officiate the service.

Her last call of the morning was to Rufus Jasper at Thomaston, Jasper, and Scallup, the law firm who Liz's boyfriend Joey said was helpful to Liz. Cece wanted to find out if he knew what legal documents she had prepared. With exact precision, Rufus answered Cece's questions one by one.

"Did Liz prepare a will?"

"None prepared by me. She was my client for other things. We encouraged her to execute one, but she did not. I bought into the partnership five years ago. If she recorded a will at the courthouse, our firm would find it. If she never recorded it, we could not know. Liz was as tight-fisted as a Scotsman and did not see our counsel for seniors as helpful. In hindsight, finding a will can save you or any family from this trouble. You and the family should look for one and if she has none, plan to distribute assets, intestate, to the heirs."

After a pause, he added, "You might find something at her home."

"How do I arrange her funeral without funds?"

Rufus said, "Until you find a will and probate it, someone in Liz's family needs to approach the proper judge in Georgetown to become administrator of the estate. Then get approval to use approved funds. If you locate a bona fide will, take it to the courts and probate it. The courts may grant hardship requests for withdrawals to pay for preparation and burials up to a local limit. Banks and insurance companies will follow court orders to give funds. Yes, ma'am, I don't see why the family cannot get court approval if they wish."

"What about distributing assets with no will? How does that work?"

"First, account for the assets and debts. Assuming you do not find a will, the family petitions the court that Ms. Perkins died intestate, without a will. A formula exists with rules for distributions of assets to heirs."

"So does that mean I handle everything long distance from New Orleans and show up in the court in Georgetown when I make an accounting?"

"Yes."

Cece still had a bug in her gut that everything was too easy.

"Okay, who is the judge I should contact?"

Rufus said, "Just a sec, I'll check."

He gave her the name and phone number of the probate judge's clerk in Georgetown. That set Cece to think, *It can't be that hard to make these arrangements.* The call ended with Cece thanking Rufus Jasper for his time.

She remembered that her college friend Harry Caisteal was a probate lawyer in Georgetown at the venerable firm of Caisteal and Wilson. His dad had started the partnership fifty years earlier. Harry was next on the list of the morning's calls. Although they had not seen each other since their days at Driesh College, they still exchanged Christmas cards and shared the progress of their family life over a quarter of a century. *Funny, how they kept in touch. It was as if the Lord knew I would need his help one day.*

When she called, they caught up on the chitchat and personalities from school.

Finally, Harry asked, "How can I help you, Cece?"

She summarized her dilemma.

"Harry, Ross and I will visit Mary's Island and stay near Georgetown next week. You may remember me talking about my cousin Liz Perkins. We need help on her estate. Can you counsel me on serving as an administrator? And can you set up an appointment with the probate judge in the middle of the next week? Oh, I have heard the judge's name is Bonham. Our trip to the island is first to meet with the city zoning folks. We have to store personal assets from her house. I want to get the court's order on this several days later. My priority is to get Liz buried, then distribute the estate."

Cece thought, *By the time this train gets rolling, I need a full week to soak up ions from the Atlantic to keep my mind straight!*

Harry said, "Sure, but first I have to ask you a panel of questions. Can we set up an interview by phone? I will be in court the rest of today. How is 10:00 am Louisiana time tomorrow?"

"Perfect. Call me!"

Cece breathed a sigh of relief and hung up the phone. Cece then asked herself, *What in the hell is next in this mayhem.* She felt overwhelming pressure to do something, anything.

The interview the next day lasted less than an hour. Cece kept on point to Harry's questions. Harry grasped the sordid situation the zoning director had described to Cece. It embarrassed and pained Cece to describe the metamorphosis of Liz, her favorite cousin, a beauty queen, a socialite, and now, this mess. Satisfied with his understanding, they ended the call. Harry made an appointment for Cece to appear in Judge Bonham's court on Wednesday of the following week. He called Cece back with the docket details at once.

Chapter 19

Ross's Research

Saturday, May 16, 1998
New Orleans to Myrtle Beach

As Ross and she started the long drive, Cece knew she was doing the right thing. She expected to bury Liz as promised. This is her character, her DNA. This is the way her parents raised her, her family's tradition. *She will not let anything deter her, not even the awful traffic in Atlanta.*

The couple had much to talk about during their journey. Cece spoke endlessly about the neighbors' dilemmas: barking dogs, rowdy children, illegally parked cars, and what person left their spouse. It is the reality of experiencing many things that meet you head-on in a suburban neighborhood, some important, some not. Being at work every day, Ross missed enduring through the mundane details himself. Just after the two crossed the Mississippi River, Ross changed the subject.

"Let's talk about the malady Kerry, the city zoning director, described to you."

Ross questioned everything. If he did not know the why or what about a situation, he aimed to soothe his curiosity with facts. He had spent several restless nights searching the internet for information about hoarding wanting to understand the psychology and cause of the disease. As he drove, he shared what he had learned with Cece.

Ross had never experienced hoarders until now. Unless you counted the plastic wrappers bread came in when he was a child. His parents' kitchen contained a cabinet overrun with hundreds of plastic bags with the words Rainbow Bread imprinted on most of them. Moreover, they had collected innumerable plastic trays the butcher wrapped meat in at the grocery. His parents felt these items held intrinsic value for something, someday. In addition, he recalled they kept a sizable cache of frozen dairy topping containers with matching lids. Ross chuckled at his memories of a benign form of object hoarding. Maybe it stemmed from the scarcities of the Great Depression. Ross rationalized, *Neither my parents nor I were hoarders. The bread bags were harmless and covert. They only were a minor problem when a glob of them fell out of their storage area.* In his mind, Ross wondered if hoarding could be genetic, as he shuddered at what used to be in his own garage.

Excitedly, Ross told Cece, "At the library, I made a breakthrough. I found a volume the doctors and researchers called the Diagnostic and Statistical Manual of Mental Disorders or DSM-4. It is the authoritative source on mental disease. It contains all science, no conjecture."

Ross explained, "In the DSM-4, the hoarding of objects and or animals fits within the broad term of hoarding disorder. And a hypothesis exists that hoarding has a relationship to Obsessive-Compulsive Disorder or OCD."

Eager to contribute her thoughts, Cece piped up, "I have watched TV documentaries portray extreme forms of object hoarding. The conditions deteriorate such that the residents cannot maneuver in the unhealthy environment. Wall-to-wall clutter crowds each room. There is an extreme emotional attachment to their stuff. The hoarder will not give or throw it away. Stuff like newspapers, magazines, old clothes, VCR tapes,

CDS, ballpoint pens, computers and accessories, bottle-caps, candles, plants, and most anything else. Oh, yeah, they even collect light bulbs! The revered and valued objects become a hazard to life itself."

She continued, "Other TV stories exposed animal hoarders like the proverbial cat lady, animal rescue shelters, animal exploiters, and even puppy mills. The episodes cited cats, dogs, and an ark-load of other animals living amid squalor. The mess overtakes the people and the animals when they cease to be able to give care. What scared me are the many unreported or undetected cases. It sounds like Liz's place, doesn't it?"

Ross countered, "My curiosity led me to learn how it starts. I found a few things when I searched the web with key words like animal collecting, animal hoarding, and animal cruelty."

Cece made a sour face at that mention.

He added, "This behavior is cruel and harmful to the animals and humans due to the squalor, the smell, the feces, vomit, and urine, and the threat of disease. These conditions often combine with elder and child abuse leaving the residents ill and devastated. It can be costly for cities to intervene, resolve, and support.

"This branch of medical science is new. The professionals are publishing educational materials and scientific evidence about casework. Dedicated veterinarians, professors, researchers, legitimate rescue agencies, and animal-care people are working together. Make no mistake. Animal hoarding is not about the legitimate efforts for animal sheltering, rescue, or sanctuaries. Nor is it about normal healthy people with multiple pets and a capacity to care for the animals.

"The animal hoarding disease stems from a drive to amass animals and control them. This drive is greater than the owner's desire to meet the basic needs of the animals. There is a failure to assess the animals' condition so they lack proper care. Cece, I don't know. Liz sounds like she fits the sketch of a legendary cat woman. Although men or women can be animal hoarders, the typical profile fits an unmarried, widowed, or divorced older female. Most of the time the hoarder is a loner who replaces human relationships with their focus of amassing animals. Other mental illness like OCD may be present. Couples or family members might be hoarders and enablers. It affects every level of society. None are immune."

Cece yawned. Her reaction was partly from boredom, and partly from avoidance of the distasteful. She was drowning in Ross's usual detailed research. Animal collecting is too kind a term for what she perceived to be a nasty, covert secret.

"Okay, okay, I give. You know your stuff, Ross. Can you turn on the radio?"

Ross commented, "Let me tie it up this way. Your Aunt Camilla controlled Liz like a puppet to fulfill her own ambition, societal wants, and needs. Under that yoke, Liz struggled to be free. Moreover, Liz yearned for a lasting, strong, loving, father figure in her man. I wonder too, how much her four traumatic marriages contributed to this fiasco."

Cece said, "The zoning director told me that Liz's boyfriend, Joey, collected the neighbor's cats or feral cats roaming the neighborhood. He didn't appear to limit how many he collected. The more, the merrier. Joey named each one and presented it to Liz.

"Kerry said he saw and has photo evidence of the cats having the run of any room, climbing on the counters, kitchen table, and other furniture, and hiding in closets. The pictures show open bags and dishes with cat food everywhere. Uncleaned litter boxes stunk up every room. What cat waste didn't find a home in a box ended upon the floor. I guess Joey controlled them in the sense the cats did not have freedom or a decent healthy uncluttered place to live."

Ross replied, "That's exactly what I am saying. The chaos and health hazard snowballed when Joey and Liz lost their ability to monitor and protect the welfare of the increasing number of cats. He wasn't valuing any one or small group of them. He collected them like I collected baseball cards as a kid."

Cece shivered and added, "Kerry mentioned the neighbors told of Joey attributing human qualities to each cat. He claimed the animals talked to him. That surely sounds delusional, doesn't it?"

Ross thought, *Well, each animal could have a different personality.* For Ross, it ended there. To him, a cat was a cat! Ross had no credentials as a mental-health professional but he relished researching new topics, no matter how sordid.

The foul and nasty conditions confronting them sank in. *How can people live like this?* Ross stopped talking and absorbed what he and Cece discussed.

He turned the radio to the public radio station and turned up the volume on a classical piece. Ross thought, *At least, Cece managed her three cats. They were usually clean creatures trained to use a litter box and to have feedings at consistent times every day. I'm sure glad the neighbor handled the daily maintenance while we were away on trips. Yet, if their care got out of kilter, the animals pooped anywhere. A daily ritual for cleanliness was the only way to keep ahead of the game. He guessed that Liz might have fed and disposed of the waste when she was sober and off the influence of prescription drugs. Surely, her standards relaxed on days of heavier intoxication and medication. Toward the end as Liz spiraled downward, and with whatever help Joey gave, the cats became secondary. Liz and*

Joey became textbook examples of overwhelmed care-givers for the cats.

Throughout the long drive, the couple bantered multiple topics but the conversation repeatedly returned to the topic of "Liz, Cat Lady". As the convertible crossed the Georgia state border into South Carolina, Cece's tender fingers grasped Ross's elbow. She leaned toward him. He studied her red lips that grinned the widest since she learned of Liz's death. He welcomed this break in her seriousness.

"I recalled something that Aunt Camilla told me that illustrates the empathy Liz had for animals."

Ross relaxed his posture and leaned back in the car seat.

"Go ahead. I want to hear this."

"When Liz worked at the vet, remember that Camilla relented and allowed Liz to adopt her poodles. She gave me the fourth puppy of the litter. I named it Coco because of its silky brown coat. This sweet runt of the litter displayed a pronounced overbite. Coco also had epilepsy that required regular doses of phenobarbital to treat it. Without the medication, Coco experienced multiple seizures. With it, her seizures were rarer and less intense. This is a common genetic defect stemming from the profuse inbreeding of poodles over decades.

"Liz and Camilla adored their three poodles as I did Coco. In her letters to me, Liz wrote she took the dogs for walks and runs in the nearby White Point Park. She spent hours there to gain freedom from her mother and she hoped to meet other animal lovers. Aunt Camilla told me that when Fifi, the last of her three poodles died, Liz rejected cremation at the vet or a simple burial in the backyard. Instead, Liz insisted they have a real funeral. Liz and her then husband number two arranged a service at a pet cemetery. Two days later, she arrived for the funeral with her husband and Aunt Camilla. Liz stepped out of her husband's silver Mercedes draped in a tight black crepe dress. A lacy black mantilla she discovered in Spain shrouded her face and platinum curls. Wearing full mourning dress in her mid-twenties, she appeared stunning. They paced to the cemetery office where an employee led them to the small chapel. In the center under the skylight lay the human baby-sized opened coffin with Fifi in it. An organ played the hymn *All Creatures of Our God and King*. Liz wailed when she saw her beloved Fifi and bawled her heart out. A tall solemn man in a black suit paced to a lectern next to the casket. This minister shared how much joy Fifi had given to the family and offered a prayer. He motioned for them to go outside where two black golf carts draped with black crepe waited for them. The driver chauffeured them across cement sidewalks to a tent. The preacher offered more words and prayers to soothe Liz. A cemetery crew lowered the coffin into the ground, covered it with dirt, and placed a spray of pink sweetheart roses over it. When she listened to Camilla's original detailed account, Cece thought, *this was the tender heart of Liz. Her cousin so strongly believed in her animals. It was a sweet sendoff."*

The stoic Ross commented, "Another red flag, isn't it, Cece?"

That afternoon, sixty miles from their destination near Myrtle Beach, they made a planned stop at the Lawson Creek strawberry fields. This ritual carried over from her childhood days. Cece remembered when she was little, only five dollars bought a gallon of red giant juicy strawberries. They were cheaper if you picked them yourself. Today, she paid the clerk seven dollars for a gallon. At the car, Cece placed a fourth of the fresh berries in a plastic basket on the console. During the remaining drive to their condominium, she and Ross devoured her cache of berries. Despite her diabetes, she enjoyed the large red juicy ones, which were as sweet as candy. While she rationalized the aromatic fruit as the perfect healthy comfort food, she made mental plans to adjust her next round of insulin.

Cece checked her email in-box on her cell phone. A troubling email arrived from Harry, her attorney. His news carried the latest update on Liz's twenty living cats. Two continued to recover; however, the rest remained in deteriorating health at the animal rescue center. With her lips pursed and her eyes glued to the phone, Cece squirmed in amazement. Harry had sent her the itemized diagnosis and treatments filling a page for each cat. Three cats endured dialysis twelve hours per day. The others suffered from an array of distemper, hypertension, heartworms, tapeworms, hookworms, respiratory infections, fleas, infected punctures from cat bites, arthritis, ticks and fleas, dehydration, and malnourishment. Cece's brain focused on the important facts. Liz was dead. As far as she knew, Joey was not capable of pet care. Most of the cats had terminal or infectious diseases. As in the eye of a hurricane, torrents of doubts and fears swirled around the calm center of Cece's mind. Only one prudent choice for the cats stood out in her mind.

When they arrived in Georgetown, South Carolina, they stopped at Apex car rental to rent a van overnight. Their last stops were the resort condominium and a seafood dinner. As they got in bed, storm clouds rolled onto the Carolina coast. Ross went onto the balcony to watch the distant lightning.

Cece crept up behind him and asked, "Can't sleep either?"

"No, I guess this storm is too noisy. Or I fear what lies ahead of us."

Chapter 20

A Pillar Falls

Late 1994
Mary's Island, South Carolina

Revered as an icon in the thriving resort, Joey Broyer regretted the day he closed his real-estate firm. In his heyday, he focused on marketing beach and golf properties. He was the go-to broker for the sale and financing of huge villas for the rich and beach bungalows for retirees and dreamy-eyed new-lyweds. His profits multiplied with the quick churn of properties on the island. The placement of his office here proved the real estate adage of *location, location, location.* Choice location applied to Joey's vast inventory of homes for sale and his own visible business office on the main street. Deals poured into his lap, despite his slothful habits, for a while.

Sudden turmoil in the financial markets sent shock waves through the economy beginning with the stock market crash of 1987. The after-effects led to the prolonged recession of the early '90s. Unemployment peaked while home sales, prices, and commissions collapsed. Four years had passed since Joey's once good life ripped apart. His business never recovered.

The banks declined customers who used to qualify for loans due to higher banking standards, tighter credit, and companies laying off employees. Factories closed, while the out-of-work employees survived on meager savings. For the lucky employees who survived the carnage, bonuses were non-existent. Smaller bank accounts meant forgoing the dreams of buying a vacation home. With no excess cash, the public avoided the real-estate market. The number of unqualified or unemployed prospects entering Joey's office increased. Something had to change. The personal crisis gnawed at his heart.

Joey recalled the wisdom of his late father saying, "If you don't have customers, you have nothing in your business. Until a sale occurs, nothing happens."

The sentiment emphasized the lifeblood of a business: sales, and lots of them.

Joey's own investments in stock and rental properties collapsed because of the recession. Joey's financial straits led him to file for bankruptcy. In his dire situation, Joey realized his life mimicked the life cycle of a black hole in outer space. He aped an enormous star that collapses and flames out in a black mass absorbing everything around it.

It was the worst of times for Joey. After a life of frivolous spending, inopportune investments, and gambling, he sought to do odd jobs here and there to survive. He was a fair fix-it person. His friend Floyd would call him to help with repairs and renovations such as plumbing, electrical, and air conditioning maintenance. He had learned trades by watching others over the years and he applied the concepts he had learned. However, the sporadic compensation was insufficient, and he missed being his own boss. Older now, he had less agility to crawl under houses, squeeze through attic recesses, or climb ladders, as a twenty-year-old would. Over the past four years, his sedentary lifestyle and diet of cheap processed foods bloated his once 200-pound frame. His body ballooned in weight by twenty-five percent. Joey's alcohol abuse did not help.

If his doctors needed a poster child, Joey's illnesses qualified him for a starring role. His health was a mess. The illnesses stemming from his lifestyle and conditions were a laundry list of ailments affecting senior adults. The general population usually had one or two of the diseases. Poor Joey had them all. He looked at his last report from the Coastal Free Health Clinic. The list of ailments included high cholesterol, borderline Type 2 diabetes, gouty arthritis, high blood pressure, hyperthyroidism, benign enlargement of the prostate, and irritable bowel syndrome.

Joey had more worthless days than good ones at work. One day Floyd fired Joey due to the decline of his workmanship. An earlier task that Joey attempted almost caused Floyd to lose his license. The customer threatened to ruin Floyd's reputation if he did not finish the mess Joey had started. The boss could not tolerate another mistake.

The coastal sun was hot and the humidity oppressive. Joey headed toward home, but first he made one stop. He pulled his passenger van into the parking lot of the Sandy Chameleon lounge on the causeway between Georgetown and Mary's Island. He had not been here in years. His thought turned to *just one drink* before heading home over the mile-long bridge that began near the bar. Joey pleasured in the thrill of conquering the zenith of the bridge followed by the rollercoaster surge on the downhill roadway. He grabbed a stool bar inside and placed an order for his favorite, Stella Artois.

The place he now called home was the Air Stream travel trailer at the mobile home park near Mary's Island. Most of the time, Joey lived alone in the trailer. His quarters became less desirable as he often lost gastric control due to the irritable bowel syndrome. The uncleaned quarters with no air conditioning to counter heat, fecal puddles, or smells reached intolerable limits even for Joey.

He purchased the used Ford Econoline cargo van without rear seats to have room for his tools and a mattress. Joey's van life would be claustrophobic to most people. Yet with windows only in the front seat and in the rear doors, the van made a perfect hideaway for Joey. The mattress soon became useless as the truck swallowed materials that would surface never again. Old newspaper, used fast-food containers, empty bottles and cans, jars, boxes, appliance parts, and other trashy looking objects crammed the van from the back doors to the front seats. He obsessed to keep things whether he would use it or not. He told himself, *This item might have value someday, eh.* When not sleeping in his Air-Stream, Joey hung out in the squalor of the van that morphed into a large body-sized foxhole. He always slept with three companions: an M16 rifle, a Glock pistol, and a female feral cat he had rescued from the side of the road.

Sometimes he camped out in his van in a vacant parking lot. If it seemed too far to drive to the trailer park, he would pull into an abandoned grove of bushes and trees or to the hardware megastore parking lot where he slept undisturbed in the van all night. In the hot summers, it was not an ideal habitat. He was not homeless in the asset-deprived sense of the word, but his friends abandoned him and he had no decent place to lay his head.

Chapter 21

Coincidence or Karma?

The Same Day
Mary's Island, South Carolina

After her messy divorce from husband four, Carl, Liz's routine changed. She ran her daily afternoon errands without a partner to drive her. She made stops at the grocery, the Post Office, the manicurist, the bank, and the beauty shop. Finally, she enjoyed a chilled treat at the Sandy Chameleon lounge. Upon her arrival, with a slight limp, Liz sashayed across the dance floor to the lady's room in a flowing short gown. Reapplying her makeup, she hoped to attract her man of the day and engage in non-stop conversation for an hour. Liz remained an enigma, as she went no farther with the men. Marriage was out of the question for her. She had suffered enough. Liz wanted a friend for adult conversation and warmth. She remained a stunner in looks. The egos of her men jumped at the opportunity to escort her around the dive. She pulled up a stool and waited for her prey. She did not consider herself a cougar, as she did not intentionally pursue younger men and she was not looking for erotic love. Well, she would not toss away a promising opportunity. Relentlessly, she looked for acceptance, conversation, and understanding. Liz still sought military men. They were always good to buy her a drink. Then she met Joey at the bar.

In a few moments, Liz opened the door to conversing with Joey and her life changed forever. They learned that each loved animals. When it came time to leave, she asked Joey to visit her home. She had yardwork and small repair jobs in her house and he could interact with her two cats. Forever naïve, she expected Joey's main role was to converse and help her.

As his daily visits took place over four years, her brood of cats grew. He tracked new cats, which he brought to her home and proudly pronounced a name for each one. Free of her mother's restraint, she welcomed the pets. He found them in the narrow lane behind the house. Others he captured running across the driveway as he exited the van. He selected one at the humane society shelter, but he rationalized why pay for them when you can get them free? Several new ones entered the property through the holes in the fence surrounding the pool. Some of the former pet owners had spayed a few of the creatures in their earlier lives. Most of the critters usually arrived in a fertile state.

To help care for the animals, Liz rationalized it would be helpful to ask Joey to stay at her place. Her mansion had ample room, and he needed a residence. The number of cats had grown from Liz's original two to a number that even Liz did not know. *That is Joey's role,* she thought. They both appeared to have thrived on animal hoarding with so many cats under their control. The important thing to her was that God's little creatures seemed to be safe in her care. Her mental state assured her that there was always room for one more. Like a cat, Joey was free to come and go from her home as he wished. Joey never told Liz his marital status, and she never asked. Distant from his wife, he had separated but had not divorced. The painful nagging in their home exhausted him. His wife asked him to leave because he was broke, refused treatment for his medical conditions, and he collected animals. She wanted to be free of his baggage. His children and brothers did not communicate with him.

Liz's budget shrank as she fed the unknown quantity in their feline army. She laid down the law and asked Joey not to bring any more home. He violently argued otherwise, but Liz held her ground. They agreed to spay and neuter the unfixed ones.

When they carried their chosen cats to the local veterinary clinic and animal rescue center, the vet's nurse asked, "What have we here?"

Liz said, "We need help!" Because there were so many, the vet offered a significant discount to help control the population. The ten cats they brought for the procedure entered as eager breeding machines, and departed unable to reproduce.

Chapter 22

Lay Advice

1995
Mary's Island, South Carolina

A s male patrons walked past, they admired the attractive blonde woman seated with the unkempt man. A few chanced a second peek. Liz and Joey huddled in the reference wing of the Public Library. Half focused on her work, she acknowledged her admirers giving a nod coupled with an occasional wink. Liz still possessed crowd appeal.

Joey convinced Liz that she could create her own will. She had only known him a year but he seemed so confident and bragged about his business often. Hence, she neglected consulting with professionals about the document she now typed. As she struggled with the unfamiliar keyboard, he attempted to show her how to create the document online. He coached her every click on the computer. Her pace went slower than he wished and he grew impatient. In his past life in real estate, he prepared his own documents for the simplest transactions. If his client resisted, he acquiesced to go to the professionals. He could not afford to lose business so he added the cost of an attorney to their closing settlements.

Joey rationalized his use of the document applications by citing cost savings, efficiency, and satisfaction with his own work product. As a buzzing printer spit the documents out, they looked and seemed valid to him. He had never prepared a document as complex as Liz's Last Will and Testament. A risk existed that off-the-shelf computer programs did not follow the applicable law of a state. Specific requirements of each state applied to a will's validity and rules differed from state to state. In the general case, the law required the simplest of wills to contain valid signatures of the person creating their will and two witnesses. Using an attorney left none of the other details to chance.

When the affected parties probated a will, the judge of the court with jurisdiction decided if the terms of a document met the law's requirements. Legal professionals understood that complicated transactions required one to dot *I*'s and cross *T*'s. The absence of simple details often led to unintended consequences.

Chapter 23

The Authorities

Monday, May 18, 1998
Mary's Island, South Carolina

A property developer created Mary's Island, a secluded planned community, on an actual island forested with gnarly live-oak trees. It lay between the Atlantic Ocean and the intra-coastal waterway. Airy clumps of Spanish moss hung from the ancient oaks. To enhance the beachy charisma of the property, the developers added saw grass and royal palm trees. Two serpentine championship golf courses wound around the upscale homes. Just over an arched bridge, the entrance to the stately country club welcomed golfers and visitors.

The wide main road circled through elegant homes to a retail village compound and the city offices. Over five hundred homes made up the quaint community. While half consisted of retirement dreams, the remainder was passive investments in a second, third, or fourth house owned by wealthy landlords. The posh development oozed exclusivity and privilege. The developers enforced a strict covenant ordinance system to protect property values.

In the center of the island, City Hall rested on a slight rise. A red brick building in the federal style, it contained the offices of the mayor, city council members, and bureaucracy common to small towns. The local government erected similar buildings nearby to house the fire, EMT, and police departments.

Ross and Cece exited the van and walked to the front door of City Hall. Cece glanced at her watch. It was 8:55 am. The perky brunette sitting at the reception desk welcomed them to the City of Mary's Island.

"How may we help you today?"

"Hello. Where is Kerry Tyler's office?"

"Oh, he said he is expecting you. Follow those signs."

They followed the hallway until they came to a door that had a plaque with the words "Director of Zoning, Kerry Tyler" on it. Ross knocked on the frame and the door opened. A balding, thin man of forty-five invited them into his office. Behind his wooden desk stood a twig coat rack on which a tweed sports jacket and a white cowboy hat found a resting place.

"Can I get you water or coffee?" he offered.

Ross said, "Yes, coffee with creamer and sweetener."

Cece asked, "Any chance you have a Diet Coke?"

"Sure."

When he came back and handed them the drinks, he sat behind his desk and looked at them with a solemn mien.

"Cece, on behalf of the mayor and people of Mary's Island we offer you our sincerest condolences."

Cece nodded and murmured a soft answer, "Thank you. Tell me how I can help."

"As a formality, we note you are here on official city business at our request. The city is asking you to enter Ms. Perkins' residence to gather and protect the things the family deems important. I will give you documents with our request. This protects you from charges of illegal entry. Mary's Island does not have non-compliant homes often. When they do, my boss, the mayor, expects me to handle the matter. We thank you for your kind help to resolve this situation. There are things the family should keep secure in their possession until distribution, so today we hope you can remove the valuable items. We want to help you any way we can. We sealed the house for now; but we will let you in to collect these assets to protect them from damage, pilfering, or thievery. While you are there, decide what documents you need. I saw piles of them. How is the progress on her funeral?"

Cece shared her plan to approach the court later that week to assume the administrator role and free up money to have a funeral.

Kerry added, "I don't think you can fathom the condition of Liz's home. My job is to make sure each home on the island meets code. Unfortunately, your cousin's house does not. We considered condemnation proceedings. If you and others in the family cooperate in good faith, then we can avoid complications of a regulatory or legal nature. The family must hire a reputable restoration company to get the property back to code. We will inspect it for any deficiencies."

Cece replied, "This restoration is a big job. But we can do it. Since we are not from here, do you have a cleaning firm you can recommend?"

"Let me explain, Liz's home is more than a simple cleanup. There will be removal of furniture, carpet, drapes, and trash, sealing of the subfloor, gutting of the interior walls and contents, installation of new floors and sheetrock, and repainting. No, I cannot recommend a specific company. I will make a copy of The Yellow Pages that list the available companies. You may call them and see which one suits you."

"But what firm do locals use more often than others? Do you know of a firm that has been in business for a while?"

Cece remembered the ordeal of cleaning up after a stove fire at her parent's home. That restoration company left a mess with incomplete work. Yet, she guessed good firms still existed.

Then Ross changed the question. "If this were your parent's house, who would you use, Kerry?"

Ross's question unlocked the door.

Kerry responded, "Well, I cannot endorse or recommend a firm, you understand. If I needed help, I would call Gus at Synergy Restoration. I have seen the work he and his people do. But again, I am answering the specific question the way you asked it."

Kerry feared a political backlash or accusations of favoring one firm over another.

Kerry continued, "Let me paint a clearer picture of what you are undertaking. Your cousin Liz met with a premature death. Also living in her home were the cats. We understand from neighbors that her boyfriend Joey Broyer collected the cats from the neighborhood. Joey called 9-1-1 to report Liz's death. He was shaking when our police and the EMTs arrived, and he paced the responders through the house to the back yard. They observed and photographed him, Liz, and the house, including the pet waste.

"A week later, the neighbors complained of a stench emanating from the house. They summoned the police for a residential welfare check. The police found Joey lying on the floor amid beer cans in an upstairs bedroom. His comatose body lay next to an open mini-refrigerator. With so many cats and the mess, the police sounded a pet-welfare distress situation. Animal control and we arrived at once and collected the cats. We found squalor everywhere including the cat's urine, vomit, and fecal material. Animal control delivered the living cats to the county animal shelter. When the police gave us the all clear, we sealed the house.

"We must warn you that the scene is ghastly, and the odor is overwhelming. It is impossible to do so, but you must prepare yourself mentally. You must wear protective gear such as heavy-duty gloves and masks. We found it best to mask the smell and make the nose insensitive to the foul odors by applying Noxzema skin cream between your lips and nose. Have you bought the protective materials I recommended earlier?"

Cece shook her head, "No, we were still in a state of shock. Can we get a complete list from you? We saw the hardware and drug stores close to here. We can go there before the house."

Kerry scribbled the items on a legal pad.

"There is just one more thing."

"What's that?"

"Joey Broyer is a sick man. I hate to say this but full disclosure is necessary. With his colon issues and irritable bowel syndrome, Joey was out of control, too. I repeat, I regret telling you this, but I must warn you. There is much human waste throughout the house. This is not a pretty sight. These components create a situation bordering on a gross biohazard. Now, do you know the house address?"

"Yes, Liz has entertained us there several times. It is a beautiful place."

"It was a beautiful place. Do you have questions?"

Cece asked, "Where is Joey?"

"After the police found him passed out, an ambulance took him to the hospital for his health issues. Oh, yeah, he was barefoot too. The cats were hungry. They had zero food for a week. The EMTs found cat bites on his body and. . . ."

Ross interrupted Kerry with a loud groan. Only a few months before he tried to give one of their cats pills from their vet. The pet would have none of it. The cat bit Ross's thumb, which swelled from the infection. Ross recovered after two rounds of antibiotics. He knew firsthand that pet bites were a serious matter.

Kerry continued, "The little critters cannibalized Joey's toes and feet for at least three days. Infection and gangrene ravaged him. The hospital amputated both legs. The orthopedic staff fitted him with prostheses over this weekend."

The horror and ghastly image of poor Joey sank into their consciousness as Cece and Ross glowered at each other. Ross groaned aloud again. His imagination filled with hallucinations of flesh eating alley cats.

Cece panicked and asked. "Will Joey be at Liz's house today?"

"No way, because he is in the hospital for at least three weeks, but I will re-check."

Cece said, "While we are at the house I want someone from the police to protect us if he or someone else surprises us in a belligerent mood. How can we arrange that?"

Kerry opened his phone and dialed a number. He talked for a moment, and then turned to Cece.

"Sergeant Joe Anthony can meet us there at twelve. There is a charge for a personal security detail by a uniformed off-duty officer from the Georgetown police department. Plan to pay thirty dollars per hour. Mary's Island does not have spare officers."

Cece was thankful for the security. The last thing she wanted was a neighbor or, God forbid, Joey crashing the scavenger hunt she expected that day. As usual, her personality pushed her to avoid conflict.

Cece, cognizant of the never-ending expenses, bellowed, "We need that guard!"

Kerry continued, "My police connections said they had been summoned for domestic disturbances at that address several times, maybe a dozen. I don't know, but it makes sense that Liz was the likely caller."

Cece shuddered to think how Liz suffered at the hands of somebody. How could she put up with torture or abuse again?

She said, "Kerry, can you share any details on what happened the night of Liz's death?"

Cece remembered gossip from years ago that had passed her way from other relatives. It tied into Kerry's comments of the domestic violence calls. Liz had told the family she once had to jump through a bedroom window, shattering the glass and getting deep cuts. She went to the ER and explained it as an accident occurring when she was cleaning windows. *God knows the prima donna never had to clean a window in her life.* She gave a typical cover-up as an abuse victim.

Kerry told Cece what he heard about the night Liz died. Cece listened as Kerry shared his observations and others' remarks during the investigation and follow-up. He saw he was upsetting Cece, so he ended it by asking, "When do you plan to work at the house?"

Cece looked her watch. It was 9:30 am.

"How is noon? We can run our errands in two hours. First, we will pick up the protection and packaging material. We rented a van to transport the items. Our assumption is we will find enough stuff to fill a van. Is that true?"

"A van is perfect. When you leave, it will be full of silver, papers, and family heirlooms."

"Kerry, I want to thank you for your time and your very helpful insight. Anything else we need to know?"

"No ma'am. You are the helpful one. Thank you."

Chapter 24

Liz's Mansion

Monday, May 18, 1998, Noon
Mary's Island, South Carolina

Bright sunshine poured out warmth as the temperature rose. That morning the weatherman had predicted a high of eighty-five degrees. City work crews scurried around the city cleaning up after the massive storm the prior night. Lines of automobiles were turning into the small public park near Mary's Island beach. Past the town center, Cece and Ross continued until they reached Liz's home.

At 12:10 pm, they pulled into the driveway. A black Georgetown police car and two vehicles parked near the house. Next to the police cruiser rested a gray van and Kerry's white pickup truck displaying the City of Mary's Island logo. While a man talked on a cellphone in the passenger seat of the city truck, Kerry stood outside gathering his things.

Cece chuckled, "Ross, I bet the neighbors have pulled their binoculars out by now."

Ross nodded and answered, "Afraid so! Everything else looks normal here. Other than several weeks' growth of grass and bushes which need trimming, the place looks tidy."

Cece chided him, "Don't be too hasty."

One by one, the police officer, Kerry's helper, Ross and Cece got out of the vehicles and gathered with Kerry. The officer introduced himself as Sergeant Joseph Anthony. Ross guessed that the officer was

forty years old. His stature and shaved head commanded attention. Kerry introduced his helper Rob,
an aging but agile senior. Cece and Ross introduced
themselves. No one was very excited to experience
what would happen next. The wrought-iron benches
placed under the oaks looked inviting. The crowd
headed there. Cece placed the bag of supplies she
carried on a bench. It looked as if five people had met
to discuss a real-estate transaction. Bright yellow tape
with the words "Police Barricade" crossed the doors
and every window but one door on the first floor of
the brick home.

Ross asked, "Kerry, who owns the gray van?"

"It belongs to Joey Broyer."

Cece turned to Sergeant Anthony and said, "We
appreciate your help today. There are two areas of
concern where you can help us. Discourage neighbors
from interrupting our work or entering the house or
asking questions. Second, the owner of this van may
return and we may need your protection from him.
Have you ever experienced this kind of situation?"

Sergeant Anthony replied, "Yep, several times over
the years. This stuff happens more often than you
would think."

The policeman walked around the van and peered
inside the front window without touching the van. The
contents were a mess. Sleazy layers of trash, mail,
newspapers, jars, fast-food containers, bottles, and
clothing continued from the floor to the ceiling. Ross
thought, *I wonder how the archeologists will analyze
this person and his collection two thousand years from
now.* With the windows cracked, foul odors emanated
from the van. The officer was not just looking for sordid contents. He might find other things. Without a
search warrant, he had reached his legal boundary.

Kerry shook his head.

"Mrs. Turner, don't worry. Joey will not be going anywhere today. I checked his status. He cannot get out of his hospital bed. Next week he will receive his prosthetic devices. Joey will not leave the therapy unit for at least two weeks after that. He will undergo retraining exercises."

While she knew Joey's healing period remained, she felt an irrational fear. Her stomach churned. Out of habit, Cece nodded. She wanted to leave nothing to chance.

Chapter 25

Let's Roll

Minutes Later
Mary's Island, South Carolina

Kerry asked, "Are we ready to tackle this? If so, prepare your supplies."

The police officer returned to his car and sat. He pulled a stack of paperwork from the prior evening to complete.

Rob went to Kerry's truck and retrieved a hammer, power screwdriver, crowbar, fabric facemasks, an indigo blue jar, and gloves.

In an instructive voice Kerry said, "I suggest y'all put your protection on now. Let me show you how to apply the Noxzema cream before we open this place. Be careful; keep it away from your eyes."

He put a teaspoon of the thick potion on his index finger and raised it to near his nose above his top lip. The others followed his lead.

Ross made a face as his nose, then lungs, engaged with the overpowering aroma.

Cece stared at Ross and giggled. "You look as if you've been eating ice cream and missed."

"How does this stuff work, Kerry? Does it help with the germs?"

"No, Mrs. Turner. It has no health benefits. It is not protection from biohazards if they are present. The cream only masks the odor. This smell may not be a strong enough cover for you. The surprises inside the house have had time to ripen. We shall see soon. Put on your mask and gloves, please."

Cece retrieved the bag she had placed on the iron bench. With his heavy-duty gloves and masks, Ross thought they were ready for the upcoming chore. He set down ten unassembled packing boxes, sealing tape, bottled water, hand sanitizer, and sanitizing wipes, marking pens, newsprint paper for wrapping and a carton of black heavy garbage bags by a van tire. As they brought valuables out, the plan was to inventory and photograph each item and place it in the boxes. They could put non-breakable miscellaneous items and loose documents in the garbage bags. Then they would take everything they collected to a storage unit for safekeeping.

An eight-by-ten foot plywood board concealed a side door, their entryway. Three-inch wood screws held the wood to the doorframe.

Pointing to a planter box several yards from the door, Kerry said to the Turners, "Please stand there."

Whirr. Whirr. Screw by screw, Rob gunned a power drill to remove the plywood sheet. As each screw unfastened, a hint of the squalor wafted out. The efficient screwdriver loosened twenty-two screws spaced around the perimeter of the wood. Seconds later, Ross got a good whiff. When the last screw popped out, the wooden seal opened, and the rotten air from inside the house pushed outward under pressure. The acrid, putrid smell of death, cat feces and urine, and human feces surged out of the house. The ammonia-laced atmosphere burned the eyes and stung the nose. Kerry was correct that Noxzema and the masks were of limited help. As Ross peered in, he held onto the doorframe. He remembered entering this house so many years earlier. However, today, the stench was too much. He gagged in a reflux moment.

He exclaimed in anger, "How in the hell did this happen?"

Kerry shrugged. He replied to Ross, "We don't know yet. Are you game?"

Ross gave Kerry a dubious smirk hidden by his mask.

Then Kerry barked, "Let's roll!"

The three men entered the home and performed a reconnaissance of the family heirlooms. Kerry and Rob led the way. Ross followed, trying to watch his step. At least he was wearing old training shoes he did not mind trashing. He hoped for new trainers for his birthday. He made mental notes and a few photographs of the layout of the first floor. After ten minutes, the three convened with Cece outside to compare their thoughts.

Ross pulled his mask off and coughed. "Cece, you would not believe it. I have gone to hell and back. You owe me more than new shoes for this!"

"What do you mean, Ross?"

Ross found it impossible to express fully the horrible sights and thoughts that filled his mind. He pulled out his camera that captured the mess.

As he showed her the digital pictures, he exclaimed, "Yes, it is definitely a hoarding situation. I found trash everywhere, cat and human poop everywhere. The cleanest rooms on the first floor are the living and dining rooms. That is where the silver pieces are and it is where I will work first." Ross continued, "My priority will be all cabinets, the documents in the kitchen, items in the family room, and hall, and then I can explore upstairs, especially any closets and drawers."

Cece replied, "Good, I'm ready."

She had assembled boxes, unpacked her own camera, and stacked two tablets and pens to prepare an inventory.

"Okay, let's make this quick."

Kerry said, "Good luck. Rob and I have another situation so we will leave you two with this. Lightning struck a family's home in that storm last night. The fire marshal asked us to help investigate. Call me if you have any issues. Thirty minutes before you are ready to close it up, call us to reseal the house."

Ross quipped, "What can you do for the stench?"

With the house opened, the ventilation helped. Ross re-entered the side door, and a hallway that led to the combined living room and dining room. His eyes panned from wall to wall toward two ecru dining-room cabinets in front of him. It was here years ago he first saw Liz glide into the room as an ethereal illusion so pristine and sterile. The chandelier that hung over the table still had its bows of pink over each arm. Now the rooms reeked like a medieval dungeon. As he leaned against heavy folding doors from the hallway, he presumed Liz must have kept the cats out of the room by closing the doors. But after she died, the cats left a sordid trail.

He walked to the large arched breakfront on the opposite wall. Locked glass panels sealed the upper three shelves containing sterling silver and crystal. Below the visible shelves were four wooden doors hiding other treasures, for sure. With his gloved hand, he pulled on the main door. It did not budge. He spotted a tassel and key on an open shelf of the breakfront and inserted it.

Click.

The door sprung open. He counted twenty-one objects of silver. Twelve were silver trays.

These will be easy to stack.

Ross checked the two cabinets, setting out items he judged were of value. Silver pieces and crystal filled the shelves. He guessed they were not worth a fortune at the current depressed silver prices. As he placed them on the dining room table, he layered the trays, and carried them to the doorway. Cece had assembled half of the boxes.

Ross commented as he handed the items to Cece to list, "Your turn!"

On a pad, Cece listed each item, including the manufacturer. She photographed the keepsake and added the photo's number to her list. She chuckled to herself; *Ross did not know the difference between sterling silver and stainless steel.*

Three of the trays were not valuable but she would list them, regardless. The truth was Ross had only one goal in these conditions, to grab what looked to be important stuff to store. They could sort out the details later.

Ross returned to the dining room where he surveyed the other silver he placed on the dining table. Their design reminded Ross of the style of a sterling-silver punch bowl from Portugal that Liz and Carl had given them for their wedding present. Item by item, he delivered the sterling silver to the doorway to Cece: a soup tureen, sugar and creamer set, coffee urn, several footed chafing dishes, a champagne bucket, and other items. He looked at his wristwatch. Only sixteen minutes passed while he emptied the top of the breakfront. He felt the house getting warmer and stuffier.

He popped open the heavy doors in the bottom of the sideboard, wondering what treasures he would find. More silver serving pieces including many casserole holders with legs and dinner accessories. He moved out everything worth keeping to the table first, and then carried it to Cece. He turned to the second and smaller sideboard. Examining each crammed drawer took time. In this cabinet, Liz stored her dinner linens and Christmas decorations. The ornaments showed signs of wear and tarnish. He found no important papers, jewels, or money. Ross determined nothing in the second cabinet was worth saving but he would ask Cece.

Chapter 26

Tarnished Tiara

An Hour Later
In the Front Yard of Liz's Home

When Cece finished wrapping and listing items that Ross had brought to her, boredom overtook her. It seemed like forever since Ross and she last talked. As her curiosity piqued, she walked to the doorway and gazed into the hall. The putrid smell and the sights overcame her. She backed up to where the outdoor air was void of the noxious odor. She yanked off her mask, gagged, and then puked.

Cece sipped on a bottle of water and regained her composure. *When is Ross going to bring me more?* Her brain pulsed with the repeated thought, *I hate to waste time.* She peered at the turquoise gloves protecting her hands. Imprints of dirt and smudges of who knows what else blotted each finger. One by one, her gloves plopped into the garbage sack. After lathering her hands with antibacterial lotion, she pulled out her cell phone. She called the restoration companies on The Yellow Pages list Kerry copied for her. With four companies to choose from, she hoped to get the best price. She dialed the companies in Georgetown, and on the causeway. Each explained they did not do severe clean-up work. They were basic house cleaning services. The last listed firm, Synergy, satisfied her search. Synergy possessed the technology and ability for the job. The owner, Gus Fence, listened to

Cece's vivid assessment of the conditions, based on her short foray inside and the images Ross and Kerry had shared.

Gus said, "Stop in our offices to pick up a contract."

She replied, "Good, I'll know my starting budget soon. I will drop in, but I will call first. See you next week."

The schedule is getting tight, she thought. *I guess we can leave for New Orleans after we sign with him.*

She dialed the number of the storage center they noticed on the highway outside Myrtle Beach. The clerk confirmed units were available for rent.

Cece asked, "If I rent a unit, can I drop stuff off at once?"

"No problem, ma'am."

"Thank you, good-bye."

Cece became braver and more curious.

What is Ross finding? Where is he?

Feeling better, she dabbed a fresh coat of the pungent cream above her lip and replaced her mask. She stepped up to the door to check the hallway. When her mind and senses took in the carnage, she retreated. As Ross described, the conditions were hellacious.

Gathering her courage, she moved forward again as she pushed herself to walk eight feet into the hall. A tall gold-leaf curio cabinet loomed ahead of her. There! She spotted it. Within the cabinet laid the tiara Liz had worn in the Miss South Carolina Glory contest. Her thoughts flashed back to the pageant in Columbia, what forty something years ago? As she leaned to inspect the crown closer, she noticed the cabinet's door was open. She reflected, *Someone had tampered with the contents recently.* With a tarnished metal finish and dull, dusty jewels on the crown, the once magical sparkle had vanished. The lackluster crown now looked like a child's misused toy. Cece's heart broke at the sight. The tiara represented Liz's legacy, now in its abysmal state. Ross poked his head around a corner and asked if she was okay or needed help. She revealed her newly found but disappointing treasure. The sight flooded Cece with emotion. She ran to the open door. She burst into tears. *How could her beautiful cousin come to this condition?* Ross followed Cece outside for fresh air.

Cece screamed a feeble cry of loss and misery. She pointed and whimpered, "Ross, that tiara was a symbol of fulfillment. It identified a kind of nobility among the group of young women in the competition. They were the best of the best, during their pageant and in their future dreams. The tiara of the queen exemplified the winner's elegance and promising future legacy. It isn't true they all live happily ever after, is it?"

In this case, choices, fate, companions, family, and her cousin destroyed the dream.

Liz's tiara appeared irreparable and dull, tarnished as Liz was. As Cece's copious tears continued, Ross's heart ached to embrace Cece, but not in this situation. With what was on his body and clothes, especially his hands, he himself was a biohazard. He hated to see Cece in this pitiful circumstance. His nostrils pulsated tighter and tighter. He felt light-headed.

"We need to take a break. Let's talk about what I found."

Cece, calmer now, responded, "Everything here is so damn crazy and surreal. I never dreamed it would be this sordid."

Ross had not heard Cece's phone calls to the local vendors. The couple shared what they had completed so far. As he stood up to reenter, Cece asked him to take extra care when he collected the fragile worn tiara and items in the curio cabinet.

Feeling stronger, he returned to the living and dining rooms and performed a 360-degree scan. Only a smaller cabinet, the dining table, and chairs needed checking. Doubtless, the furniture would smell, so there was no use in saving it.

Ross ambled to a new workspace. Liz's kitchen and huge great room united as one massive room. The scene was a wreck. Filth and squalor overwhelmed Ross. The heart of this once beautiful, magazine-worthy home sat in shambles amid an icky field of cat and human poop, dried hairballs, trash, used paper towels, stacks of newspapers, magazines, pill bottles, empty and partly eaten bowls of cat food, litter boxes, and multiple bills layered a foot high. Piles of Joey's random discarded and soiled clothing draped the mess.

How can a human stay in this filthy sty? Ross started in the kitchen. The refrigerator reeked of the contents of expired and rotting foods. Dishes and glasses, many unwashed and still containing decayed food and crumbs, used paper plates, prescription drug bottles, and paper covered the creamy granite countertops. On the circular kitchen table and the surrounding four chairs, more unopened mail consisting of bills and ads lay in heaps awaiting somebody's attention. One chair held Liz's worn, unzipped purse. He bent to the floor to pick up several pill bottles. The first was half-full of phenobarbital. The next two contained generic oxycodone and tramadol. On a whim, he counted more than fifteen medicine bottles of the same drugs on the floor. A small portion of the prescriptions came from the animal clinic to medicate the cats. Some were Liz's pills. The rest had labels with Joey's name. On a side counter stood six one-liter bottles, two of Scotch, and one each of bourbon, gin, tequila, and vodka, and empty beer cans. Ross mused, *She and he preferred Scotch and beer. Damn! A few drinks of this tonight would be handy to help forget this mess! Not that anyone could ever forget it completely.*

The furniture and ecru plush carpet had brown spots and shriveled piles every five or six inches marking where the cats or Joey had left urine, vomit, and feces. Ross maneuvered through the filth and health hazards trying to avoid tracking residue from many piles. The wanton destruction of property through intent and negligence angered Ross.

The ripe odor was stifling. Sunshine poured in the windows, raising the house temperature to uncomfortable levels. Ross wrestled with his facemask but his adjustments for comfort proved futile. His one-size fits all mask did not conform to the contours of his smooth face. Sweat wept from his pores as the mask crept up and interfered with his work. Ross pulled off the sweaty covering. Without the annoying mask, he moved easier and faster. Later, he regretted this impulsive action. He continued through each room, one by one, gloves on but unmasked.

In the kitchen, Ross cleared the counters of their long-term coverings. He opened the large garbage bags and stuffed them with the piles of bills and paper. Sorting useful items from trash proved to be Ross's most time-consuming task that day. He set aside, as best he could, the advertisement flyers, newspapers, and magazines in a trash pile. To keep the bulging bags clean, he placed them on the chairs and table. He figured Cece would scan the contents to decide the relevance of each item at her own speed later. *Surely, clues as to Liz's financial assets and debts filled the bags.*

The adjoining two-story great room once pulsed as the heart of entertainment in the huge house. The old television console faced a plush couch and an arc of three massive writing chairs. Ross reminisced about the times he had gathered with the family here in a stream of happy, lively conversation. Now, the room stagnated as a cesspool of deafening silence.

Between the chairs and couch, a short table stood with stacks of books, including two Bibles and self-help and spiritual books by Norman Vincent Peale and Billy Graham. Ross chose the cleanest of the three adjoining chairs. He rested his aching legs and struggled with breathing. An adjacent closed box hugged the small table. The plainness of the cardboard parcel appealed to him. Feeling curious as if he were a modern day Pandora, he popped open the flaps. Inside, a ream of documents and originals caught his eye. As he sifted through the papers, he found insurance policies, legal documents, and uncashed checks. *Wow, I may have found the needle in the haystack, right in front of me,* he thought. A grainy packet of six pages of legal-sized paper drew his attention. To Ross, the document resembled a will, except for scratchy, odd handwriting that bled ink throughout the typed font. He placed everything back into the box with the six page document on top.

One by one, he lifted the books on the adjoining table and scanned through them. He wondered if there was cash buried inside, as he found that night so long ago. One volume was an old family Bible while the other must have been Liz's Bible. The inside cover page said *Presented to Elizabeth Perkins on the occasion of her Holy Confirmation, Bayview Methodist Church, Charleston, S.C., April 10. Happy Easter! Love, Dad.* Ross observed notes scribbled on the margins on most pages. Her dated notes showed that Liz searched for God's will, for peace within, and for a happy life. Now, she was absent from the pain and hurt that tormented her. Ross placed the books and Bibles on the box and made a mental note to retrieve his cairn of documents and books before they left the house.

The incredible squalor and bedlam baffled Ross. Someone overturned small furniture throughout the house. He walked to the wall that once contained Camilla's library. The entire collection of classics and best sellers, which had filled the built-in shelves, now covered the floor. The books in haphazard piles resembled preparations for a bonfire. It was as if someone looked through the pages of the strewn books for something and did not replace them. That someone must have taken out Aunt Camilla's money. Smelling their urine on the books, Ross thought, *Damn cats have marked this as their territory, too.*

The brick fireplace and floor-to-ceiling picture windows formed the entire back wall. Ross saw the family crests of the Perkins and the Davies families that hung on the sides of the hearth. When he examined the hearth, Ross noticed that tarnish and corrosion covered most of the brass filigree fire screen in front of the mammoth stone fireplace.

With his anger and rage boiling at the situation, Ross muttered aloud, "Damn cats peed on it too."

Above the mantelpiece, photos, mementos, and candlesticks still comprised the shrine to Liz and her once promising legacy. On the left side of the mantle, Liz had added a two-foot marble replica of Michelangelo's David that gazed into the room. Ross saw the irony surrounding this Biblical figure who with his slingshot battled against a giant successfully, while Liz's efforts against her enemy giants proved futile. On the other side of the mantel stood an equal-sized statue of an adult angel in a peaceful pose. An inscription on the base proclaimed *Fear Not!* Six massive candlesticks on brass holders nestled between the two marble sentinels. At the center of the mantelpiece, a short crystal bowl contained a multi-colored rock formation that looked unusual to Ross. *Was this a magic totem of stones?* Ross felt superstitious about such stuff, but he dismissed it.

No, there is no reason to mess with that! He felt a chill run through his body just thinking about what might happen if he disturbed the display.

Above the mantel hung the massive oil portrait of Liz in her empire style pageant evening gown. The painted Liz held court, standing regal over the turmoil of the room and the house like Emperor Nero peering over Rome while it burned.

Ross nosed around the room. He thought, *What a hoarder's nightmare, filled with trash, stacks, and squalor.* Only the document box and a few books, in the room appeared worth saving. Most everything on the floor was tattered, messed on, or rendered useless. He took the portrait, coats of arms, brass candlesticks, and the two statues to Cece.

When he returned, he glanced out the picture windows next to the fireplace. First, his focus went to the hot tub where the paramedics said they found Liz's lifeless body. He lowered his head for a moment in respect. Beyond the swimming pool, the three Buddha statues roasted in the warm sunlight. Overgrown bushes in Liz's tea garden had withered to brown stalks of woody stems. The weathered pool furniture looked uninviting amid rust, dirt stains, and discoloration. Empty pet food dishes lined the poolside, an earlier source of nourishment for outdoor feline visitors or visiting vermin.

He stirred from his momentary stupor as he detected movement along the brick fence. Two new cats entered the yard through a hole in the fence. Stealthily, a caramel tabby with splotches of white led a chubby black and brown Persian. Ross thought, *They were lucky! They must have sensed someone had arrived to feed them.* He considered opening the door, when a bead of sweat ran down his forehead. Changing his mind, he returned to his search. An arched doorway opened to the main hallway and foyer. Gingerly stepping into the hallway Ross came to the cabinet that contained the pageant tiara and other keepsakes. Before he picked it up, he studied the crown as if it were a biology lab specimen. He placed it into a small box. All the other items he stacked into a larger sturdy box. As he carried the salvageable remnants to Cece outside, he found her perched on an iron bench.

She exclaimed, "Wow, Ross, you are exerting such an effort. Is there much more to recover?"

"Under the conditions, I'm going to give no more than an hour to the upstairs rooms."

He climbed the stairs leading up to four bedrooms and three baths. Ross thought, *Lord, how much more squalor is there?* He watched where he positioned his shoes as he moved up the carpeted staircase.

The first and largest room on the second floor was Liz's spacious master suite. Ross grimaced, as he thought about what he would find. He swung the door open and observed the organization and cleanliness within her bedroom and bathroom compared to the rest of the house. Liz protected this personal space. The closed door normally prevented the cats from destroying her private suite. Yet someone had intruded with tracks of residue from the piles of poop on the stairs and first floor. Ross paused. *The intruder could have been the police, EMTs, animal control, Joey, or Kerry and his crew.* Ross re-shut the door to block waves of the stifling odor from pervading the room. Drawer by drawer, and within closets, inquisitive Ross made a thorough sweep of the suite. Cece had asked him to look for jewelry and Aunt Camilla's heirlooms. When he thought he found the treasures, he was disappointed. Liz's three-foot-high jewelry cabinet was empty except for a few trinkets. He had his suspicions who cleaned out the chest, but he left it to Cece to reach her own conclusion.

An opulent designer bathroom filled one corner of the suite. The dressing alcove featured three floor-to-ceiling mirror panels inset into gold frames. A padded chair and ottoman rested in front of the angled mirrors and vanity table. Ross flipped several wall switches. He slid a rheostat to its highest setting. Overhead, the light from a crystal chandelier joined the warm glow of four golden wall sconces to cast perfect makeup lighting in the room. *I will have to show this corner to Cece. It looks like a glamorous Hollywood movie studio where Liz must have applied her makeup daily.*

Liz pulled her vanity chair closer to the mirror. A half-full glass of chilled Chablis sweated under the heat of the lighting. The mirrors did not lie. Her body, covered with her soft robe, reflected wrinkles and added pounds. It had become difficult to maintain her former image. She ran her hand through her silken platinum curls. Then with her brush, she arranged the curls in gentle motions. Thanks to Michele, her go-to stylist, she maintained a close semblance of the hair color of her younger days. Michele is the best! On her aging face, Liz applied makeup base, filler, mascara, eye shadow, rouge, and finally her go to flaming red lipstick. Joey was coming over that night. She smiled into the mirror. From her full closet, she located the sparkling frock she wanted to wear for their evening at the Sandy Chameleon. Her eyes brightened as she slipped on the backless gown. She believed, *Despite my flare-up of arthritis in my back, this will be a special night. I'll just pop an oxy pill.* Little did she know where the darkness would take her.

Ross shuffled through six drawers in the makeup station but found nothing of worth. He stepped to a massive claw-footed bathtub with gold faucets that stood on a platform of white and gray Carrara marble. Under the counter and sink, he searched through more drawers that yielded no valuables.

The bathroom opened to a twenty-foot-by-twenty-foot walk-in closet full of glamorous clothes befitting a Hollywood starlet. Liz stored her valuable furs in sealed garment bags, protecting the contents from the odor and cat hair. Racks of clothing hung in similar bags. An alcove with six shelves held boxes of shoes. Other than the furs, Ross guessed Cece would have little interest. *The ladies at the battered women's shelter could use these garments.* Satisfied he had checked each nook, and had taken enough photos, he pulled the door shut behind him.

Next to Liz's room, three smaller bedrooms and adjoining bathrooms beckoned Ross to explore. With most of their doors closed to the hallway also, he hoped the odors had eluded these rooms. Ross examined each piece of furniture. *Can Cece salvage these pieces? Maybe someone could sell it or give it to charity?* A set of twin beds, a bureau, two nightstands, and two lamps occupied the first bedroom. Ross thought, *The stark white furniture is so simple and amazing.* The sterile white walls and contents contrasted with the bedlam found outside the door. As he perused the closets, and furniture, Ross found nothing to share with Cece.

He discovered a few surprises in the next room, which Liz had decorated for a young girl. Wall-to-wall shelves of Barbie dolls still in their original boxes obscured the walls of pastel pink. A comforter with cerise roses covered the brass bed. On the center pillow lay an antique Baby Toodles doll in perpetual slumber. The packed drawers of the furniture contained more clothes to donate. An enlarged, framed black-and-white photograph hung above the bed and drew Ross closer. In the center of the nature scene, a five-year-old girl sat on a swing in a lush park.

Ross exclaimed, "Wow!" as he recognized Cece on the swing.

She will love this. He lifted the frame off the hanger and set it by the door.

Ross continued to a final bedroom where the door was half-open. He guessed, *This room was Joey's hideout when he stayed here.* The floors and bed contained evidence the cats either invaded or invited themselves here. *On the other hand, Joey may have brought them up here.* Ross switched the overhead fan on for ventilation. Not that it would help much! He observed the unmade bed and piles of dirty clothes lying on the messy floor amid wall-to-wall neat stacks of magazines, paper, and books. The disordered clothes contrasted with the tidiness of the books and magazines. The clutter and squalor overwhelmed Ross as he studied the contents. Between two windows, he noticed a wooden chest draped with more clothes and opened drawers. Ross went through each drawer. Nothing exciting or of value, just tattered clothing.

Another tall cherry-wood chest stood in the corner next to one side of the bed. In the top drawer, he stumbled onto a cache of Playboy magazines, odd things for Liz to keep in her home. *To whom did these magazines belong?* No mailing labels with names or addresses appeared on the magazines.

Ross wondered, *If these were her magazines, did Liz aspire to pose as a model. Or . . . ?*

With no answer, he sorted through the remaining magazines. He opened the next drawer. Ross found legal documents for a malpractice suit against a surgeon who botched Liz's breast-augmentation surgery.

Were the magazines a pattern for her surgery? Was her surgery a failure?

Ross was not comfortable getting into the deepest personal effects and behavior of Liz, the deceased. But he found himself in the thick of it!

He pondered, *There has to be a better way to dispose of deeply personal or tainted things, your skeletons, when you die. Uh, why can we not take care of business ourselves while we are still healthy?*

He shamed himself for the thought. He and Cece had not yet placed their own final affairs in order. Why should he be so quick to judge someone else? He vowed, *I swear we are going to correct our own situation when we get home!*

Another drawer held papers for a lawsuit for injuries Liz incurred while tripping over a concrete parking block at the front end of a parking space. The lawsuit claimed Liz suffered a broken arm and bruised hips.

A disheveled stack of postcard ads rested in a drawer. The ads invited parties to join class-action suits. The bright papers reflected every stripe of injury stemming from the ill effects of pharmaceuticals, medicines, and surgeries, asbestos, black lung, and mesothelioma illnesses, and accidents involving eighteen-wheelers, incorrect and faulty tires, and car seat belts. Only the expired ads lay here. He found no evidence Liz took part in any of the lawsuits.

When Ross told Cece about the lawsuit documents later, she exclaimed, "These are surprises. I never knew about her fall nor the breast surgery. I assure you she didn't need augmentation!"

Around Joey's bed, empty beer cans and liquor bottles littered the floor. A small refrigerator served as a bedside nightstand. He popped the refrigerator door open, spreading the empty cans beyond the door's path. Cold cans of Stella Artois beer filled the shelves. Ross thought, *Hand it to Joey; at least he had good taste in women and beer.*

He studied the floor where he stood. The realization struck him. *Damn, this spot is where the EMTs found Joey and the cats feasting on his gangrene-infected toes.* Stains of puce blood globs and sienna feces soaked the once ecru carpet. The compound soiled his shoes. The oozy viscous material adhered to anything that touched it. Ross jumped out of his skin as his psyche registered an awful ick feeling! Shaken at the gross spectacle, he backed up three steps. He struggled to wipe the putrid mess off his shoes unsuccessfully while gasping in the noxious vapor. His wry humor registered the thought, *This is beyond Cece's job description for me.*

He sighted a closet with hangers holding men's clothing. As he raked across the rack of clothes, he found nothing of value. In the adjacent bathroom, he examined each drawer but found only personal hygiene items.

Ross headed outside for a break. The stench in Joey's room was so odious he worked only for minutes before he needed fresh air. When Ross described the spare rooms to Cece, she cried, "Oh, Ross retrieve that photo, the Barbies, and 'Toodles, the Action Doll' for me. I want to keep them."

Cece giggled as she remembered playing with Toodles and Barbies at the family gatherings in Charleston. For hours, she and Liz posed Toodles in moves that would make a contortionist jealous. The two girls pretended the Barbie dolls competed in make-believe beauty pageants. Of course, Liz's doll always received the crown. When they played, they had to use "Liz's rules" which meant Liz won.

As he explained each room to Cece, he showed her the photos he made. She agreed she and Ross needed to walk through so he could point out all of his findings. Cece trusted his judgment, but she might want something else from the house for the family. She thought, *Let's face it. Sentimental family items meant nothing to Ross. After all, he is a man.* At that, she chuckled. She expected the restoration company to sort the rest for charity or trash. At 3:30 pm, Ross's body told him he had done his duty and was nearly finished. With the stress, odor, and optics getting to him, he estimated he had no more than an hour's effort left in him. The loss of family, stench, and hoarding of pets created an emotional pain that yearned to get out. This day etched deep in his mind. He hoped he would never witness such a scene again! His mind repeated an indelible thought, *This mess is the most God-awful thing I have ever experienced in my life.*

She and Ross agreed that the three-car garage was the only major room that remained. Ross entered the garage from the kitchen. Here in two of the bays, Liz habitually accumulated thirty or forty huge garbage bags full of refuse for days before she or Joey would take them to the dump. *Surely, Liz could have afforded a sanitation service!* Ross noted another red flag that life's cares, duties, and procrastination overwhelmed Liz. The ripe aroma from used cat litter and decayed food saturated the garage.

Ross stood behind the car and pressed a wall button to open the overhead garage door nearest to it. Liz's red BMW sat with four flat tires. Ross went back to the kitchen to retrieve the car keys from Liz's purse. He tried the key. No luck, the battery was dead. This Beamer was going nowhere. Ross wondered when Liz drove it last. Cece entered the garage through the opened door.

He asked, "Can you make a note to find the BMW dealer's phone number? Check the glove box. Maybe you can find an old receipt. That dealer can send a tow truck and assess the car for resale or even parts."

Liz loved her red Beamer. Never mind the scrapes and bumps she amassed from other cars in a parking lot or the doorframes and walls of her own garage. Somehow, she kept the auto on the road while the wind fluttered in her platinum hair. As people stared at her, she felt her ego inflate. She felt like a celebrity again as she tried to keep the car in her lane.

He closed the garage doors and returned to the great room. Each time he walked through, Ross had noticed the Bibles and spiritual books, Liz's purse, and the box sitting by the three writer's chairs. He carried the stack of items out to Cece. On the side of the box, she wrote in big letters, *Documents to Review.*

When Cece conceded they had mined the valuables the best they could, Ross sat on the shaded grass. He stared at the accumulation of things in the front yard, lying in six neat rows, each ten feet long. Cece walked through the artifacts, objects, plastic bags of papers, and boxes. She completed her inventory of the items and made more photographs should they need evidence for the court. It was 4:00 pm.

"Cece, let's get Kerry to close up after a walk through, then we will split."

She nodded, and they re-entered the house. Making the circuit, they reviewed the interior room by room, turned off lights, and closed doors.

Chapter 27

The Visitor

While Cece and Ross Were Inside
Mary's Island, South Carolina

Officer Anthony stood by his car under a shade tree.

A voice from his left said, "Hello, hello, is anybody home?"

His hand moved to his hip holster as he turned to where he heard the voice.

He said, "What may I help you with, ma'am?"

The curious neighbor said, "My name is Donna Bell. We live next door. We were sorry about Miss Liz's death. My husband called the police here last week. Exactly what's going on, officer? Is there a problem today? How is Mr. Broyer doing?"

"No, no problem. I don't know Mr. Broyer."

"Will there be a garage sale soon? We saw all that stuff in the yard. Liz had nice things."

Officer Anthony thought, *Yeah, the operative word in that sentence is "had".*

He said, "That is a family decision. In the meantime, I am asking you to leave the premises."

Mrs. Bell was out of sight by the time Cece and Ross exited the house. Each one carried a kitchen chair. Ross reasoned that sorting the bags of papers could take hours, maybe a day. They needed a chair while they worked. The two walked over to the officer.

Officer Anthony said, "Mrs. Turner, you were right about the neighbors. She seemed nice, yet nosy. She wanted to buy some items here."

He gave a quick recap of Mrs. Bell's questions. Not having to talk with neighbors pleased Cece. She was under enough stress. The court hearing loomed. The unknown future troubled her.

Cece stepped up to Officer Anthony and whispered, "Thanks for the report. I am sure she meant well. We finished our work. If you help us load these piles into the van, we can let you go soon. Find gloves on the bench. I'll call Kerry to return to reseal the house."

She breathed an exaggerated sigh of relief. Cece removed her surgical gloves and spread a lavish helping of hand sanitizer on their hands. She wanted a hot bath. With her phone's speed dial, she called Kerry Tyler.

"Kerry, can you meet us now? Yes, we collected what we needed. Thanks!"

"He will be here in ten minutes and then you can leave, Officer."

With new gloves on, they loaded the van with their collections in minutes. Cece raised the hand sanitizer again. This time the three scrubbed their arms up to their elbows. Ross wanted a shower, too. Cece found her checkbook in her purse and paid the officer as Kerry's pickup truck was turning into the driveway.

"Sergeant Anthony, can you sign this handmade receipt so I can get reimbursed? I'm sure the court will ask for something that proves I spent this money on security."

Cece gave him a hand-printed receipt and the police officer signed the paper. Graciously, she dismissed him with a twenty-dollar tip. His presence gave her peace of mind.

Kerry and Rob exited the vehicle. Rob pulled his power screwdriver from a cabinet on the truck.

Kerry asked, "How did it go today?"

She replied, "Considering the condition of the house, okay. Our mental and physical states need a rest. Should be no problem sleeping tonight. Thanks for coming back so quickly. I have talked to Gus Fence about restoration. Will it be difficult for them to get access to the house? Is your oversight needed during the renovation?"

"We need to be here only the first time, Mrs. Turner. They will show us your authorization in writing. It's part of their contract. The daily opening and closure of the house is theirs to handle. At the end of the job, you need to hire an environmental engineer to sign off on removal of biohazard risks. When they finish their work, my team will inspect the property."

"It may take time before the restoration starts, as the courts have to approve the release of money."

"No problem. You have proven you are making an effort."

Ross knew it was time to go. He had had enough! He resolved not to hang around this mess any longer, as he had exhausted his energy and patience.

Replace that damn plywood board over the front door and go! Quit the small talk, Cece.

Kerry and Rob matched the board to the screw holes made earlier and replaced the screws to re-block the doorway.

Whirr. Whirr.

"I'm unsure when we will meet again Kerry. Call if you need help."

"Thank you for your help, y'all!"

Ross and Cece removed their old shoes and pulled out spare ones before getting into the van. They tossed the ruined sneakers into a trash bag. *There is no need to contaminate the van,* Ross thought. As the two drove back on the beach causeway to their condo, the residual stench of decay and cat smells on the papers and objects filled the van. They planned to look at items in their room. The odor in the van convinced them otherwise. Ross set the van's air conditioner fan to high and opened the windows.

Drained, Ross said, "It will be best to wait until tomorrow to deliver this stuff to the storage facilities and then you can review it."

He sneezed five times in a row. His head ached. His nose was running.

Each took a long steaming shower. Then, each consumed two glasses of Cabernet on the condo balcony. They stepped downstairs to the Hermit Crab Cafe for a light dinner. By eight-thirty, they were ready for bed. Usually, Cece closed the balcony blackout drapes before sleeping. But she did not that night.

Chapter 28

Regrouping

The Next Day
The Condominium

Tuesday morning the bright sun shone early into the one-bedroom condominium overlooking the Atlantic. Cece had slept poorly.

The entire night, nightmares and questions ran through her head. She dreamt of visions of purple Liz lying in the freezing cold morgue. Cece scaled walls and ran like a rat negotiating a maze while pursued by a gang of cats. The questions bombarded her. *How will I know I found all the financial assets? Should we sell Liz's house as is or restore it? Should I have it gutted and fumigated, or bulldoze it?* Then her psyche reverted to the horrible conditions amid the squalor.

Ross slept no better than Cece. Despite taking an antihistamine, his sinus cavities felt as if they would explode and his head ached. He grew angrier with the situation at the house. In his nightmare, his body swam laps in the middle of a biohazard. No matter where he stepped as he dreamt, he could not escape cats, their residue, and trash. Civilized people do not live this way!

Between the sun and the distress of their confused minds, they both awakened by 6:00 am. Both experienced the effects of the prior day's trauma. Ross had coffee brewing when Cece walked into the kitchen, yawning.

He demanded, "Exactly what is your plan for today, Cece?"

"The storage center opens at 8:00 am to sign new renters. Let's try to get there, unload the van, and sort through the papers before it gets too hot. Assess what we have in the bills and documents. Maybe afterward, hit the beach and the pool."

Ross thought, *Always holding a carrot over the old mule, himself.*

She added, "Get dressed. Strawberries and cereal for breakfast, and then we'll head out."

Chapter 29

Sorting

An Hour Later
Mary's Island Storage Center

Ross pulled into a parking place in front of the massive storage facility. Ten rows of buildings each with ten garage doors stood as if castle ramparts on raised ground. Ross guessed the higher ground base was to protect against possible tidal surges during a hurricane. Constructed of poured concrete, the walls appeared massive. A ten-foot security fence topped with concertina wire ran the perimeter around the units. *They should have called this place Bulwark City. It looks like a modern fortress.*

The two walked inside where a young man behind the reception desk greeted them. Cece introduced herself. She told him she had inquired the day before about a unit's availability.

"We need to store the items for a year until an estate is settled. I need the smallest unit you have."

"Sure, that is our eight-foot by eight-foot model."

"What's the rental rate?"

"We are running a 'special' for a six-month contract. This one is just forty-five dollars per month. After the first six months, you can renew every month, or you can quit with thirty days' notice. Keep your payments current. Any lapses over two months and we will donate your items to a local charity. Access here is twenty-four seven."

Cece said, "It's a deal. Where do I sign?"

The clerk printed a booklet of forms for Cece's signature.

"Here are two keys for unit twenty-nine, at the end of the third row, and here is the magnetic card to get into the front gate on our fenced property. Return these security tools when you move out and we'll refund you one month's rent."

Ross and his morning coffee buddies at the university had discussed the week before that there were at least two recession-proof businesses in existence: laundromats and storage rental units. He could see why. People needed clean clothes which meant a steady flow of coins from customers that did not have operating washers and dryers. Likewise, a storage facility provided a perpetual flow of cash interrupted only when the user or renter decided it was time to move on, soon replaced by another soul needing the service. The mass culture found it easier to store something they might need instead of donating or trashing it. People held onto their stuff, often for unexplainable or irrational reasons. They were happy not to make a decision to keep or dispose.

Cece rode on a golf cart with the attendant to the unit. Ross followed in the van. With the large overhead door up, three full walls remained. Seeking to have organization amid the chaos, Cece suggested they position the loose items and breakables on the back wall.

"We can line one wall with the boxes of silver and unbreakable items. And along the opposite wall, lay the six bags and the box of documents on the floor."

They each pulled on surgical gloves and emptied the van of the stinky contents. Ross placed the two kitchen chairs facing the boxes, which gave them a sorting surface.

Cece ordered, "I want the life-insurance policies and related information in one stack, bank statements and checks in another stack, stock and bonds in another.

Separate stacks for electric, gas, cable, water, and so on as needed. For items that are not financial documents, we can decide how to sort each. Meanwhile, make piles for those dogs and cats as they occur."

Ross grimaced at her unintended pun. *I hope we have no animals in those bags!*

Piece by piece, they arranged the smelly papers. The paper trail represented months of billings, statements, advertisements, and random mailings. In the middle of the mess, Cece found cards and letters she sent Liz over the years. Repeatedly, she noticed many receipts for the same taxi service and for the Sandy Chameleon lounge. An idea flashed through her brain that she could do some detective work herself. She pulled one receipt for the taxi and the bar and set them by her purse.

For each set of bills, they focused on two key items, the billing date, and the sender. Without looking closely at other details of each page, they found they could sort through a bag in an hour. The rubber gloves stymied their efforts to grasp the aged, dusty paper. Cece sorted the stacks of bills and located the latest statement for each vendor.

Then the details of the selected bills became important. She set aside the most recent statements to capture the account number, phone number, and balances. When they visited the court the next day, she expected they would need a copy of each vendor's latest bill to authorize payment from Liz's funds. Before they left town, she expected to return the originals to the storage unit and carry another copy home with her. If the court named her administrator, Cece had to call each creditor to end the account and services. She planned to make copies of the bank, insurance, and stock statements as well. The details on these identified how much cash was available to use for Liz's funeral, restoration of the house, taxes, the unpaid bills, care of the cats, the morgue, storage units, car evaluation, and attorney fees. She guessed the list of amounts owed would grow nearly as quickly as the national debt. She hoped the estate had leftovers to distribute to the heirs. Her mind flashed the first action she planned if she became the administrator.

Ross looked at his watch which showed 1:00 pm. Only one task remained. He lifted the box on which Cece had written *Documents to Review* and placed it on top of the other boxes. Cece opened the flaps.

Within the box, original documents and their copies merged. As Ross had described to her earlier, Cece found the grainy packet of papers that appeared to be Liz's Last Will and Testament on top. Under it lay a receipt from a local copy center for the copies in the box. The paper had the same date as Liz's death. *Hmm, we can go there to copy my stuff. I wonder what they were doing copying these important papers that night?* Cece put the copy receipt with those she had selected for the taxi and bar. She uncovered two life-insurance policies, multiple stock certificates for the power company and an oil company, corporate bonds, and a receipt for bank Certificates of Deposit. Next, legal documents including a divorce decree came out of the pile. Cece pulled out a stack of uncashed checks payable to Liz. When she totaled them, she realized she held four thousand dollars. Cece whistled at the thought that the checks were nearly enough to pay for the funeral. She thumbed through the stack of checks again looking at the payers to gain clues about Liz's investments. On the bottom of the box rested a safe deposit key envelope for the Mary's Island National Bank. Cece looked at Ross, her eyes widening.

She said, "Is there more?"

Ross replied, "I don't know, but it looks like it. Look, I'm sick of this. We have looked over everything. We can get Harry's advice tomorrow. Let's ditch the van and head to the pool."

Cece placed the items she wanted to copy in the van. The remaining documents they moved to boxes within the storage unit. From the six bags of papers they started with, they sorted out enough trash to refill two emptied bags. Ross carried the waste to the trash-bin behind the main office. Cece pulled the hand sanitizer from her purse. The two doused their hands and arms up to their elbows.

Ross started the empty van and opened the two windows for fresh air. By the time, they reached the auto rental office, only a trace of odor remained from the booty of their scavenger hunt. They returned the van and retrieved Ross's car. She placed the four-inch high stack of smelly billing statements and financial documents in the trunk of the car.

In the copy store, Cece asked to see the manager.

Showing her Liz's receipt, Cece asked, "Do you know who may have made these copies?"

"Let me see. Yeah, that is my code on the receipt. I remember those customers. I had to pull the night shift when the regular clerk got sick."

Cece felt like jumping up and down.

"Sir, I need to make copies of these receipts and to ask you some questions. Is that okay?"

When they finished, she asked Ross to make several other stops before they went to the condominium. He looked at his watch. It was 2:00 pm.

"I thought you promised beach time this afternoon."

"Ross, give me a few minutes at two more places, please."

Ross dutifully drove Cece to the Sandy Chameleon and the taxi company's office.

While they were in the bar, Cece said to Ross, "Thanks for your help. I'll treat you to a drink and lunch."

Cece waved her hand at the barmaid to come to their table.

"Can I ask you some questions? I see that the lunch crowd has cleared out."

"Sure, what's up?"

The waitress pulled up a chair and told Cece everything she saw the last time Liz visited the bar.

"I'll tell you what I told the detective several weeks ago. I don't want any trouble, lady."

Similarly, when they confronted the taxi driver at the cab company, they learned more. Cece thought, *This is all very interesting, yet inconclusive.*

In the early evening hours, Ross and Cece attempted to relax at the condo swimming pool. They took a long walk along the beach. The respite refreshed their minds as they coped with the ordeal they had endured over the past two days. Cece pondered her appearance in probate court the next day.

That night, a weather front brought turbulence to the sea. The storm repeatedly awakened Cece, compounding her sleep-deprived condition. For a second night, she had awakened in fits of confusion, doubt, and second-guessing herself. She was at physical and mental war! Again, she dreamt a nightmare of purple Liz freezing in the morgue. The nightmare transitioned to a battlefield of decay and odor in her cousin's home. Tall stacks of unopened mail transformed into paper soldiers jabbing at her. The final surreal dream included a cadre of twenty cats standing in a chorus taunting her with a refrain of *Catch Me if You Can.* Simultaneously her head suffered an onset of nasal congestion and coughing. Why had she done this? She felt sad she subjected loyal Ross to her family's problems. He was a jewel. In the bed, she rolled over to give him a love pat. No one was there.

Chapter 30

Professional Advice

Wednesday, May 20, 1998
Georgetown, South Carolina

The mayhem in her mind forced her to arise at 6:00 am. She smelled a pot of coffee brewing in the kitchen. She filled a large mug and walked into the living room. The sliding doors to the condo balcony were wide open allowing a strong breeze to enter the room. Menacing clouds covered the sky.

Cece asked, "What's happening out here?"

Grumpy Ross exclaimed, "You tell me first!"

They gazed at each other wondering why the week was so difficult.

Cece broke the silence. "I'll 'fess up first. I had insomnia from our encounters. And I suppose I lost sleep over going before the judge today."

Ross replied, "You'll be fine. Just answer your attorney's questions."

Cece panned a glance at the other one hundred and twenty balconies attached to the building.

"Your turn, what were you doing out here?"

"I'm praying that the Lord will take this cup from me!"

He wiped his nose with a paper towel. Cece sat on the other chair, slipped an arm through Ross's, and leaned her head on his shoulder. He patted her back.

Ross asked, "What time is the appointment at Harry's and the court?"

Cece said, "Nine and eleven."

He replied, "Stay here a few minutes and finish your coffee. Then, we'll get dressed and find a mom and pop café downtown for breakfast before we meet Harry. Bacon, eggs, and cheese grits sounds good to me."

Following their meal, Cece and Ross walked a block away to the front of the law offices of Caisteal and Wilson, Attorneys at Law, at the corner of Screven and Front streets. Across the street stood the storied century-old courthouse that had braved many hurricanes without a scratch. An attractive blonde middle-aged woman greeted them as they entered the reception hall.

"Hi, I'm Cece Turner and this is my husband, Ross. We have an appointment with Harry this morning."

"Hello, I'm Dianne. Yes, ma'am, Harry is expecting you."

Dressed to the nines, stylish Dianne led Cece and Ross through a winding hallway where a non-stop window looked onto the murky, choppy ocean. The high winds had not abated and dark ominous clouds covered Georgetown. They stopped at an interior conference room.

Cece asked, "May I use the ladies' room, please? I want to work on this hair."

The relentless wind had played havoc with her perfect hairdo when they walked to the office from the Talk of the Town cafe.

At 9:00 am, Harry Caisteal knocked on the door to the conference room. He enthusiastically announced, "Good morning, Cece, Ross."

To Cece, Harry made the same sterling impression now as when they had classes together. Since then, he kept his body buff at a gym. He looked dapper in his three-piece pinstriped suit. A receding hairline and twenty extra pounds added an air of gravitas and maturity to his features. Otherwise, he had not changed since their college days. He earned his Juris

Doctor degree at another university after his under-
graduate studies.

Ross sat next to Cece to lend support and editorial
comments when Cece appeared to need coaching.

Harry offered the two of them something to eat or
drink.

Cece replied, "We enjoyed breakfast moments before
we arrived here. That met our limit for coffee for today.
Maybe water?"

Harry opened a small refrigerator and retrieved
two bottles of water.

Cece asked, "Harry, what is your secret to keeping
young?"

"Fish and lots of it!"

They laughed.

"You look great, Cece. I am very sorry for your loss.
Pleased to meet you, Ross. Cece talked non-stop about
you in our school days."

Good-natured Ross nodded and smiled, "I heard
about you, too!"

Then the social niceties ended. It was time for
business.

Harry opened a folder and said, "Cece, this should
not be a difficult situation for you today."

He had a relaxed manner and put Cece at ease.
He exuded experience and knowledge.

"Before we see Judge Bonham, let's review your
intentions, sign the court petition and other papers,
and answer your questions."

Cece's insides were churning.

She answered, "My goal is to give Liz a proper
funeral, to get her buried. To do that, we need to free
up her money. Add the matter of whether she had a
will, and if so, is it valid. Then, manage her assets,
the house, bills, stock, bank accounts, and those cats.
There is just so much. A lot to keep all of us busy."

"Relax, Cece. Take one-step at a time. This morning we only ask the court to name you the administrator. We will petition access to money to pay for the funeral, morgue, and specific things. The rest will take time. Refresh me about what has happened so far."

Harry listened to Cece's concerns, her ideas on the funeral plans, their experiences in Liz's home and at the storage unit, her conversation with Joey, the assets in Liz's estate, a preliminary list of potential creditors and the amounts owed, and the evidence they brought to Harry. Within the evidence, Cece pointed out the copy of the grainy packet that masqueraded as a will. Cece impressed Ross in her thorough briefing of the attorney in the short time. It helped that Cece had her stuff together. Ross thought, *She is the most analytical person I have ever known, even more than I am.* As if a sponge, Harry absorbed the information in his professional way.

At 10:10 am, Harry said, "You have done what you needed to do. There will be no issues with Judge Bonham this morning if you answer her questions as you responded here. I do not know this judge or anything about her personally. But I reviewed most of her earlier rulings and I saw fair treatment in her courtroom. Now, let me give you information detailing your responsibilities should you accept them. Are you ready to make notes?"

Cece nodded. Not showing any signs of nervousness, she focused on her goals. Harry had calmed the earlier tumult inside her.

Cece's pen scratched across the parchment grade paper. She thought, *Boy, these attorneys only use the good stuff. No wonder they are so expensive.* In detail, Harry reiterated her potential duties as a court-appointed administrator. She listened and paraphrased his comments.

When someone dies, the administrator is a detective of the deceased's finances. The administrator identifies who the deceased's creditors are, and pays the debts, taxes, and for the funeral. To pay for these things, an administrator locates funds from the deceased's cash, bank accounts, investments, insurance policies, and sales of property. They must answer to the probate judge for their actions.

If a will exists, the administrator, or another party submits it to the probate court at a proper time. When the judge rules the will valid, the executor named within takes over the administrator's duties. The executor performs other duties as outlined, but their main duties are making payments to the government, creditors and named heirs. The court appoints another executor if the designee named in the will has died, disappeared, or refused to take part. When the parties cannot find a valid will, the administrator distributes what funds are left; the state law sets forth the pecking order of the heirs and their share.

Harry stopped his comments and Cece looked up from her paper.

She asked, "That's it? I think I captured what you said. I could not write as fast as you talk so I simplified your comments. My notes are close enough, I guess. It looks like I have accomplished some of this by gathering the documents, eh?"

"Yes, you are doing well. Next, we need to sign a few papers for the court and Dianne will notarize them. When you finish signing, please try to relax. We'll walk over to the courthouse in about ten minutes."

Soon, Harry said, "Let's go."

Chapter 31

First Court Appearance

Minutes Later
George County Courthouse

As they crossed the cobblestone street to the courthouse plaza, the sun burst through the storm clouds and the wind abated to a gentle breeze. Cece breathed a sigh of relief. They climbed the worn front steps of the red brick and turreted courthouse. Cece thought it resembled an ancient castle. They entered a wide hallway and proceeded to the courtrooms. Imposing heavy portals led to the massive chambers. As the centerpiece of law, the county leaders built the place to stay. The ancient wooden doorways glistened with the smell of a fresh coat of pine-oil furniture polish. A bailiff posted the court schedule of the day on the bulletin boards hung on the brick wall surrounding the wood. The bulletin boards at the other courtrooms displayed added helpful information about the judge and the court. At the room where they stopped, Ross noticed only one item, the day's schedule; no other documents, pictures, or certificates. Harry held the door open for his clients.

At 11:00 am sharp, the bailiff addressed those gathered with a brief litany of procedures. Twenty people sat in the courtroom.

The bailiff thundered, "The Honorable Judge Janie Bonham, All Rise!"

The judge entered the courtroom, sat down, and motioned to the audience to sit. Work began on the morning's docket. The clerk of the court scheduled two other probate cases ahead of Liz's matters. When her turn arrived, the bailiff called Cecilia Turner to the bench. Both Harry and Cece approached the judge. Her Honor leaned toward Harry and asked for the papers.

Harry had expedited the proceedings since he had completed the documents in advance. Judge Bonham queried Cece about her relationship to the deceased, her competence, and her involvement with the estate, the money requested, the source, and purpose. Then the judge signed the order Harry had prepared. Judge Janie Bonham decreed Cece to be the administrator of Liz's estate and allowed her to spend specific funds from Liz's accounts. Cece's list included $6,000 for the funeral home and cemetery, $800 for the morgue, $1,000 for legal expenses, and $1,500 for Cece's item-ized expenses for the past week. To make it easier for Cece to pay future estate expenses and bills, Judge Bonham consented to opening an operating fund checking account at a local bank.

The clerk of the court handed Cece a list of probate instructions. As she scanned the sheet, Cece noticed that large draws on Liz's money required prior writ-ten approval from the judge, and that the clerk of the court audited estate expenditures. Cece understood, *The clerk of court carried significant power here.* Cece was thankful another set of eyes was responsible for accuracy. Her attorney could ask for more funds as needed. Harry told Cece it was fortunate that South Carolina law did not require the administrator to buy a surety bond as other states did.

Chapter 32

Cece's Thoughts

Minutes Later
Downtown Georgetown

To celebrate Cece's successful hearing with Judge Bonham, the three agreed to regroup thirty minutes later for lunch. Harry suggested the Starwood Cafe, a "meat and three" restaurant across from the courthouse. In the South, a "meat and three" referred to cafés where the entrees consisted of the patron's choice of one item from a listing of several meats and three items from multiple vegetable options.

Famished from her work that morning, Cece felt hunger pangs. However, she realized she must make four phone calls. She dialed Tom and Sharon Lee at Cooper River Gardens. Tom's calendar showed the next Tuesday, the day after the Memorial Day holiday, available to have Liz's funeral. Tom arranged Liz's move from the morgue after Cece paid the morgue fees.

Then Cece called Ross's father, the Reverend Matt Turner, to confirm his availability to officiate at the graveside ceremony.

Cece remembered Nancy Mayer's offer to get the word out to Liz's classmates because she was so well connected. Cece called her next. Nancy wanted to hear what had transpired since their first phone call in the middle of the night a month ago. Then, Cece discussed the funeral arrangements.

Cece asked, "Nancy, would you honor Liz by giving a short eulogy during the service?"

Nancy replied, "Yes, I want to do it!"

Finally, Cece dialed the Georgetown Animal Rescue Center.

"Hello, May I please speak to the manager?"

Seconds later, a woman's voice said, "Hello, Kay here, who is calling?"

"Cece Turner here. The probate court named me to serve as administrator for the estate of my cousin, Liz Perkins. Kay, your clinic has been caring for her cats since she died. Yes, those cats! How many are survivors? Oh I see, just fourteen out of the twenty. I am so sorry. In how serious a condition are they?"

Kay recited a brief status on the cats.

With all the courage she could summon, Cece said, "I hate to do this, but I am calling you to pull the plug on all the surviving cats. I have concerns over their quality of life. Yes, I understand. Well, unless you can find a home for the two healthy ones by Monday, you have my order now to euthanize all of them including the healthy ones. *Pause.* Yes, every one of them! *Pause.* Yes, I will sign the form this afternoon. Thanks, Kay. Good-bye!"

It was a humane and simple business decision. As she walked toward Harry and Ross, her mind repeated, *I am not a heartless woman! I am not a heartless woman!*

Before that day, Harry focused on preparations for the hearing. His curiosity about the circumstances surrounding Liz's death piqued during their lunch. What had Cece learned about the events before and after Liz died?

The would-be detective Cece pieced together the puzzle and told Harry a plausible timeline of the night Liz died.

She began, "You can say the proverbial *night had a thousand eyes.*"

She and Ross gathered her patchwork story from observers in Mary's Island, the police, locals, and her memorable conversation with Joey. At each of Liz and Joey's last stops, witnesses contributed snippets of what they remembered. The information the people supplied astounded Cece.

She whispered, "I think I did a decent job retracing most of their steps that evening. Joey told me that he and Liz enjoyed several cocktails before they went out carousing."

Harry commented, "This sounds good."

"We found many receipts for taxis. For about a year, Liz used Palmetto Taxi for local transportation. The same driver's name appeared repeatedly on the receipts. I had a hunch we needed to visit him. With her car inoperable and no room for a second person in Joey's van, they called the cab company. The driver noted that he carried lots of passengers with luggage and groceries, but never one with a box of papers. He told me Joey carried the box out to the taxi at 8:00 pm despite a deluge. Liz got in the car next to Joey. The couple's first stop was the Sandy Chameleon, the dive where they first met. The taxi driver said he drove them to the bar often. Liz paid the driver for the short ride and a tip. Joey asked him to return to pick them up at 11:30 pm. Joey commented they wanted to make other stops later."

Cece continued, "We paid a visit to the bar, too. A disc jockey who played endless runs of oldies beach music, a young bartender working the bar, and two barmaids served as the only employees at the Sandy Chameleon. We talked to them about what they saw. The workers thought it odd that Joey carried a boxful of documents as he entered. He placed it in their usual corner booth. The couple ordered more drinks to top off their earlier consumption. A rain shower chased people inside, which crowded the dance floor more than a normal night. The polished wooden floor in the center of the old-fashioned honky-tonk allowed the talented and not so talented to dance nightly. The bar workers noticed the platinum blonde and the old man getting applause from the admirers in the audience. Liz and Joey danced the shag with moves adapted from the East Coast Swing. One of the barmaids taught the patrons the dance steps on nights when business was slack. Weeks before, Liz convinced Joey to take lessons of the in-vogue dance with her. Liz told the barmaid she loved dancing, however her limp hindered her. She said she relished searching in her gown closet to find something that sparkled and caught the eye when she danced. She still coveted a stage presence. But Liz complained to the dance teacher that her back ached for hours if she overdid it. Liz added, 'It's hell to get old!'"

Ross winked and added that the server told him, "Liz's mantra for years was if you got it, flaunt it baby!"

Cece said, "At 10:00 pm, Joey went to the men's room. Liz walked over to the dj and complained about arthritis pain in her lower back that never seemed to ease. She told him she had no choice but to end her dancing for the night. The young dj asked if she wanted him to massage her back. She voiced soft purrs and moans as the thirty-something's hands caressed her bare shoulders, and then around her lower back. She thanked him and strutted back to their booth.

"When Joey returned, a late-night snack and more drinks appealed to both. Joey ordered his usual, a greasy burger, and fries. Liz had her favorite, grilled red snapper with asparagus tips. Forever concerned about her figure, Liz had no dessert, but she agreed to one more nightcap before they moved onto their next task. At 11:25 pm, Joey checked outside for the cab. It was waiting for them."

Harry interrupted Cece, saying, "Amazing what people will tell you, isn't it?"

Cece nodded and added, "The taxi carried the inebriated couple to a twenty-four seven office supply and copy center in Georgetown. Ross and I went there as well. Joey made copies of everything in the box of documents. The condition of the couple plus the quantity of documents copied at that hour surprised the clerk behind the counter. Joey had to ask for help with the copier often. She said she would not forget him. The store's charge for copies totaled $200. Liz paid for it with a credit card. The taxi returned in the promised two hours to pick them up and carry them home safely."

Before Cece continued with her story, she took a sip of water. She looked at Ross, then Harry.

She whispered, "Harry, my Momma always said nothing good happens after midnight!"

Quiet Cece relished this audience. Her voice cracked as she continued the saga.

"I had that illogical conversation with Joey one night. He told me that Liz wanted to soak in her hot tub. She put on her swimsuit and headed to her backyard. I am not sure what happened next. Joey babbled that he left her so he could go to the bathroom. Instead of returning to the hot tub, he said he went to bed. The next thing he knew it was morning. He awakened to find Liz face downward with her head in the spa and her feet on the sidewalk."

She added, "Joey declared he was frightened and anxious. He called the local police who examined the scene and pronounced her death an accident. His friend, confidant, lover, cats' momma, and latest soulmate had died. Gone. It's so sad. The coroner took Liz's body to the morgue for autopsy and then storage. Then Joey did nothing to bury her. Joey's indecision and fear bound him."

Cece interrupted herself, "Harry, did you know the labs have not released the autopsy yet?"

He shook his head. Harry sat with lips tightened as he listened to Cece's summary. He guessed correctly that she replayed the scenes repeatedly in her mind. He could not imagine how she tolerated living out this awful tragedy.

The waitress asked if she could clear their table of empty plates.

Harry responded, "Yes, ma'am, can I have the check?"

He turned to Cece and said "Stay strong, girl! Call me if you find out anything else."

The three finished their last comments and said their good-byes. As the Turners left, Harry told them he planned to be at Liz's funeral.

Chapter 33

Final Rites

The Next Tuesday
Cooper River Gardens

Ross and Cece arrived at the funeral home and cemetery as planned two hours before Liz's service. Despite the occasion, Cece found satisfaction in her efforts. She mustered the energy to handle the paperwork, pay the balance for the funeral, change clothes, and freshen herself. She had no clue who would attend. *Would Joey come to the funeral?* Cece did not think so. Ross's mother and father, and Bill and Nancy Mayer arrived an hour before the service. The director, Tom Lee, requested all of them to be early to review the order of the simple graveside service with them. Cece felt an enduring sadness for Liz's passing and the incredible life she lived in the good and bad times.

Following their meeting, Sharon Lee requested they move to their cars. Led by a polished silver gray Cadillac hearse, the procession wound through the massive graveyard followed by the family and others. It was a pleasant sunny day. Being the day following Memorial Day, rows of small American flags fluttered over the graves of veterans. The crowd of fifty people already gathered at the gravesite surprised Cece. Harry Caisteal stood in the back. Cece expected no curious outsiders.

Ross's dad, Rev. Matt Turner, took the dais. He was eloquent with a booming bass voice. He sought to remember the beauty who represented the state so long before and who almost won a national title. The preacher paused in his comments and asked the attendees to offer a verbal remembrance if they wished. Several people spoke of her love and beauty. After them, Reverend Turner nodded to Nancy Mayer to make her comments.

Nancy and Liz first became friends in the Shakespeare class. She knew when Cece invited her to take part that her choice should be the emotive obituary from the Bard's *Cymbeline*.

Fear no more the heat o' the sun,
Nor the furious winters rages;
Thou thy worldly task hast done,
Home art gone and ta'en thy wages;
Golden lads and girls all must,
As chimney-sweepers, come to dust.

Fear no more the frown o' the great,
Thou art past the tyrants stoke;
Care no more to clothe and eat;
To thee the reed is as the oak;
The scepter, learning, physic, must
All follow this, and come to dust.

Fear no more the lightning-flash,
Nor the all-dreaded thunder-stone;
Fear not slander, censure rash;
Thou hast finish'd joy and moan;
All lovers young, all lovers must
Consign to thee, and come to dust.

No exorciser harm thee!
Nor no witchcraft charm thee!
Ghost unlaid forbear thee!

Nothing ill come near thee!
Quiet consummation have;
And renowned be thy grave.

William Shakespeare "Cymbeline"
Act IV, Scene 2

Cece mused to herself, *Nancy gave a touching trib-ute; I wish I thought to use that.*

Reverend Turner said, "Now I will read the Twenty-Third Psalm from the Bible written by David, the shepherd that later became the King of his country."

Cece wept as her thoughts conjoined with the comforting words. A fleeting image of the David statue from Liz's mantelpiece came to her mind

The LORD is my shepherd; I lack nothing.

As she heard the sentence, Cece pictured that her cousin had lacked nothing in the material or talent or beauty sense. In the early years, the socialite had owned life! *However, baggage came with those good attributes.* A glamourous woman, Liz possessed looks, charisma, the paid-for mansion in the paradise setting of Mary's Island, and a portfolio of ample funding. Everything the world offered.

He makes me lie down in green pastures.
He leads me beside quiet waters.
He refreshes my soul.

Cece, still sniffling, considered that Liz is at rest now. Cece had fulfilled her duty to Liz. In a measured cadence, Reverend Turner's voice carried the ancient passage.

He guides me along the right paths for his name's sake.

Cece's sorrow turned to anger as she saw in her mind the four husbands, the destroyed mansion, the cats, the bottles, the pills, the squalor, the mess. . . .

Even though I walk
Through the darkest valley,

Cece's brain raced over the odors, squalor, and unpleasantness in the house the prior week and the depths where Liz fell. The teardrops became a river, then a flood. Cece cried out. Ross moved his arm tighter across her shoulder and patted her back. How she hated his patting.

I will fear no evil.
For you are with me,
Your rod and your staff,
They comfort me.

The words enveloped Cece with a sense of peace. She started her closure of Liz's death. She pictured Liz's entrance to heaven, dressed in white linen, with a pink sapphire necklace. A jeweled crown nestled on her hair. Liz earned a new crown to replace her tarnished one.

You prepare a table before me
In the presence of my enemies.
You anoint my head with oil.

In her early years, Liz seemed to be the anointed one among her competitors.

My cup overflows.
Surely your goodness and love will follow me
All the days of my life,
And I will dwell in the house of the LORD *forever.*

Cece thought that at last Liz was experiencing the goodness and love she always sought. She was now in a mansion in the Lord's heavens.

The poignant service ended with a final prayer. Ross's dad intoned the last Amen and then walked to Cece and Ross and hugged them. Cece mingled with the crowd mourning Liz.

Someone tapped Cece on the shoulder. She turned around to see her only living first cousin, Richie, the geek who now lived as a bonafide social recluse. At the end of their short conversation, Richie asked Cece if she would handle his final affairs also. She thought, *Well, what is the worse that could happen?*

She replied, "Sure, Richie, I've got experience now."

When Ross and Cece noticed that most of the attendees had left, the two plodded to the grave bier. The workers lowered Liz's remains into the cavernous hole. They shoveled dirt on top of the concrete vault containing the steel gray coffin. Cece reached to the single funeral spray of red roses and picked up a blossom. She paused, bowed her head, and the tears flowed once more. The flower triggered her flashback to Liz's rescue of Cece from the dangerous snake in the park. She and Ross walked toward their car as her sobbing subsided.

In the corner of her eye, Cece spotted a bystander walking toward them.

Out of earshot, Cece whispered to Ross, "Another of Liz's suitors, perhaps?"

Dressed in a gray business suit with a red necktie, the tall stranger spoke, "Hello, Mr. and Mrs. Turner. My name is Allen Schafer."

Allen was a tan, handsome preppy man with a buff athletic build, smooth face, and a head full of hair like a silver fox. Despite his age, late fifties, she guessed, he had taken care of himself. Cece imagined he could be a stockbroker or CPA. He talked about his and Liz's years at the university.

"Liz and I dated and fell in love. I always loved her, and I know she loved me. In our freshman year, she was my fraternity's sweetheart. And my sweetheart also."

Then Allen whispered, "Beginning around this past New Year's, Liz and I restarted communications with each other. First, I called her and then we wrote each other. My friends regard me as a dinosaur because I do not use a computer for personal correspondence. I prefer a handwritten romantic letter approach. Now a widower twice, I have been seeking a new companion. Yes, I wanted a wife. I mailed my last letter to her two weeks before she died. It contained the characteristics I thought a perfect wife should have. Added to that, I wrote the traits of a faithful husband. Then I compared the two of us to these lists."

Allen added, "A perfect match. I ended the letter asking Liz to marry me. I am not sure if she received the letter because she never replied."

Allen's voice became deeper and louder, as he asked, "How did this happen? What happened?"

Cece replied tersely, "We don't know yet, or if we ever will."

"I hope that SOB who lived with her didn't cause this. If you hear of treachery, let me know and I will make it right for Liz. And me."

Cece reached toward Allen, hugged him, and said, "Thank you for coming to this service and sharing your experiences. I know it is such a tremendous loss for you also. Good-bye and I will let you know what I hear about the situation."

Cece steered Ross toward the car. Allen's comment about making it right unnerved her. Pangs of anxiety churned within her chest. *Had she and Ross unknowingly tumbled into the midst of a lover's triangle?* She felt apprehensive until she made it to the safety of the trusty Mercedes. Dueling suitors were not how she wanted to remember Liz. She hated conflict.

Cece watched through the windshield as the last shovels of dirt mounded over the vault. While the worker placed the red roses atop the grave, Ross pulled into the road to exit. Cece had not experienced full closure yet. She held a conviction about Liz's legacy she wanted to get off her chest. It welled up inside her, stronger and stronger. For sure, she wanted to avoid a repeat of Liz's legal mistakes in her own life.

Before leaving town, they stopped at Gus Fence's restoration company. When Ross stopped in the Synergy Restoration parking lot, Cece ran in and picked up the contract. She met Gus and they chatted for several minutes. Feeling good about the firm, and Gus, she thought, *What other choices do I really have?* He asked Cece to fax the signed contract back after he sent her his estimate.

Ross drove to the parking lot of Mary's Island National Bank. Cece met with a bank officer, conducted her business, and then they left, headed for New Orleans.

Chapter 34

Home Sweet Home

Two Days Later
New Orleans, Louisiana

With the business issues completed for now, Cece and Ross drove back to New Orleans over two days. Cece had gathered her data, secured the assets, arranged restoration of Liz's mansion, ordered the demise of the cats, and buried Liz. Despite what he thought was the start of a cold, Ross drove the entire way home. Devoid of energy, Cece coughed non-stop, as she lay curled in her seat. She wanted to climb in her own bed again. Her forehead burned with a fever.

Word of Cece and Ross's return spread quickly. On the second day after their drive, Cece's entire neighborhood book club gathered in Cece's home. One by one, the ladies poked their head in the Turner's front door. Janet Lawrence, Bobbie Hunter, Di Porter, Jean Osborne, Nancy Wayne, Starla Adams, Trudy Cantrell, Jeanne Willis, Ana Scott, Linsey Jones, Emi Johnson, and Cindy Miller each hugged Cece in a show of love and concern. The aroma of Louisiana coffee and Janet's fragrant homemade cinnamon rolls wafted through the rooms.

Before they had left for the East coast, Cece avoided sharing with her friends the details about her cousin's death so the ladies met to catch up on the interesting situation. Cece's home barely accommodated the unusually large crowd. Between sentences, she continued her incessant cough. Her head ached. While she never mentioned her fever nor complained to her friends, they observed her discomfort. Their regular scheduled meeting to review their latest literary conquest would occur the next week. Regardless, she set aside today as a time for coffee, a snack, and her latest news. Her eager audience clamored for facts, news, and gossip. Cece's three rescue cats heard her calming voice. They jumped onto plush pillows, lying in a warm bay window in the next room, safely out of the sightlines of the human gathering. First, Cece summarized Liz's plight and the gross condition of the mansion, and then she vented her new conviction.

Trudy commented "Heck, Cece, this is better than reviewing a book. What did you find most interesting?"

"Boxes of stuff including legal documents, bills, valuables, furs, a safe deposit key, and the mess I mentioned."

Trudy responded, "Did you locate a will?"

Cece shook her head, "We are not sure if the document we found is valid. The attorney is reviewing it."

Without blinking an eye, Cece continued, "Oh yes, we stored Liz's crown, but it was in terrible shape. What a symbol of her life. Tarnished and ruined. Something went terribly wrong in Liz's affairs. At the end, things about her seemed warped; like her mental and physical capacity, personal relationships, and her legacy. You know, before they die, a person should try to put their stuff in order. I am convinced we must be proactive to avoid this predicament in our lives."

She had misgivings that she was too judgmental towards Liz, but the Herculean effort to clean up someone else's mess had zapped the two of them.

As the flashbacks curdled in her mind and on her lips, she quizzed the group, "Why aren't adults responsible?

"The person need not finish every detail, but the important ones are necessary. Before you go bonkers or become ill, at least consider your end-of-life choices. Decide early where you want to live in your last days and what to keep in your domain. Get rid of the trash, clutter, and extraneous stuff before you cannot move yourself. Limit your current responsibilities to what you can handle in your lifestyle, including pets. Name a reliable person to care for pets in your demise. Above all, do the correct legal paperwork! So when you die, people are clear about how you want your money and stuff distributed, even little things. Prearrange your funeral to include specifics, tell the family what you want ahead of time. Write it and save it in a safe place. Tell them."

Starla interjected, "I know, I know. Most people cannot accept the finality of dying. They believe it will not happen to themselves soon. Not me, I will not die today or this week. A sense of invincibility surrounds our generation."

Cindy added, "This effort seems so overwhelming. Where does one even start?"

Cece replied, "Ross has a friend who is an elder-care attorney. We scheduled an appointment to get our paperwork in order next week. She mentioned creating documents such as an updated will, a trust to protect against confiscatory taxes and lawsuits, other papers, and a preferred disposition method for our remains. Both of us opted for cremation. We still need to find a final resting site, too. All these decisions are manageable if the person chooses to face them. Pre-thought relieves the family from a lot of pressure and indecision."

The recent events weighed heavy on her mind. She continued to expose her new convictions.

"You and I received and bought stuff over a lifetime.

We placed extreme value on much of it, yet at our demise most is just worthless stuff. It may have had a high price, but to a dead person it is worthless. Liquidating assets is becoming more difficult for the survivors. I read the old stuff we coveted has no appeal to today's younger generation, so the market is smaller. Ross and I sorted that out, too. We agreed to declutter our stuff and dispose of it the best we can."

Cindy said, "One day, our children will recognize the lunacy of our generation's over-purchasing and storing of stuff in basements, garages, bedrooms, and rental storage. Things we had to buy, but we never used. Stuff too dear to dispose of ate up valuable space while gathering dust and mildew. Just stuff. This is insanity."

Di piped in, "Your comments remind me of William Wordsworth's poem about that. Have you heard it?"

No one raised their hand or nodded yes. Di had a penchant for matching common situations with the masterpieces of English literature.

Starla countered, "Tell us, now that you have baited our curiosity."

The former high school teacher recited, "The world is too much with us; late and soon, getting and spending, we lay waste our powers."

Bobbie said, "Cool, Di. That's catchy!"

As they talked over the morning hours, the conversation churned over Liz's situation. Janet passed out the last of the cinnamon rolls.

She asked, "How do you think this happened, Cece?"

My Momma said blood is thicker than water. Family takes care of family. Values cement inside at an early age. That means when the going gets tough, you help the down and outers. You give to those who need help, especially if they are dead. Sometimes you get in a hole with a relative and you have no clue where the darkness ends. You hope and pray something will help."

Janet was half-smiling, half-sad in her expression.

"No, no, I didn't mean how *you* helped her. I meant, how did *she* turn out this way?"

Cece chuckled and continued, "Excellent question, Janet. It's so complex. The love of a father and mother are so important to their child. The repeated tone of voice, their touch or lack of it, the praise, the correction, the nurturing that the child receives from the parent replays repeatedly as the child grows older, positive, and negative. Did the drama and excessive control of Liz as a young child push her to seek fulfillment on the dark side? Alternatively, did the abusive husbands take her to the edge? Maybe she sought to fulfill her passions in her men, but she never found a permanent good one to counter the lifelong criticism of her mother. For some reason, she rejected human love and replaced it with animals."

Ana changed the focus, "Do you think it was accidental, an illness, a stroke, or self-inflicted? Was her death assisted suicide? Did she have heart trouble? What was it?"

"I don't know and I refuse to play a guessing game about it. Sorry, no, we have not seen an autopsy yet."

"But, but, someone said she was face down in the hot tub. If she fell wouldn't she be lying outside or inside the tub, not partly submerged?"

Ana's questions rattled Cece. Part of her wished this long-time friend had gone to South Carolina as her resident gumshoe. Cece admired her curiosity. But at the same time, Cece didn't want to go there.

Cece smiled as she quipped, "Oh, come now, Ana. You've been watching too many detective television shows."

The circle of women hooted and cackled at the good-natured gibe. The focus of Ana's favorite television show centered on police departments that investigated special victim crimes in large cities. She craved books steeped in mystery, blood, and mayhem.

Cece continued, "The police ruled the death accidental. What can explain it? That is up to the authorities. We must accept what they find."

Bobbie asked, "Have you heard from any of her exes?"

"No, I understand they are all dead."

Jean piped in, "Cece, you can't make up this stuff. Did you follow up on the safe deposit key you found?"

"Oh yes, that last day before we left the coast, we drove to Mary's Island National Bank. We opened a checking account for the estate and tried the key. We met this interesting bank officer, Marie Seren. She recalled Liz right away. 'What a piece of art Liz was,' exclaimed Marie. She said Liz always liked to stop at Marie's desk and talk about boyfriends.

"Marie added, 'One of the last times she was in the bank, Liz arrived in a frazzled state. She had trouble using her key to start the car as she was leaving. I helped her. I was walking back into the bank when I heard a loud bang. She backed her car into another car in the parking lot. Can you imagine a tussle between a BMW and a Mercedes? Shook up Liz asked me to call a taxi company for her.'"

Jean said, "But what was in the safe deposit box? Did you find valuables? Gold bars, coins, jewels, or useable stuff?"

Cece replied, "Liz's safe deposit box was the largest size the bank rented. We found policies for the insurance companies we identified earlier. Then, there was a metal box like a fishing tackle box but flatter. We took the container out of the safe deposit box and gave it a good shake back and forth! The one item inside rebounded with a thud each time I turned it. We had to visit a locksmith to pick the lock on the box, which cost ten dollars. We expected a bar of silver or gold. No! Wrapped in a hand towel was a pistol, a Smith & Wesson. A gun dealer who examined it told us it is a compact semi-automatic weapon. Ross locked the gun and ammunition at the storage unit. Anybody want to take shooting lessons with me?"

The women shook their heads collectively, except for Nancy.

"Cece, I'll go with you. I wanted to learn to shoot since I was eighteen."

"Great, let's do it!"

Cece reiterated that a good administrator scoured the details of their findings for clues that led to other assets. She said she and Ross scrutinized every corner, nook, and cranny. Then she had another coughing spasm. Linsey jumped up from her chair.

She asked, "Cece, where are your lemons, bourbon, and honey? Let me prepare my sure-fire remedy for that cough."

Linsey's family recipe helped calm the hacking cough. The ladies left except for Emi, who stayed to keep an eye on Cece. When Ross returned from work, he felt her flaming hot forehead. Emi told him that the poor girl slept all afternoon and she needed a doctor. He checked Cece into a nearby hospital. For a week, Cece burned with fever from the effects of bacterial pneumonia.

Chapter 35

Administrator

Three Months after Liz's Death
Mary's Island, South Carolina

With her health issues and physical location in Louisiana, Cece struggled to complete long-distance transactions in South Carolina. Over time and with experience, she became more efficient. She transferred funds from redeemed insurance policies, certificates of deposit, savings accounts, and stocks and bonds into one new bank account. She worked an hour each day to check the status of the assets. Cash rose to a half million dollars from the liquid assets and earned interest. Cece began the work to restore Liz's house. She signed a flexible contract with Gus Fence's restoration company. Gus explained the cycle of remediation of damage and repair in his home jobs. The firm carried a certification in disposal of hazardous material and mold. In hazmat suits, his workers removed the furniture contents, carpet, and soiled interior sheetrock. The experts soaked the remaining skeleton of walls, subfloors, and ceilings with anti-microbial spray, and anti-mold solutions. The few surfaces not demolished received a coat of Kilz paint to seal in potential contaminants. Environmental engineers tested and attested to safe living conditions. When the clean-up phase was complete, the workers had rebuilt the home interior. Gus peddled salvaged items for cents on the dollar. He did not need to explain the limited market for items over-exposed to biohazards. Most of the stuff ended up in a secure dump. Kerry Tyler's team of inspectors pronounced the house fit for human habitation. Cece made plans to put it on the market.

State law dictated the pecking order of heirs of an intestate person. Cece reported the known beneficiaries of the estate to the court. The closest surviving relatives in Liz's bloodline were her cousins. There were only two: Cece and Richie. The deceased siblings had no heirs. Cece understood the state's rules that she and Richie each would receive half of Liz's estate. *Simple,* Cece thought.

Chapter 36

Summons

Six Months after Liz's Death
Georgetown, South Carolina

A pile of unopened mail from the prior day lay on Harry's oak credenza. In the stack of envelopes, he found his usual bills, ads for continuing education classes for attorneys, and recurring summons. At the bottom of the stack rested a legal-sized envelope addressed to Harold Caisteal, Esq. Harry slid his ancient envelope opener under the flap and pulled out the papers. He read "The Honorable Judge Janie Bonham in the case of the Estate of Elizabeth Perkins." *What the. . . .*

With his attorneys, Joey Broyer had filed a petition to probate Liz's estate despite all of Cece's efforts over the six months since Liz died. The summons proclaimed that the law firm of Thomaston, Jasper, and Scallup represented Joey. Harry quizzed himself. *Of course, Cece mentioned this firm. They claimed not to have executed the questionable document. Our base assumption is that whoever did create it did so improperly, right?* Immediately, Harry called Cece with the shocking news. He related that the court summons announced a hearing for Joey to probate Liz's estate. They had two weeks to prepare for the hearing where none other than Her Honor, Judge Bonham will preside. Harry felt blindsided.

Harry told Cece, "First we need to set up a video conference to review the case with you. Can Ross arrange that at his office? We must get it done this week."

"I think so."

"This hearing is in Georgetown. Can you come to it?"

That idea suited Cece well. When the hearing ended, she could enjoy the beach again.

Harry called Rufus Jasper four times over the next two days. No one answered the phone. He thought a firm with three lawyers would at least have a reliable secretary to take calls.

The voice mail recording played over each time, "Your call is important to us. We cannot take your call now. Please leave a message with your phone number and we will return your call as soon as possible. Thank you."

The first time Harry called, he reacted to the recorded phone greeting with an entreaty for Rufus to call him back to discuss the proceeding. With no response on any call, coupled with Cece's permission, Harry filed an opposing response for the family with the clerk in Judge Bonham's court. He asked the judge to allow Cece to take part in the probate case. In response, the court sent Harry a notice of Cece's eligibility to participate.

By the end of the week, Harry met with Cece and Ross in a teleconference. As he perused his pad of notes, Harry reviewed the notion that Liz or Joey executed the do-it-yourself will improperly. Sourced from common software that created legal documents, the DIY will contained language that sounded official and legitimate, but Harry shook his head. *I*'s not dotted nor *T*'s crossed in this document. Harry pointed out to Ross and Cece that the signer did not initial all pages as required, confusion reigned over the actual witnesses, and dates did not match.

Harry turned back to the first page and held it up to the video camera.

"And look at this mismatch. Liz's signature here does not match this other one. Neither resembled her driver's license signature. Just saying, it looks phony to me."

Harry contended the key snag was the abundance of witnesses, three.

He continued, "The witnesses included a shoe-store clerk, a desk lady at a hotel in Nags Head, NC, and a party with an interest in the will. On the original document, Joey signed his name in the margin below the other two witnesses. Beneath his name, he hand-wrote the word 'witness'. Do you see it right here?"

Harry pointed at the scratchy penmanship.

"It is unclear why and when he signed. Was he shouting to the world his involvement? Combined, irrational behavior and ego is a strange thing. The additional witness created confusion. Judges do not tolerate confusion. Did he add it later? Had he coerced Liz to accept something she did not want? Who are the other two witnesses?"

Watching the video monitor, Cece's abdomen churned while her heart smiled. *Harry said it appeared to be invalid. Chances looked good for the family. If Liz had listened to a professional, the lawyer could have executed a valid Last Will and Testament.*

Harry continued, "I've seen these canned wills. Liz or somebody inserted words into the basic format. These edits ramble about extraneous things. An impartial reader might conclude she was not of sound mind, nor sober when she executed the document. Your best hope is for the judge to rule the document invalid. Then, the rules for distribution to the heirs are as if Liz had died intestate."

Harry set up their next meeting in his office on the morning of the hearing. Ross turned off the video screen. Cece sat in her chair staring at the black screen. She thought, *What could happen next?*

Chapter 37

Probate Court

Two Weeks after the Summons
Georgetown, South Carolina

Ross and Cece packed their car for the long two day journey from Louisiana to South Carolina. They drove over miles of interstate highways, passing bayous, long-needled pine trees, fertile farmland, piedmont hills, coastal plains, and low country terrain. After their arrival at the rented condominium, the two ate dinner and went to bed. As the gears of uncertainty and fear meshed in her brain, Cece endured yet another sleepless night.

They met with Harry at his office several hours before the hearing. The lawyer asked Cece which strategy she wished to pursue. Her brain raced through Harry's questions.

If Judge Bonham ruled the document as a legal will, would Cece fight it? Was she open to appeal? How long would she dispute the validity of the document?

What about the other first cousin, Richie? What did he want? Fortunately, Richie asked Cece to represent him at the hearing. Whatever she thought best, he would accept.

Did she and her cousins want to contest an award to someone other than family?

What grounds would Cece cite, other than the technical faults? To honor the family was a lame reason.

Joey's incapacity?

What is Cece's tipping point to settle in the court?

How big a fight are you up for, Cece?

In the conference room, Cece glared at Harry. She wanted to ask him, *Aren't you the lawyer? Help me here, Harry!* Exhausted and emotional, Cece cried. How she hated this conflict!

With Liz buried, Cece's next goals were to sell the house, pay remaining bills, to repay the massive expenses Ross had funded up front, and for the two cousins to share the residual assets. *It was what Liz intended, wasn't it?* However, she figured that repayment of the expenses and her administrator fees were the least she could accept if things did not go her way.

Harry reiterated three obstacles in the document that harmed the chances of the family sharing Liz's assets:

- Joey Broyer can live in the house as long as any of the original cats are alive and he can care for them and himself;

- If Mr. Broyer's health prevents him from staying there, the cats receive perpetual care;

- The residual funds are distributable to a charity in Charleston that cares for animals.

Harry warned, "If the judge accepts any of these conditions, your family can kiss the benefits goodbye."

The team of three walked into the Georgetown Courthouse twenty minutes before the start of the day's hearings. The essence of a fresh coat of pine-oil furniture polish from the wooden portals permeated the hallway. At the end of the wide passage, they reached Judge Bonham's courtroom. They read the docket posted on the bulletin board for court activities on that day. Ross and Cece examined a massive new portrait on the left side of the schedule. It filled half the wall. In the painted likeness stood the Honorable Judge Janie Bonham, in her court robes, with a cat in each arm.

They looked at each other. *What omen is this portrait?* A sense of foreboding fell over them.

The bailiff nodded to Cece and Harry as they entered the courtroom. He said, "What are your names?"

After their reply, he added, "The Judge wants to see the administrator and her attorney in her chamber for an impromptu unilateral case management meeting."

Judge Bonham wanted to assess Cece's penchant for settling. Ross gave a puzzled look at Harry and Cece and whispered, "Where do you want me to go?"

Nervous, Cece pointed a crooked finger to a chair in the well where the parties to a case assembled.

She shrieked, "You sit here!"

Damn, is she instructing a two-year-old? He slid downward to a bench. He sensed that the courtroom atmosphere rattled Cece.

Cece followed the bailiff and Harry to the chambers.

After Judge Bonham stared directly at Cece, she stated, "Thank you for your participation in today's probate hearing. I appreciate your continuing role as administrator of the Perkins estate. As we go through today's proceedings, realize that you may continue to contest or you can settle. Whatever, it is your choice, so please keep your counsel apprised of your decision."

While Cece and Harry discussed matters with the judge, Ross noticed Kerry Tyler, the zoning department director, entering the courtroom. Ross waved. Kerry walked up to him and they exchanged pleasantries. Harry had asked Kerry to serve as a witness. Participants in the day's proceedings paced in and out of the courtroom as they prepared for their cases. An entourage of three males dressed in gray pinstripe

suits entered together. Ross guessed they were attorneys. Behind them followed a young person pushing
an elderly person in a wheelchair. The youngster had
the same attire as the lawyers, dressed in a gray suit
and conservative blue tie. The older group excluded
him from their banter.

Ross wondered, *Is that Joey Broyer in the wheel
chair?*

Ross and Cece had never met Joey, nor seen a picture of him. In stark contrast to the chair pusher, the
passenger wore walking shorts and a dirty t-shirt. The
shorts exposed his prosthesis replacing the sections
of both amputated legs and feet. The devices appeared
to be the new sleek transtibial above-the-knee models
used by the military for wounded veterans. With its
carbon fiber innovations, the intricate mechanism
allowed the wearer to not only walk, but also run, jump,
and even drive a car. The combined dramatic scene
of exposed prosthetics and a wheel chair generated
compassion for Joey. Ross watched with sympathy
as Joey tried to be comfortable. Ross admired the
strained efforts the dude had to make.

In their tight huddle, the attorneys stood shoulder
to shoulder as they reviewed their strategy near the
first row of seats. The wheelchair, its occupant, and
the novice lawyer rested at the end of the same row.

Harry and Cece emerged from the chambers about
five minutes before the day's sessions were to begin.

Walking nearly to where Ross and Kerry sat, Cece
asked her attorney, "If I settle, could I get my expenses
and the restoration costs reimbursed?

Harry replied, "Probably, but realize it is a
negotiation."

When Cece looked at him, Ross winked at her.
Then he nodded his head toward the army of attorneys
and Joey. Looking at Cece, Ross mouthed the name

without making a sound, Joey Broyer. Cece nodded her understanding.

Harry asked Kerry, "Ready with your comments?"

"Yes, sir, more than ready."

"Great, I will call on you first to set our stage. Just answer the questions I ask you."

Chapter 38

First Witness

Minutes Later
The Probate Courtroom

The bailiff, in drill-sergeant style, shouted the judge's obligatory set of courtroom rules to the audience. He droned on and on, "No outbursts, no photography, no smoking, no chewing gum, no applause, no wearing of hats. . . ."

The bailiff brought the audience back to attention when he thundered, "All Rise!"

Judge Janie Bonham strode to her chair and looked sternly at the standing audience, and then she smiled. She fancied contested wills and there were three on the docket today.

She scanned the documents and said, "Oh my, I love to discern difficult wills. They are so interesting. We have winners and losers in this court. Regardless, we strive to do the best we can to assure the outcome resembles what the decedent's wishes are. Let us begin this session."

The bailiff announced the first case, *The Estate of Elizabeth Perkins vs. Cece Turner, et al.* As expected, the court merged Joey's petition to probate with the family's response. Harry prepared the response to include both of Liz's cousins as parties.

The bailiff barked, "Counsel will cite the responders' statement."

Harry stood with a copy of the do-it-yourself will in his hand.

He pleaded, "Your Honor, under the laws of our state, the petitioner filed for probate based on an invalid will. It is incomplete. Key characteristics required by the laws of the state are absent. These errors render this document invalid, even inadmissible. Ms. Perkins' family submitted a response taking the position she died intestate absent a legal and complete will."

Harry called Kerry Tyler to the stand first. Kerry carried his cowboy hat under his arm. He used it for protection from the sunny weather in the Low Country.

The judge commented, "Son, you are prudent to shield yourself from the harmful effects of the sun."

Kerry nodded and said, "Yes, your Honor. Melanoma runs in our family. I go nowhere without a hat."

Through this simple brief exchange, the judge had determined Kerry was not a hostile witness, at least not to her.

Harry's first goal aimed to show Joey's physical and medical incompetence to care for the cats. If Harry succeeded, it removed one of the three obstacles to winning the case. Cece and Ross listened with rapt attention to the arguments.

Harry asked, "Mr. Tyler, please inform the court who you are and your involvement in this hearing."

Kerry cited his position and responsibilities with the city including reviews of conditions of real estate and covenant enforcement.

Harry questioned, "Now, please tell the court what you observed about the condition of Elizabeth's Perkin's house."

Kerry depicted the homes in Liz's posh neighborhood. Then, he shared a vivid and scathing description of her house before and after Liz's demise. Beauty contrasted with squalor. The commentary of his word pictures painted a nasty canvas. He spoke so vividly that Cece's husband re-experienced the day six months before, including smells, sight, and disgust. Then, Ross sensed nausea. The judge asked Kerry how the house interior changed after Liz's death.

"Your Honor, I present these pictures as evidence. The first set came from the Mary's Island Police Department after Ms. Perkins death. Later when my team assessed the conditions, we took the second series of photos. Together, the two sets of photos support my opinion. The squalid conditions worsened after her death. Whoever occupied the house, took the foulness and filth to another level. Pardon my gross description, Your Honor, but the sole human resident pooped in most rooms of the house. There was gross damage from felines due to the uncontrolled animal hoarding in the residence. Blood, urine, and feces intermingled on the floor. Trash, piles of paper and food waste also filled the squalid rooms. In summary, we are dealing with a biohazard here."

Murmurs broke out in the audience. Joey Broyer squirmed in his wheelchair. As if a meteor, Joey sprang upward. He stood between one of his attorneys and the chair pusher. The lawyer's fist grasped a rolled-up issue of the latest national bar journal.

Joey took two steps towards the witness stand as if miraculously cured. He pointed at the witness.

Joey hollered, "Damn liar!" as he shook his fist in the air.

The judge said, "Order in the court. Who is that? Quiet or I will hold you in contempt!"

All eyes in the courtroom pivoted to Joey in unison.

In an immediate response to the disruption, the wheelchair pusher sitting next to Joey shoved him back into the rolling chair with a loud thud. He secured the seat belt around Joey's torso. The other lawyer raised the rolled document and bopped Joey on his head.

He whispered to Joey, "Shut up, you fool."

In a hushed voice, Kerry said to the judge, "Your Honor, please note for the record the disrespect and verbal abuse hurled toward me by this person in the audience. I feel threatened by this outburst."

Judge Bonham said, "So noted Mr. Tyler."

With fire in her eyes, Judge Bonham stared at the assembly. Angered, she declared a fifteen-minute recess. She acted swiftly to quash foolishness in her courtroom.

She pointed her finger at Joey Broyer and barked, "I want to see you and your team of attorneys in my chambers now!"

On her way, Judge Bonham shouted, "Bailiff, get yourself in here in case we need you."

Whispers of the audience rose to a crescendo of deafening verbal speculation. *What was happening in the conference room?* Harry and Cece conversed among themselves. In her chest, she sensed the familiar spinning of butterflies. Ross and Cece traded anxious glances.

While Joey Broyer and his attorneys sequestered themselves with Judge Bonham, Liz's friend met his fate. Firsthand, the judge observed Joey's behavior. Joey protested loudly and refused an appeal for voluntary treatment of his conditions. The judge requested the bailiff handcuff Joey to protect the conferees. At the end of their discussion, she ordered an intervention. The judge stood and approached a floor-to-ceiling mirror. With a frown and hand motion, she dismissed the attorneys, Joey, and the bailiff back into the hearing. Staring into the mirror, she brushed her hair back with her hand, adjusted her robes, and sighed.

As the bailiff exited the chamber, he stopped and shouted, "Quiet, please!"

A hush fell over the room.

"All Rise!"

During the entire recess, Kerry Tyler had remained in the witness chair.

The attorneys and Joey Broyer returned to the courtroom. A moment later, Judge Bonham returned. Joey's face scowled.

Judge Bonham said, "Audience, you may sit. Now Mr. Tyler, thank you for waiting. I have one more question before the petitioner's attorneys ask their questions."

The melee that transpired next played out in less than ten seconds. It seemed an eternity to Cece.

"Where are the cats now?"

Kerry uttered, "They are. . . ."

This time, Rufus Jasper vaulted up, interrupted Kerry, and pointed his index finger at Cece.

"Your Honor, *that* woman had them all killed!"

Cece pounced up and shouted, "No! Your Honor! I did not kill any of them! I asked the county rescue center to euthanize them, but they disobeyed me."

"Order in the court. Order in the court please!"

Cece was red-faced and angry. In her entire life, no one had accused her of malicious behavior. The allegation stung. She was not a murderer of cats. *Weren't they dying on their own? It was humane to take them out of their misery.*

Harry sprang up as he retorted, "Your Honor, I object to this false accusation of my client!"

"Sustained, counselor."

Judge Bonham banged her gavel. She was showing signs of losing her temper.

"Mr. Tyler, please go ahead!"

Kerry said, "The surviving cats are at the county's animal rescue shelter. They are not all dead. Some of the deceased cats died of natural causes, or unnatural, depending how you look at it. The manager of the shelter euthanized none of these poor suffering animals, despite the administrator's specific order to do so. The shelter charges money for daily boarding and medical care for each cat. It is prudent to conserve funds of the estate."

"How many cats are there?"

"Twenty were alive, Your Honor. Two others had died in the house. The police and humane society evacuated the live ones. Ten died at the rescue shelter since May. That leaves ten survivors. As in most cases I have seen in animal hoarding, the survivors suffer from a range of diseases."

"Are any of the animals healthy?"

"Yes, Your Honor, two are healthy. The shelter quarantined them after their first exam. However, they and other unrelated pets in the clinic are at risk of contracting the highly contagious illnesses that Mrs. Perkin's cats brought with them. Loyal customers of this vet are upset about the risks to their pets. You would be concerned if your pet boarded there. The quarters are tight at the shelter."

"How ill are the other eight, Mr. Tyler?"

"I'm not a veterinarian, Your Honor, but the Georgetown County Rescue Center provided me this list of the ailments yesterday."

He offered the list to Harry first, who handed it to the judge.

"Three cats are now on dialysis. Other cats that had heartworm and a very contagious form of the distemper virus still suffer from aftereffects. These diseases are of concern to the rescue center. Some of the other diseases on the list I can't pronounce, plus fleas."

The judge asked Joey's attorneys if they wished to question Kerry Tyler. But this witness and the ensuing discussions wedged bad karma into their case.

Irreparable damage occurred with the interruptions by Rufus and Joey. Quizzing Kerry would harm their side more. They declined to question him further.

Judge Bonham asked, "Mr. Tyler, tell me why I should consider the family's interests in this probate hearing, despite the specific instructions given in the submitted will."

"Your Honor, this family came from New Orleans to do their civic duty, at our request, to collect, secure, and inventory Ms. Perkins' assets and debt. Mrs. Turner arranged for Ms. Perkins burial. She is restoring the home to sell it. I commend her for her service. Her health deteriorated from this nasty work. Since childhood, Mrs. Turner stood by Ms. Perkins in her good and difficult times. If the so-called will was executed improperly, isn't it a matter of law to disregard it?"

Judge Bonham thanked Mr. Tyler for taking time away from his busy schedule at City Hall and dismissed him. Kerry trudged from the witness' chair to Ross and sat with him. He wanted to hear the verdict. The judge turned her attention to Harry.

"Counselor Caisteal, do you have other witnesses?"

"Yes, Your Honor, Mrs. Cecilia Turner is next."

The bailiff asked Cece to swear on a Bible that she would tell the truth.

She said, "I swear."

Harry began his line of questions with, "Mrs. Turner, please describe your relationship to the deceased, Elizabeth Perkins."

"She was my oldest first cousin. We stayed close all of my life."

"What has been your role with Ms. Perkin's estate since her demise?"

"Many years ago dear Liz asked me to handle her final arrangements. I applied to this court for administrator status, which you granted. I am the closest next of kin. The city asked our family to find and secure the assets and bills so I stepped up to the plate."

Judge Bonham studied Cece for signs of credibility. "Go on, please."

"The state should distribute the estate to my family per the intestate law. Six months ago when we searched the premises we found among the many papers one do-it-yourself document which my legal counsel advised would not likely qualify as a legitimate will. It's non-conforming to the state law about wills and is confusing."

Cece pointed at the stained form on the evidence table.

"Liz promised to me that everything in her estate belonged to her first cousins. My role as administrator required that I complete specific reports which I did. Moreover, I researched how to pay for Liz's burial. With enough cash for a funeral, I submitted requests to this court for authorization to withdraw funds. Personally, my husband and I encountered the biohazard conditions in the home.

"Our health deteriorated due to the disgusting filth. I remained in the hospital for a week at my expense. I had contracted bacterial pneumonia and I almost died. The long-term effect is that my lungs burn from this experience. My husband had recurring sinus infections requiring massive doses of antibiotics. After our long-term recovery, I worked to restore Liz's home. In the inventory and appraisal reports, I submitted to this court the financial and tangible assets, and outstanding creditors. My and my husband's personal funds paid for many estate expenditures because accessing Liz's funds over long distances was difficult during our illnesses. We request reimbursement for these significant personal advances before final distribution of the assets. We performed the requirements asked of us and more."

Though her demeanor appeared calm, Cece felt nauseated. The butterflies had returned to her gut.

Harry asked, "Mrs. Turner, why are you contesting this do-it-yourself paper?"

"My roots of loyalty go back to my childhood when Liz protected me from physical harm. Liz told me she wanted me to share her assets with those she loved and those who loved her. For the record, to reintroduce the cats into the environment of the home and under the dubious care of someone unable to care for them is futile."

Cece cast a disapproving glance toward Joey. She shuddered as she recalled her weird phone call with him.

"But with funds from the sale of the house and investments the two remaining healthy cats can be supported in a good and loving environment. Euthanize the others to end their suffering. It is right that the family who cared for and loved Liz be the recipients of the estate, as she herself said. She never gave an inkling to the family that it was her intent to give her estate to charity when she was alive."

Harry looked at Judge Bonham and said, "That is all, Your Honor."

The judge turned to Rufus. "The witness is yours to cross examine, Mr. Jasper."

"Mrs. Turner, have we ever met?"

"No."

"Have we discussed the will of Elizabeth Perkins?"

Cece nodded, and then said, "The only contact between you and me was a phone call after Liz died. I remember you saying you had never prepared a will for her. I had no knowledge then of any other document including this do-it-yourself version."

"Since we have her wishes expressed here, why do you disagree with the written intent of Ms. Perkins?"

"Pure and simple, I can give you two over-arching reasons. We are the family of Elizabeth Perkins, who stood with her in life and now in death. Liz had verbally expressed her desire for her family to be her heirs. Second, the document submitted has technical errors and fails to meet requirements in the law. There are major questions whether this document is valid and whether Liz wanted this document to guide her final disposition. Did she understand what she was doing? Is it possible someone coerced her? There are three witnesses on this document, including the petitioner. Isn't that strange?"

She paused for effect and continued, "One of these witnesses is an interested party."

Rufus snapped back, "Let me ask the questions, Mrs. Turner. Do you have any other reasons?"

Determined, Cece replied, "When Liz and her fourth husband moved into her mansion, my husband, my mother, and I visited her. She pulled me aside. She whispered that she wanted to leave her estate to her two cousins. She had no children and no other family. Liz spelled out her intent clearly. Liz also asked me to arrange her funeral and burial, which I did per her wishes. It was a sweet service, if I say so myself."

She dabbed her green eyes with the tissue.

"Is that all, Mrs. Turner?"

"She elaborated that her mother's home and antiques, Liz's home, cash, and investments were to go to us."

Rufus pursed his lips. He showed no emotion.

"So as I understand it, you want the court to take your word that Liz's intent in a conversation is more valid than her will?"

"Yes, the conversation was real."

"I see."

"Did you record this conversation?"

Cece snapped back at Rufus, "No. It was a personal conversation. I don't make a habit of recording my personal conversations."

Ross observed that Cece was becoming nervous for the third time that day. He knew the tone of Rufus' questions provoked her.

"That is all, Your Honor. The petitioner rests."

While calling for a fifteen-minute recess, Judge Bonham banged her gavel. She asked Harry and the three petitioner attorneys to confer in her chambers. Joey sat in his wheelchair, next to its attendant.

Ross walked up to Cece and hugged and kissed her.

"You performed well. Good job."

Chapter 39

Verdict

The attorneys exited the judge's chamber into the courtroom. The audience quieted without prompting from the bailiff. Stern-faced, Judge Bonham entered a moment later. She took her time to position herself in her chair.

She proclaimed, "Please remain seated."

As every person focused on the judge, she exclaimed, "I am ready to issue a ruling on this case now."

Judge Bonham lifted the do-it-yourself document from her desk.

"My opinion is that this paper represents a valid will. Ms. Perkins owned so many pets. I imagine as she aged, she rationalized she could do more good trying to care for her beloveds and other cats in the world. Her written intent in the will overrules the insignificant technical mistakes. Based on our conference, I order the following directives:

"As to her estate and her wishes for her cats, I order Rufus Jasper to serve as the executor of the Elizabeth Perkins estate. The decedent's instructions are to award the residual funds to the Charleston Animal Humane Fund. I order this payment to occur after the surviving cats have all died. Before this award occurs, the executor will liquidate assets and pay all expenses and debts. Mr. Jasper will perform other duties customary to the role of an executor. I order the estate of Elizabeth Perkins to pay executor fees to Mr. Jasper as allowed by the state.

Second, I order that the will created a trust upon Ms. Perkins' death to provide care for the living cats owned by her. As long as any of the cats that survived in this home remain alive, in whatever condition, the Georgetown County Animal Rescue Center or GCAR controls their physical care. The trust funds this upkeep. Care includes food, daily medical examination and treatment, and spacious living quarters. The trust pays for the rental of a mobile living unit for the Perkins' cats if cramped conditions continue at GCAR. Adoption of a cat removes it from future trust benefits unless the new owner returns it. I name Clovis Thomaston as trustee for the cats. I order the estate to pay trustee fees to Mr. Thomaston as allowed by the state.

"Third, I declare that due to his present state, medical and psychiatric professionals evaluate Joey Broyer's condition. I appoint him as a ward of the state with twenty-four seven care pending the evaluation results. If the conclusion warrants his permanent committal, I so order. He cannot live in the Perkins' house. I name Winston Scallup as guardian of Joey Broyer. I order the estate to pay guardian fees to Mr. Scallup as allowed by the state."

Cece glanced around the courtroom, reaching out to Ross for reassurance. He gave her a kind nod. She had lost the battle, and the law firm of Thomaston, Jasper, and Scallup was in the driver's seat of Liz's estate and Joey's future.

The stern brown eyes of Judge Bonham connected with the soft green eyes of Cecilia Turner. *What does she want from me now? Oh, my queasy stomach! What is she going to say?*

The judge continued, "Fourth, the executor will reimburse any expenses and administrative fees substantiated by Mrs. Turner. Mrs. Turner, I commend you for your diligence in the administrator role under these trying conditions. A death in the family alone is a cause of pain and torment. I applaud you for incurring the added trouble. Your term as administrator ends now. I did not know your cousin Ms. Perkins. She sounds most enchanting, if not unusual."

Cece relaxed her shoulders and sighed. Her role was complete.

"Please send to the court and the executor any inventory and appraisal records of the estate you collected. Account for your expenses and fees, and the estate will reimburse them. When estate documents are silent as to fees, you receive none. But Ms. Perkin's document insists on payment for whoever works on her estate. Please send an itemized statement for your work to the clerk of my court. She will assess the fee you receive. You should suffer no loss of money for stepping forward to do your family duty. Since you did this work on behalf of the family, are there any estate mementos we can offer to you to remember Ms. Perkins and this experience?"

Cece looked at the ceiling, thinking. She had seen so much, it was hard to decide. Did she want the David statue? Clothing? Or silver pieces or china?

"Your Honor, I know what I would like to have. The two items I want most are Liz's tiara that she received in the state beauty pageant and her mink coat. We have photographs of these two things. I remember Liz's crowning as I was there. The tiara is badly tarnished now, but it is the best memory I can have of Liz. Thank you for reimbursing our expenses and fees."

Rufus Jasper stood up and shouted, "Your Honor, I object!"

"Objection overruled! This award to Cece Turner is so ordered. Mr. Jasper, please arrange for her payment and have the tiara and mink coat shipped to Mrs. Turner. Is there any other business?"

Rufus uttered in a testy voice, "Yes, Your Honor. My staff and I reviewed the earlier accountings provided to your court by Mrs. Turner. The document included a credit-card receipt for a meal at the Royal Catch Restaurant in Murrell's Inlet. You know yourself; Royal Catch is a pricey restaurant. As executor, I assert that reimbursement of Mrs. Turner's thirty-five dollar meal is imprudent. In fact, I researched that a supermarket operates not a half mile from where Mrs. Turner stayed. The estate contends Mrs. Turner should have purchased a hot dog or a piece of pizza instead of this extravagance. Please strike this receipt from her reimbursement."

"Mr. Jasper, what did you not hear after your last objection? You are overruled, Mr. Jasper! We are fortunate we do not share the same fine taste in food you do. Include the restaurant cost with her other expense and fee reimbursement."

The judge rolled her eyes. *Goodness! If he had the opportunity, he would snatch candy from a child!*

"What items have we not addressed?"

Silence. No one said a word, wary of the wrath of Judge Janie Bonham.

Judge Bonham banged her gavel. "Case closed!"

A huge sense of relief filled half of Cece's soul. The tension in her shoulders evaporated as she removed this albatross, this never-ending drama. Her smile returned. She cleared the hurdle of reimbursement of expenses. She felt that was fair. Besides, the judge granted her fees for her work. But betrayal and anger welled up in the other half. Her promised inheritance, which carried a sizable windfall, evaporated before her eyes. Instead, almost all of it went to care for cats that never set eyes on her cousin. She did understand the exact words Liz had stated. However, Liz had not kept up her end of the legacy bargain. Exhausted, Cece could fight no more.

Cece, Ross, and Harry stepped outside the courtroom and looked at each other. The butterflies within Cece filled her insides. Harboring second thoughts on her loss, she reacted with silent anger. She became quiet and withdrawn. Harry invited them to his office for refreshments. They needed to vent and review the proceedings. No one had an appetite for lunch.

Chapter 40

Collateral Damage

The Remainder of Cece's Life
New Orleans, Louisiana

In addition to Cece losing her expected financial windfall, she and Ross encountered wave after wave of serious health issues that slowed them from the active life they knew. Their time spent in the untreated biohazard had blindsided both of them.

The bacterial pneumonia that ripped through Cece's lungs induced lethargy, sleep, and no appetite for a week. Although she overcame the pneumonia symptoms with the help of heavy-duty antibiotics, she had long-term repercussions. When the hospital released her, she went home with a nagging cough. Her hacking persisted upon awakening each morning. Her stamina nose-dived. Walking moderate distances and climbing stairs at home presented obstacles to her. Cece had walked 5K and 10K races in the years before Liz's death. Now, Cece shunned all exercise due to exertion and fatigue. A simple walk to the car was a struggle.

Cece insisted her continued condition stemmed from the pneumonia and her exposure to the bio-hazard. During her annual physical, Cece's internist referred her to a pulmonary surgeon. Her medical costs mounted with extensive studies over months. The expensive tests included a lung biopsy, weekly blood tests and X-rays, and quarterly MRIs, CT, and PET scans. The specialist diagnosed Cece with idiopathic pulmonary fibrosis, IPF. He explained that idiopathic meant *we do not know the cause.* He told Cece she had permanent leathery scars around air sacs in her lungs. The scars restricted movement of air between the tiny air sacs.

He warned that breathing would continue to be difficult, as IPF is progressive. For now, he prescribed medications, physical therapy, and oxygen to aid her stamina and to treat symptoms. He explained that in the future she might have other options. She ballooned twenty-pounds almost overnight from a heavy dosage of prednisone. Over time, the dosage declined, and she lost the excess weight. Cece enrolled in the clinic's physical-therapy routine. In her biweekly sessions, she started walking only short distances on the treadmill. As her stamina improved, she progressed to three-miles-per-session while aided with oxygen. To increase the oxygen in her lungs, Cece purchased a concentrator machine to transform oxygen from plain air. While she slept, the machine forced oxygen through her nose mask. When she traveled, experienced exertion, or exercised, the battery-powered concentrator provided a continuous flow of pure oxygen. As if a life-giving ball and chain, the portable device journeyed with her everywhere. While a necessary nuisance, the oxygen machine allowed her a further range of mobility than without it.

The exhaust of countless automobiles provoked Code Orange days during the summer months in New Orleans. When the air quality of the city worsened, the bad air remained sealed within the nasty dome of atmosphere of the city. From the ground, one could not discern the mess, but Ross's airline pilot friends talked about encountering the murky haze daily. Because of the noxious pollution cloud on days of bad air quality, Cece suffered breathing difficulties necessitating repeated visits to the Emergency Room for steroids and breathing treatments. Then the steroids played havoc with her blood sugar. She faced a vicious cycle that took days to calm her system down.

Ross suffered a serious and lengthy series of sinus infections and bronchitis, which eventually healed. He sought the best ENTs and changed doctors three times before settling on one. The last ENT went to the source via cameras instead of just treating symptoms. The nasal probes did not hurt, but were annoying. The specialist successfully prescribed regiments of antibiotics to treat Staph bacteria that had grown in Ross's head and chest. As he grew older, Ross suffered from sarcoidosis that attacked his immune system. His physicians repeated biopsies, and CT and PET scans in periodic cycles. Deposits of benign tumors called non-necrotizing granulomas attached to body organs and his joints. His treatment consisted of heavy regimens of steroids, which resulted in weight gains. Cece and Ross's doctors directly attributed their health declines to their hazardous encounter on Liz's property.

Chapter 41

Commitment

After the Probate Hearing
Georgetown, South Carolina

Immediately after Judge Bonham's court session, an off-duty bailiff and a deputy transported Joey to his new home. The transfer van pulled into the entrance portico of the Santee Delta Medical Center, a modern two-story clinic and residence nestled in a wooded area west of Georgetown. A young man with a linebacker's frame, standing six-foot-five inches and weighing 250 pounds, greeted Joey at the door.

The young man spoke in a reassuring voice, "Hello, Mr. Broyer. Welcome to Santee Delta. I am Lloyd, your primary caretaker. I will see to your comfort here."

Lloyd sniffed. Apparently, Joey had a digestive accident on his way from the courthouse. A stain marred the back of his shorts.

"Let me get you checked in and you can shower and change clothes."

The bailiff and deputy left Joey and the court's paperwork with Lloyd. A woman behind the desk handed Joey a package of three khaki uniforms, underwear, pajamas, black socks, and sneakers, the uniform of the day male patients wore. Joey thought, *Due to my condition. I surely do not need these shoes and socks.*

The linebacker led the new resident upstairs to the men's ward that comprised the east wing of the complex. Female patients lived in the north wing. The two wings adjoined in a common area.

The sheer size and strength of Lloyd intimidated Joey. Eventually, Joey relaxed enough to allow the caretaker and him to use first names. *Maybe this was not so bad. Somebody finally cares.*

Lloyd said, "Here's your new home, Joey."

"Where is my key?"

"The doors in the living area do not have locks. Don't worry, you are safe here."

Lloyd opened the door to the small bedroom on the second floor. The room contained a single bed, a bathroom, an open closet, and a window. The bathroom came stocked with toothpaste, mouthwash, a brush, comb, soap, and shampoo. Joey glanced at the one posting on a bulletin board, a list of his daily routine of required activities. His new digs were sparse and utilitarian, but comfortable. Lloyd explained that residents ate in the dining hall in the common area. For leisure activities, the residents used a central activity room, and the exercise center.

"Shower and change into your clothes. Then, our medical staff would like to talk with you. I will return in fifteen minutes."

Fifteen minutes later, the imposing human frame filled the doorway.

Lloyd said, "Ready to go, yet?"

"Okay."

The two men meandered through the hallways. Lloyd pointed out the common facilities that Joey could access. He quizzed Joey to create a bond and to gain information to help the doctors.

Lloyd introduced Joey to the medical and psychiatric team. The group consisted of an internist, a gastric specialist, an endocrinologist, and a psychiatrist. They began their probing work immediately.

Rufus Jasper and Winston Scallup came to see Joey at the mental facility three days after the probate hearing. Protocol disallowed visitors for a period after commitment to allow the patient to adjust to their new surroundings. The attorneys' visit was ill timed. Joey seethed that he must return to Liz's house.

Winston sternly chided, "That's not going to happen Joey. It will be irresponsible to let you into the house. Judge Bonham ruled it impossible."

"Well, damn Judge Bonham. But what about my cats?"

"Dude, your friends are in good hands."

Winston's vague comment increased Joey's rage. Winston lacked a bedside manner. He remembered Joey's unexpected outburst during the probate hearing that led Judge Bonham to call a recess and order the intervention. The lawyer observed that this client might be a danger to society or to Joey himself. Joey did not understand his illnesses or their consequences, his addictions, or behavior. He disregarded the dangerous effects of his diabetes, his irritable bowel syndrome, and mental state. Joey denied it all. He failed to grasp that if the state's evaluation meshed with the judge's observations, then the court ordered commitment to a mental-treatment facility forged into a permanent arrangement.

Immediately, Lloyd stepped into the doorway to the room.

"Is there a problem in here? I think you gentlemen best leave now. You are upsetting my patient."

The mere commanding presence of Lloyd brought calm to Joey. The two attorneys left.

The committee of four doctors ran tests during the first week. Blood work, X-rays, exams, and questions focused on Joey. Then, dialogue, observation, and mental testing. Head to toe, the professionals studied the body and psyche of Joey. Multiple results funneled into a one-page summary resting atop topical summaries and a ream of data gathered by each physician. The individual doctors met with Joey, face to face, to discuss his treatment. The internist, gastro, and endo doctors each explained they found no new physical issues that Joey had not heard about from his visits to the free health clinic. The doctors agreed upon a healthy diet, physical therapy, and prescriptions to corral medical issues. They assured him he would soon feel much better physically.

The psychiatrist explained Joey's mental state to him.

"Mr. Broyer, you are a very smart man, however, you suffer from severe clinical depression, and conditions we call schizophrenia and OCD or obsessive compulsive disorder. However, my remedy holds promise for you. Same physical therapies as the other doctors have prescribed. You will do lots of exercise. I will counsel you twice a week for a while. Lastly, I am adding daily doses of anti-psychotic and anti-depressant medications. These drugs are in a class known as selective serotonin reuptake inhibitors or SSRIs. Mood enhancers are their common name. They will affect the balance of serotonin absorbed in your nervous system. You can expect side effects, but it's worth it."

Within a short period, the exercise, healthy food, and drugs proved effective in improving Joey's mood and created a sense of well-being in him. He found that time passed quickly in his daily routine. After a few months, with good behavior assisted by medications, the staff allowed Joey to volunteer as a sous chef in the kitchen. He found pleasure working with the food preparation. He remained under the watchful eyes of the chef and learned new dishes that fed the staff and other residents. He exhibited symptoms of OCD when he repeatedly rechecked the ovens and stoves after the chef turned them to "off". Joey found pleasure in rearranging the canned goods and spices in alphabetical order each week.

In most patients, the dosage of medicine Joey took carried a half-life effective for three or four days. However, the drugs' affected Joey longer than most people. The medication improved Joey's outlook, but he tired of the effects on his still problematic gastric system, continuing headaches, and weight gain. While he kept a good mood, he felt bloated and lethargic on most days.

Still obstinate, Joey dug in his heels. For three weeks, Joey intentionally dodged his medication by not swallowing it. His actions were invisible to others. He clenched the pill in his teeth and spit it out moments later, or he pretended to take the pill, but kept it in his hand. He dropped each uneaten pill into the toilet or sink. As each day passed, the doses consumed in the past became less and less effective. Soon he had none of the drug in his body.

Another week passed. Wave after wave of depression rolled over him as if a dark ominous ocean. Sleepless, night after night, he recounted his many losses: beautiful Liz, his beloved cats, his health, Liz's house, his family, his wheels, and his freedom. The multiple defeats crushed his will to live. One gloomy morning he pondered these burdens as he sat on his bed staring out the window from his second-floor room. He tried to read a newspaper, but the day's stories added to his malaise. The weather spoiled his demeanor, as the sky filled with dark blue thunderheads. Lightning flashed in the distance. He judged that the storms would move there in less than thirty minutes.

Then he saw it! Joey watched a gray van resembling his own van roll into the complex near the front lobby. Moments later the driver walked inside to the security desk. Joey strained his eyes to see the logo painted on the van. The decal contained a picture of a water facet and the words "Beach Plumbing." When the visitor returned to the van, he drove to Joey's work area, the kitchen, on the same side of the building. There, the van remained visible from Joey's vantage point. Joey hatched an idea that might work. This could be his ticket to freedom, but he had to be quick and act carefully.

Since he volunteered, Joey's access points within the mental center had increased over time to include the kitchen galley twenty-four seven. The kitchen's locked exterior door normally prevented his voluntary exit. He observed the doorway as the plumbers entered and exited. They left abundant equipment and supplies outside propping the door wide open.

He glanced at his clock. In twenty minutes, the schedule called for him and the lunch team to cook a meal. Joey thought, *Maybe I have enough time. It is worth a try.* The kitchen supervisor, who had other duties, often arrived late for meal preparation. Joey snapped on his prosthetic legs. He quickly descended the steps downstairs to the first floor, while desperately trying not to attract attention. At every turn, he looked behind to see if anyone followed him. He knew the security cameras were rolling. He milled around the kitchen, moving pots and pans back and forth from the preparation table to the stove and back again. He wanted to avoid suspicion with the plumbers and to look busy in case other preparers entered. He nodded to the one plumber standing above the other, whose legs protruded from under the problematic sink. Joey feigned curiosity for several minutes as he waited for his opportunity.

The plumber in the prostrate position barked at the other, "Now go outside, and turn on the main water supply."

The helper followed orders. The time arrived for Joey to move! He crept fluidly like one of his cats would and edged out of the open door. A tall, bushy camellia provided cover as he assessed the situation. When the helper returned inside, Joey circled the van. Out of everyone's sight, he opened the driver's door. What luck! The key rested in the ignition. He looked back at the kitchen. No one noticed his absence. *Would his prosthesis on both legs enable him to put enough pressure on the brake and gas pedals?* Joey sealed his fate in this moment. He pressed on the brake with his left limb and turned the key. Suddenly, the van started. *Freedom!* With his right leg extension, he controlled the gas. He had no time to spare. As he backed out of the parking spot, he assured himself he could out-drive anyone on foot that might chase him.

He knew exactly where he was going. He had rehearsed the repetitions of leg motions in his mind and body many times. During his past sweaty exercise in the gym room, while pretending to drive, he conceived his plan. The repetitive workouts yielded their expected dividend in his legwork. Stifling heat enveloped the van. When he reached the main coastal road, Joey tried to turn on the air conditioner, but it did not work. He pushed the buttons to lower the two windows. Hot but fresh air poured into the sweltering truck. Drops of sweat fell from Joey's temple. He looked back in the rearview mirror. No one behind him.

The clouds overhead, and in his mind, swirled in torment as the darkness turned gloomier. Faster and faster he drove, but still under the speed limit. His memory held fast to the thought, *Only a short distance to my goal.* He had driven this roadway many times. The Sandy Chameleon lay ahead. Tears of anxiety dripped on his cheek. Without looking at it, he raced past the Sandy Chameleon. The dive was only a blur in the corner of his eye. As he started on the one-mile bridge, ahead he saw the spectacular eighty-five foot rise that allowed tall boats to pass under it. He guessed, *Less than a quarter mile to go.* Only two cars preceded him. The van dashed up the incline. He glanced in the mirrors repeatedly, just in case. No other traffic and no police chased him yet. Joey felt a steady gale blowing into the windows. The speedometer gauge clocked ninety-miles-per-hour. At the apex of the bridge, Joey jerked the steering wheel sharply to the right in a violent motion. Sparks flashed, clouds of smoke rose, and flames ripped the van. At the point of impact, the burning van somersaulted over the railing. A twelve-foot chasm opened in the guardrail.

At that moment as if in slow motion, reality struck Joey. It was too late. The sinking spiral of his mind's darkness mirrored the van's plunge off the bridge. The plumber's van bobbed as if a cork in the murky waters of the swirling river. Within seconds, the van with opened windows sank beneath the surface. A huge bolt of lightning flashed against the ominous indigo sky. Automobile and boat traffic ceased as other helpless drivers watched. In his troubled mind, the pain of Joey continuing his life had outweighed the benefits. He had no hope left. Now it no longer mattered to him. Nothing mattered.

Chapter 42

Contentment

From all signs, most of the Turner's lifestyle resumed to normal in their cottage. However, several things were different now. Their observations of the grotesque condition of Liz's mansion provoked Ross and Cece to declutter and then remodel their home. They had made few updates over the years, so Cece opted for a Tuscan feel to her new décor. Ross hired a part-time efficient housekeeper to help with the housework. Daily, Ross dropped the morning paper on Cece's writing chair before he left for his morning classes.

At times, a simple stroll outside to pick up the mail exerted Cece. Conversely, at other times, she walked several flat city blocks with the help of her oxygen source. Everyday brought different challenges. However, her long-term prospects were good. Her pulmonary specialist told her she appeared to be an excellent candidate for a lung transplant and he would add her name to the organ recipient registry if she allowed it.

She refused to surrender to a life of incarceration in her home. Tonight, she and Ross planned to enjoy their monthly date night. The enjoyment she expected held more importance to her than the momentary discomfort. The golden evening sun burned through the matrix of city lanes as Cece and Ross pulled into a handicapped parking space in the Vieux Carre. The old quarter of New Orleans glowed with fascination, glitz, and grandeur. Within moments, the two trudged to their nearby date-night haunts. Ross wheeled the oxygen concentrator machine behind him in case Cece needed it. Cece's savory, aural, and nasal senses flashed to a heightened alert. Gaslights lining the sidewalk awoke to perform their nightly duty. On the ancient cobblestone pavement, the clicking of Cece's shoes mixed with the sounds of street musicians. In the evening twilight, a refreshed regiment of street performers filled Jackson Square. Their antics charmed and wowed the crowds. The atmosphere reverberated with the beat of primal drums, ripples of panpipes, and a city of guitars. Tattooed hawkers begged to read one's hand for fortunes, while others sold handmade crafts and peddled counterfeit handbags and faux watches. Aromatic scents wafted from pans seated on the gas burners of food wagons. Scantily clad hookers stood in the shadows of an adjoining cross street. As Cece's consciousness took in the sights, smells, and sounds of the French quarter, her eyes widened and her lungs burned in the nighttime air. She paused and assembled her breathing apparatus.

After walking another city block, Cece stopped again, this time to remove her breathing mask. The two lovers stood at a street vendor's wagon where they shared their first course, a fresh ear of corn dripping with creamy butter. Cece and Ross excused themselves from Aunt Camilla's proper dinner manners, as they chomped on the appetizer mid-street. Their satisfaction trumped Camilla's antiquated rules. Ross tossed the spent corncob in a garbage can as Cece reassembled her mask. She chuckled to herself as she thought, *I would be equipped for Mardi Gras if I added a few feathers on my mask.*

The duo slipped around a corner into a dueling pianos bar and enjoyed the cocktail hour. The musical pub featured a signature drink, the ubiquitous hurricane concoction. For old time's sake, Ross ordered a Scotch old fashioned while Cece nursed a cosmo. Two feisty piano players revved up the crowd. They sang and played audience choices of college fight songs, British and Australian drinking songs, and classic love songs. In between sets, their bawdy jokes tickled the ears of tourists and locals with off-color humor.

Cece and Ross stepped back onto old Bourbon Street into an open-air cafe. They heard the strains of a street jazz band forming a ritual procession like the ones they had seen on previous occasions. Each swallowed a half dozen oysters on the half shell doused in red cocktail sauce with stinging horseradish. The fresh treats mixed with saltines in a viscous slide down the gullet. The delicacy qualified as Cece's most favorite snack in the world, except for chocolate.

As they paced another city block, Cece commanded the conversation. Ross kidded her that she had already exceeded her limit of 30,000 words per day. Undaunted by Ross's wry humor or her nasal mask, she chattered about her favorite bloggers and books, her friends and work associates, and the latest cooking star on television. They entered a new style eatery recommended by Cece's friends. The artsy menu offered neo-Cajun dishes such as lobster gumbo, grouper arnaud, and cheesy shrimp and grits. When their entrees arrived, the soft burn and the brash flavors teased Cece's taste buds. *Her friends were right about this bistro! They must return soon.* With no room in her calorie count for a round of soft airy beignets and sauces, Cece pushed back from the table. Within minutes, Ross drove the few miles home. He pulled the ragtop into their driveway. Cece climbed in bed exhausted and went to sleep without her usual soaking bath.

The next morning, the digital clock in Cece's bedroom clicked to 9:30 am when the alarm rang. Cece had reached her physical limit in the French Quarter the prior night. Her body had forced her to sleep at least nine hours before she cycled into the next day's activities. Removing her nose clip, she rose and clicked off the oxygen concentrator. She felt more refreshed than usual. Usually, she made time to visit a gym at her medical clinic. Instead, she decided to forgo her workout of supervised treadmill exercise with prescribed oxygen therapy. She rationalized that last night's walking more than offset the scheduled regimen. In this moment of stillness, peace and confidence embraced her. In her robe and pajamas, she nestled into her comfortable chair. One of her three rescue cats jumped into her lap. As she stroked her pet, it responded with a gentle purr. The other two felines slept with one eye open in the bay window, awaiting their entertainment, a hungry bird landing on the feeder.

Cece reached for her reading glasses and lifted the morning's *Times-Picayune*. Since Liz's funeral, she cultivated a new habit of studying the daily obituary page. She marveled at the spectrum of legacies her town's citizenry unveiled every morning. The practice led her to question her own legacy. *How would people remember Cece?* Her natural thoughts majored on her flaws instead of her strengths.

Against her better judgment, her cerebral war targeted the events of the previous months. Cece's mind latched onto a mental picture of Liz's home in disarray and squalor. The memories of the filth traumatized her as she internalized her encounters. *The events and experiences involving Liz and me in the past intersected*

*at this crossroad in a tangled mess. Before Liz's death,
I had never engaged in something so complex. I lacked
confidence in myself. I was not sure if I had the leadership skills or the experience to do such a complicated
project as her estate. I doubted, as I was not an initia-
tor. There were so many moving parts to handling this
estate, including Liz's double-mindedness and lack
of preparation, my own motivations, and my usual
trusting self which others misinterpreted as niceness.
I must face it that Liz disappointed others and me by
failing to fulfill the lifelong destiny we hoped for her. I
lost my health. Moreover, Ross suffered too.*

Prone to discount herself, this morning she flushed
her negative thoughts instead. She struggled to item-
ize her positive traits and events. Cece felt anxiety in
her abdomen again. She realized she needed to calm
herself. Continuing a negative spiral could only hurt
her more. She remembered the deep-breathing exercise suggested by her physical therapist. With each
new gasp, she swept away the fleeting ill thoughts.
The memories that held her hostage vaporized. Then,
as she prayed, her mindset crossed the spectrum to
a positive mode.

She reached across the chair arm to the end table
and picked up the organized binder of documents created by her eldercare attorney. The binder pertained to
their end-of-life matters. As she thumbed through the
book, she thought, *I will not leave a mess as Liz had
done.* The lawyer included an executed last will and
testament, and a trust funded with specific financial
assets. The trust contained beneficiary instructions
for their home, 401-K plan, and life insurance policy
proceeds. With these written directions, Cece controlled the disposal of these assets after she passed.
The binder also contained a signed durable power of
attorney, HIPPA release, and a Living Will. Together,

these documents gave Cece and Ross peace of mind over their affairs. When her time came, the process would not be pleasant, but the path would be smoother than Liz's paper trail. In the back of the binder rested two blank pages. On these sheets, the lawyer instructed Cece and Ross to create their own obituaries.

She found a tablet and pen to start writing a draft. Deeply, she breathed again. Words flowed to her. Cece listed her late parents and grandparents and her late brother Jack. A tear and then another dripped on her cheek as she poured out her thoughts. She described her love for Ross, and his kindness and support of her ways. She applied humor as icing on her years laboring in the work force. The patchwork quilt of relationships in local organizations and her neighborhood glowed in her mind. The friendships she gained in their church and community enhanced the joy she experienced. She laid down her pen. *That's enough work for this day.*

She stood up and glanced outside to see if the earlier rain ended. Her eyes moved to the arched alcove in their newly renovated kitchen. She and Ross had carefully positioned Liz's tiara under a glass dome in the place of honor. How it sparkled and glistened in the sun's rays and a row of new LED lighting. Just two weeks before, a small box had arrived containing the tarnished crown.

Inside the box, she found a handwritten note, which read, "Per the terms of the Elizabeth Perkins probate hearing. Signed Rufus Jasper."

True to his form, Ross researched nearby jewelry restoration companies. He found just the right artisan to restore the tarnished tiara to its previous glittering state.

Cece remembered that Liz's mink coat had not arrived. She etched a mental note to call her lawyer this week. *What? Has it already been six months since that court hearing?*

Suddenly, the phone rang. This jolt interrupted Cece's reminder to herself to call Harry. The haunting question recurred, *Who would call at this hour?* She hobbled to the landline phone on the kitchen wall.

"Hello, yes, Cecilia Turner here. Oh, Kerry Tyler, hi. How are you doing? We are both fine."

Her voice broke into a coughing spasm for a moment.

"Oh, excuse me. Yes. I see. Well, I am sorry. When did it happen? Oh, that's awful."

Once again, a litany of questions and comments continued. Her questions satisfied her momentary curiosity.

Kerry stammered, "I thought you needed to know to have closure. Yesterday, a terrible one-vehicle accident occurred on the causeway bridge just past the Sandy Chameleon. Joey Broyer escaped from the mental health center by stealing a plumber's van. Do you remember the mile long bridge?"

Cece's mind relived a meme of the immense vista of swirling aqua waters and turquoise skies she and Ross witnessed as they drove up the incline many times.

"Joey plunged the vehicle off the highest point of the mile long bridge. Although there was no note left by Broyer, the coroner ruled it a suicide. That's obvious."

"Sounds like it, Kerry."

Cece had disconnected herself from the situation of Joey, Liz, and twenty-two cats. These characters represented the form of a nebulous gray rock to her now, void of stoking passion in her. She felt no emotion, remorse, or care. She had learned to forgive. Cece shed not one tear. She nodded, then looked up and sighed. As they closed the conversation, Cece hung up the phone and sat in the chair. She yawned

and repositioned her worn body. Droopy clouds of
sleepiness enveloped her. She nodded off sinking into
a quick nap.

When she stirred again, suddenly her soul filled
with vast sadness and darkness. She needed something
to cheer her up. Hope from somewhere, anywhere.
To counter, she reached for her tattered and worn
personal Bible. She started to read where she had
last placed her bookmark in Chapter 6 of the book of
Ecclesiastes.

> *[1]I have seen another evil under the sun, and it
> weighs heavily on mankind, [2]God gives some peo-
> ple wealth, possessions and honor, so that they
> lack nothing their hearts desire, but God does not
> grant them the ability to enjoy them, and strang-
> ers enjoy them instead. This is meaningless, a
> grievous evil.*

How true the words rang in her mind.

Moments later the sharp, staccato ring of her wall
telephone shook Cece from her stupor. The gruff
voice uttered, "Hello, this is the Greensboro Police
Department. I need to speak to Mrs. Cecilia Turner."

"This is she. What do you want?"

"Do you have a cousin named Richie Evans? We
were given your name by a neighbor."

"Yes sir, why?"

"We found Richie dead in his home last night. Can
you help us?"

The World Is Too Much With Us

WILLIAM WORDSWORTH

The world is too much with us; late and soon,
Getting and spending, we lay waste our powers; —
Little we see in Nature that is ours;
We have given our hearts away, a sordid boon!
This Sea that bares her bosom to the moon;
The winds that will be howling at all hours,
And are up-gathered now like sleeping flowers;
For this, for everything, we are out of tune;
It moves us not. Great God! I'd rather be
A Pagan suckled in a creed outworn;
So might I, standing on this pleasant lea,
Have glimpses that would make me less forlorn;
Have sight of Proteus rising from the sea;
Or hear old Triton blow his wreathed horn.

CPSIA information can be obtained
at www.ICGtesting.com
Printed in the USA
LVHW081551061218
599494LV00017B/1136/P